LUCY VINE

ORION

First published in Great Britain in 2018 by Orion Books,
an imprint of The Orion Publishing Group Ltd
Carmelite House, 50 Victoria Embankment,
London EC4Y 0DZ

An Hachette UK company

1 3 5 7 9 10 8 6 4 2

A CIP catalogue record for this book is
available from the British Library.

ISBN 978 1 4091 7223 9

Typeset by Input Data Services Ltd, Somerset

Printed and bound by CPI Group (UK) Ltd, Croydon, CR0 4YY

MIX
Paper from
responsible sources
FSC® C104740

www.orionbooks.co.uk

Wedding Number One: Kelly and Hamish, Saint Columbia's Presbyterian Church, Edinburgh

Theme: Floral. Unparalleled numbers of flowers everywhere you turn. Several hayfever sufferers forced to flee church.

Menu: Smoked salmon starter, followed by chicken and a meringue dessert. Veggie option: stuffed red pepper with goat's cheese.

Gift: His and hers champagne glasses @ £150.

Gossip: The best man's speech went on for forty-five minutes, dissecting the groom's very real porn addiction in horrifying detail. Grandma started crying.

My bank balance: £425

1

I've been trying to make this conversation happen for what must be seventeen hours now, and I wish so hard that I could give up and walk away. But I can't. I've invested too much time – I *have* to keep going.

'SO,' I try again loudly, cringing at the nasal fake-cheer in my voice and feeling all of life's awkwardness condense into that one stupid syllable. 'How long have you been, um, doing this . . . job?'

He barely glances in my direction. 'Huh? What'd you say, babe?' he replies, his Birmingham accent jarring, distinctly out of place on this random roof terrace under a too-hot sun.

'Oh!' I force a laugh, knowing he definitely fucking heard me, and that he just doesn't want to talk. I stare down at my feet, examining the blister forming on the side of my big toe, and consider going heavier with my chat. Small talk isn't working – everyone hates small talk – so maybe I should go straight in with *big* talk. Donald Trump's hostage wife, floppy Brexit, any dodgy uncles he had growing up.

Sweat itches the back of my neck and the glare of the sun, reflecting off his baby-oiled nipples, briefly blinds me. I sigh. Why am I doing this to myself?

I'm only twenty-four hours into this hen do – here in Tenerife for my demanding and not-even-that-nice-to-make-up-for-it school friend, Harriet – and I already hate everything. Here we are, a group of women who don't really know each other, trapped together in a rented apartment with

3

a fancy roof terrace for a long weekend, enacting an intimate itinerary of nudity-based activities. It's like an intensive episode of *Big Brother*, but with no cameras behind the mirrors.

Actually, that did happen on a hen do I saw on the news last year, but I think that hotel manager is in jail now.

So much forced fun, so many phallic-shaped inflatables, and such middle-class guilt over the Butler in the Buff beside me. That's why I am trying so hard with this conversation – while carefully avoiding eye contact with his free-swinging cock – so that he knows at least one person here sees him as a real-life human being. So far, all he's had is two hours of hens coming over, one by one, to scream in his face that he should 'take off the stupid apron already' and 'do the elephant dance, bitch'. Earlier, one of the bridesmaids spilled a bright green jelly shot all over his bum-crack and screamed that it was an arsehole waterfall. Actually, that was really funny and I couldn't stop laughing – which I think is probably why he doesn't want to talk to me now. But I really want him to know I'm a nice person. I need him to know that I do see him as more than just a piece of meat and a naked jelly-shot arse vessel. I want to tell him about the fantastic Yelp review I plan on giving him after this weekend.

I also need him to explain to me what an elephant dance is.

The Shiny Naked Man turns suddenly away from me, to catch a toppling-over woman. She is slipping about on a large greasy patch on the ground that Shiny Naked Man may or may not be responsible for. I'm not one to point fingers, but I think he is the only one who brought a two-litre bottle of baby oil with him on this hen do. She – damn, what is her name? – smiles up at him sloppily and paws at his apron, which is the one thing standing between his sad penis and this cold, cruel world. Poor Shiny Naked Man. He doesn't deserve this. He's probably a world-class heart surgeon or something in his normal life.

I quickly try to catch the eye of the bride, Harriet, sitting a few feet away, and wave frantically towards the sexual assault in progress beside me. In two hours, I fully expect to be locked up in a local police station, being grilled by Spanish lawyers as the other hens rustle up bail money. Actually, that might be more fun than this . . .

Harriet rolls her eyes at me, but staggers up, shouting at 'Jill' to leave the Butler in the Buff alone.

Jill, that's it! That's her stupid fucking name! Like Jack and Jill, except she's climbing uphill to fetch a pail of penis.

I force down another giggle, remembering our tepid introduction at the airport last night.

'Lilah, this is Jill Tide,' Harriet told me, smiling from underneath her brand new polyester veil – tags still attached. 'She was my boss until last year, and she's just been promoted to head of accounts at her new office. She's now in charge of a team of, like, two hundred people, right, Jill? It's a huge promotion.' Harriet grinned then, adding impulsively, 'So this weekend will be like a double celebration for both of us!' And then she'd looked really worried and added sternly, 'But mostly it will be *my* celebration. I mean it's *my* hen do. I think we can call this here in the airport – this little bit in the departure lounge – *your* celebration, Jill, and then not mention it again. OK? I really don't think it's cool of you to try to steal my thunder, Jill.' And then she'd made a really unenthused toast with our free airport Baileys. I tried to whisper congratulations but Harriet gave me a really livid look.

I remember worrying that Head of Accounts Jill, in her fancy grey trouser suit from, like, Jigsaw or somewhere else fancy that I never shop, wasn't going to be too impressed with the wild events planned for this weekend. But here she is, not even a full twenty-four hours later, in her red horny devil outfit, with dried tequila dribble peeling off her chin. Good old Jill.

This is, at least, better than last night. The moment we arrived at the villa we were herded straight down to the pool for a 'hen photoshoot'. Harriet had hired a local photographer to capture us all jumping around in the air, wearing our matching hen t-shirts. Then we had to do another set-up, posing in our red bikinis around the pool. Harriet kept screaming at us not to drink the cocktails because they were just props for the photoshoot. She'd put hairspray all over them to keep the straws and decorations from moving about too much in the breeze. The shoot went on for ages – almost four hours – but Harriet said we couldn't leave until all nine of us looked like we were having the exact right amount of fun. She said her Instagram followers had to be properly, spitefully jealous, or what was even the point of this weekend at all.

As you may well have picked up, Harriet, the bride, is being a proper dick about everything. And I would say you only get one hen do, but Harriet is actually having two more after this. One back in Liverpool where she lives, and then a third one for work friends the week after. She said it was for people who couldn't make it to this one, but then she said everyone here has to attend the other two as well. Which is really just truly fantastic news for my overdraft.

'No!' Harriet suddenly screams now, leaping unsteadily from her seat and knocking a sun umbrella over. She looks panicked and is pale under her heavy fake tan.

'Are you OK? What's wrong, Harriet?' I run over, the only one to react. The rest of the hens are too drunk. Jill is humping Shiny Naked Man's leg, like a horny puppy, and all his energies are focused on keeping his penis safe from her grasping hands.

Harriet looks at me but her eyes are super glazed. 'Delly?' she says, unsure.

'Yes, it's me,' I say through gritted teeth, wincing at the ancient school-era nickname. It's LILAH – how many times do I have to casually refer to myself in the third person before she gets it?

She bursts into loud sobs and thrusts her left hand into my face. 'I've lost my engagement ring,' she wails, looking bereft. 'It's gone! I can't find it. Have you seen it?' It takes me half a second to register the bare knuckles in my face. The webbing of her fingers is stained orange, but there's no sign of the usual massive sparkler that sits there.

Holy shit. This is bad. She can't really have lost it, can she? It's probably just down in our apartment? Surely?

Harriet's fiancé is a big-time wanker-banker, and I'm pretty sure that ring is worth a lot of money. I say 'pretty sure' but I mean 'absolutely sure' – because Harriet specifically told me it's worth a lot. Loads of times. She sent us a group email about it. She put it on Facebook. Oh, look, the ring cost £25,000.

I attempt a reassuring smile and put my hand on her arm. 'Don't worry. We'll find it, I promise,' I say as calmly as I can, biting my lip.

It must be here. It must be.

I really hope it's here.

It's definitely not here.

I've looked all over this stupid roof terrace, discarding a thousand willy straws and knocking over a million more sticky shot glasses, but no ring. Shiny Naked Man briefly

7

shook Jill off and helped me search, but after a few minutes he muttered something about his insurance not covering this, and wandered back over to resume being pestered. Actually, he is starting to seem fairly OK about the groping situation. Ooh, maybe he and Jill will fall in love? That would be so romantic! Wait, *would* that be romantic? I'm not sure I've got romance right.

I turn to Harriet, who is staring forlornly at her empty glass. It's hard to tell if she's more upset about the missing jewellery, or being momentarily out of alcohol. 'You're absolutely sure you didn't leave it back in your room tonight, Harri? Maybe in the bathroom? Can I not just go down and check?' I ask for the third time.

She wails again, 'I've already told you: no! Definitely not! I'm not an idiot, Delly. Oh God, I'm sure I left it at the cocktail class earlier. I remember taking it off there. Or maybe it was at the life drawing class we did? Or maybe the karaoke? Why did we go to so many different places today? I'm pretty sure it must be at one of those. I'm ninety-nine per cent certain it's at the cocktail class.' She looks at me pointedly and then adds slowly, 'I guess someone is going to have to go back over there to check.'

Oh shit, she wants me to go. I pause, thinking about retracing the many, many exhausting steps we've taken today and knowing I'm the only one here sober enough to do it.

Harriet seizes on my reluctance and starts shrieking again. 'Oh, forget it! What's the point? My hen do is ruined; everything's ruined. We might as well go home right now and I'll just cancel my wedding since clearly no one gives a shit about me.' She covers her face with her hands.

I can't believe I'm about to do this.

'Of course it's not ruined,' I say, knowing I'm being

manipulated and hating it. 'You stay here and keep having . . . fun. This is going to be fine. I'll go to the cocktail place and find it.'

I locate my bag under the maid of honour, Nina, who is flopped across one of the sofas. There's a sick bucket next to her head and a really rather surprising amount of bright green vomit in there.

'Nina, are you all right?' I ask, genuinely concerned. She lifts her head up from the sofa and nods, blearily. I look again at the bucket. 'Er, I don't suppose you have the phone numbers for any of the venues we've been to today?' I say, enunciating as clearly as I can. 'Or maybe an itinerary or something? Harriet can't find her engagement ring.'

Nina looks momentarily stricken. 'Oh no, that's . . .' She stops, confused. 'Wait, what's happened? Sorry, Nelly, what do you need?' She tries to stand and immediately lurches back down.

Nelly, now, is it? Fabulous.

I save her hair before it flops into the green liquid, and say as nicely as I can, 'OK, Nina, never mind. You stay there and keep that bucket close. I'll sort this out.'

She gives me a weak thumbs up. 'Thanks, Nelly.'

It's fine. I can do this all by myself. I will handle it. And Nelly is at least a nicer name than Delly.

Three hours later, and I am totally broken as I trudge back into the villa. I have been all over town looking for this fucking, fucking ring. I managed to figure out the names of the various places we'd been to, even without Nina's help, and got their phone numbers off Google, using up all my O2 data. But it's a Saturday night so obviously no one was really answering when I rang around. Oh, except that one

9

guy who just kept asking me what I was wearing, and when I mentioned looking for a ring, he said he wouldn't mind looking for my ring sometime. So I got a cab to each of the three places we'd visited, to search them properly for myself. Sadly, all I found were yet more drunk groups of women, and barmen who smirked and made the exact same joke about my ring as the other guy.

At some point in my travels, my phone died, and I had to admit defeat and head back to the apartment, empty-handed and miserable.

I know Harriet has been a pain, but I feel really, really awful. I told her I'd find the ring and I haven't. I've failed the bride. I've let her down. Everyone knows that's the one thing you're not supposed to do. If a bride says jump, you bloody well jump and then jump higher and then you find a lost fucking engagement ring.

I find everyone gathered back in our apartment, playing pin the willy on the donkey in the large living room. The mood has lifted decidedly since I last saw them, and I feel a pang at having missed out on so much of the fun. I was so desperate to get away from them but now I'm sad and resentful at having missed out.

I'm surprised to see Shiny Naked Man is still here. His allotted booking with us must've run out ages ago. But yep, that's definitely his apron I can see in the corner, covering those hairless legs poking out from underneath Jill.

Oh God, I hope he's not dead.

But at least that might distract everyone from my failed ring mission?

Harriet looks up, surprised as I come in.

'Where have you been, Delly?' she says delightedly.

I wince – she's going to be devastated. Come on, Lilah,

10

woman up. Just tell her the truth. It's not like you lost the ring yourself, and she'll understand that you did everything you could to get it back. She's not a monster.

She is a bit of a monster.

Deep breath.

'I'm really sorry, Harri, I couldn't find it,' I say, covering my eyes.

'Find what?' she says, and I peek through my fingers. She looks confused.

'Your engagement ring,' I say, waiting for the crying to start again. There really should be crying at this point. Maybe she's saving up the tears for telling the fiancé – that conversation will require a lot of crying to avoid shouting.

But instead, she waves her hand dismissively. The hand glitters.

'Oh, that. Don't worry, I found it hours ago,' she says. 'It was here in the apartment all along – in the bedside table. I remembered that I left it here deliberately because –' she lowers her voice – 'I thought I might want to get off with the stripper.' She gives a peeved nod over in the direction of Jill, before adding thoughtfully, 'But that didn't work out. Plus, the diamond didn't go with my horny devil outfit.'

I gape at her, as my stomach acid starts to boil.

What. The. Fuck.

It was here, all along? I asked her that – over and over. I shitting *asked* her that. I even tried to wrestle the apartment key off her to check, but she was so insistent it wasn't down here, she wouldn't hand it over. Hours I've been out there searching for this ring. Hours. I start counting up in my head all the Euros I've spent on taxis back and forth. How many times my arse got pinched and my nipple got elbowed, fighting my way through to the front of the karaoke stage so

11

I could check the sticky floor for a missing fucking diamond that was here the whole time. I asked her so many times if she might've left it here.

I wait. She waits. We look at each other. She's not going to say sorry. She doesn't even seem bothered.

The words bubble up and out of me. 'You know I've spent my whole night out there looking for it?' I say, my voice breaking a bit.

I know, I know, I'm lame, but it's the best I can do – I really don't like confrontation.

She shrugs and I feel myself go rigid.

Just leave it, I tell myself. She's the bride, this is her hen do, don't be the one who makes a fuss and ruins everything with an argument.

There's silence and I can't bring myself to say anything else. For a second she looks half repentant and then the defiance slides back into place. 'Actually, Delly, to be honest, I'm the one who should be annoyed with you,' she says in a sing-song school-marm-y voice. 'After all, we've been waiting hours to take a group selfie. You know I have a schedule to keep to for my Instagram posts. I can't have my followers forgetting about us, or thinking we're not having the best hen do ever!'

I picture forcibly removing her engagement ring right now, putting it on my own hand and then punching her in the face with it. It would feel good, wouldn't it? The impact of that over-priced rock smashing her over-priced nose job. I might have to go to jail for a while, but I think it would be worth it. When the rage in my stomach is like it is now, I honestly think I could do a murder and it would be worth it. Or maybe a revenge-suicide. Right now I could happily throw myself in front of Harriet's car, just to make her feel bad for killing me. I think it would be worth my death if I could make a shitty person feel shit, if only for a few minutes.

'What's going on?' shouts Nina, who's staggered over, leaving a trail of blood on the floor. She's barefoot and, for some reason, still clutching the bucket of green sick under her arm.

'Nothing, it's all fine,' I say, swallowing down my fury harder than anything in my life. There is no point getting into an argument. There's no way I'd win. And, thinking about it a bit more now, I proooobably shouldn't kill myself or murder anyone just to make a point.

Before I can say anything else, Harriet suddenly looks angry, turning to Nina. 'Delly's in a massive huff with me because I thought I'd lost my ring and she volunteered to look for it, even though I didn't ask her to,' she says defensively. 'I found it myself but now she's in a giant mood with me for no reason. Even though I'm the bride and this is MY HEN DO.' She shouts the last part and Nina turns to me, the liquid she's inexplicably carrying with her like a souvenir slopping about.

'What the fuck, Nelly? Let it go. It's HARRIET'S HEN DO.'

I shake my head. This is stupid. 'No, no,' I say tersely. 'I'm not in a mood, I'm fine. I was just surprised for a second. Can we leave it and get back to the games?'

'You should be happy she found the ring!' Nina goes on, getting in my face. The smell from the bucket is making me gag. 'You know it cost Jamie twenty-five thousand pounds? I can't believe you lost it in the first place, Nelly. You should be fucking relieved Harriet found it, or you would've had to replace it, love. Do you even have twenty-five thousand pounds? Because it cost twenty-five thousand pounds, did you know that?'

13

Harriet nods aggressively in agreement.

I feel my brow furrow. 'Hold on, I didn't lose it,' I say, my voice shaking. The anger in my stomach has drained away and now I'm just desperate to get away from this pointless drunk anger. 'I was trying to find it because Harriet thought she'd left it at the cocktail class earlier. I was helping her. Why would I have to replace—'

'OH, IT'S MY FAULT NOW, IS IT?' shouts Harriet, whose drunk logic has suddenly shifted gears.

'No, no!' I say again quickly, thinking, yes, yes, it is your fault, you stupid idiot.

Oh crap, what's happening here? Why am I the one in trouble now? I didn't even do anything. Oh Christ, I hate this.

The Shiny Naked Man, who is much less shiny, and Jill, who is a lot *more* shiny now, have joined us and are listening interestedly.

'WHOSE FAULT IS IT THEN, NELLY?' Nina bellows at me, and panic starts building in my stomach. I can't handle being shouted at in any situation, never mind something like this with a group of semi-strangers. And I know she's that kind of drunk where no amount of reasonable explanation is going to calm her down.

'Oh God, look, guys,' I try desperately, 'please stop shouting at me. This is over absolutely nothing. We thought Harriet had lost her ring, I went to look for it, but it was here in the apartment all along. It's a good thing! I'm really sorry I upset you, Harri. Let's get back to having fun, shall we? Can we? Please?'

Shiny Naked Man interjects. 'Hold on, have you been out looking for that ring this whole time?' He pokes a finger at me. 'Fookin' hell, babe, I wondered where you'd gone. And them shouting at you, that's hella out of order.' He turns to

Harriet and Nina, who are black-faced with fury. 'Why's you two shouting at her when she's just been trying to help ya? She shouldn't be sayin' sorry to you; youse two should be apologising to her.' Beside him, Jill glares at me jealously, her fingers turning white as the iron grip she has on his arm tightens.

Fuck. I really appreciate Shiny Naked Man trying to help – and, honestly, it feels really good to finally, properly have his attention – but he's clearly now made everything worse. Harriet and Nina will feel cornered and fight even harder. That's how angry drunks work.

'WHY ARE YOU EVEN STILL HERE, YOU FRIGID BITCH?' Harriet shouts at Shiny Naked Man, taking a step towards him.

Jill immediately switches her attention to Harriet, elbowing her shiny man out the way to scream in the bride's face for her to: 'STEP THE FUCK OFF, HARRIET'.

I glance around the shouting group, my heart pumping hard in my chest, as the rest of the hens join us. I note distractedly that one is still blindfolded from the pin-the-willy donkey game.

Nina steps closer too and we're all now practically forehead to forehead, anger bouncing like an electrical current around the circle. 'MIND YOUR OWN BUSINESS, DICKHEAD!' she screams, and suddenly everyone in the room is shouting at each other about rings and strippers and donkeys. It's absolute bedlam and I'm at the centre of it, wondering how the hell this happened.

Oh, and there goes the bucket.

When I finally get to bed an hour later, showered and broken, I remember my dead phone and reach for the charger. I stare at the ceiling for a moment, thinking how horrendous today was and how it's only the beginning of a hellish year. I slowly count up how many weddings and hen dos I've said yes to. It must be ten. At least ten. Last week I was at a dull-as-fuck ceremony up in Scotland, and I've got another one coming up next week for my mum's middle-aged cousin. Can I really handle dealing with this kind of drama over and over and over again? Why do I always say yes to these things?

I'm just drifting off, completely exhausted, when my phone turns itself back on and begins frantically vibrating.

Blinking blearily at my phone, a message flashes up:

You have 44 new WhatsApp notifications.

They're all from Lauren. Fuck, what's happened? My heart speeds up and I'm suddenly wide awake again, adrenaline pumping. I sit up in bed, thinking how shit all comes at once. Has something happened to Granny Franny? Surely not? Lauren wouldn't WhatsApp me if my favourite person in the world – the woman who basically raised me – had died. But death is always my immediate assumption. I've written off everyone I know at some point.

I open the app.

Lauren: OMG OMG OMG OMG ANSWER YOUR PHONE
Lauren: Y ARENT U ANSWERIN UR PHONE
Lauren: FFFFFFFFSSSSSSSS LILAH
Lauren: I have such massive neeeeeews!!
Lauren: OK screw it, I'll just tell you. Charlie
    prooooopoooooooosed!
Lauren: IM ENGAGEDDDDDDDDDD
Lauren: I'm trying to send you a picture of the ring. It's shitting
    massive.
Lauren: It won't send.

16

Lauren: Trying to FaceTime you.

Lauren: Why aren't you answering!!!

Lauren: Oh, you're on that stupid hen do, aren't you? I forgot that was this weekend. I can't believe you went, you never see that girl Harriet anymore. I didn't even reply to her email about it.

Lauren: Ah, no worries, I'm probs going to bed in a min. We've got all the time in the world to celebrate, and there's no rush to start planning it. I promise I'm not going to be one of those mad brides!!!! Going to bed now, love yooooou.

Lauren: I wish you were here. I'm so happy! I can't believe I'm engaged! It feels so weird. I can't wait to start organising the day. And the hen do! Wah!

Lauren: It was so romantic, Lil. He took me to the restaurant where we first met, and got down on one knee in front of everyone. The whole room started cheering and they gave us free champagne for the rest of the night!

Lauren: Did you know he was planning it? Did you help him choose the ring? It's exactly what I wanted. Thank you so much, I love it.

Lauren: Although I may have to swap the diamond.

Lauren: And the band.

Lauren: I think we'll just do something small. Small weddings are totally in right now and that's what I always pictured. A small wedding feels right. Maybe just like 50 of us, tops?

Lauren: Maybe we could have it on a beach? A really secluded beach in, like, Florence.

Lauren: Wait, does Florence have beaches?

Lauren: We should've paid more attention in Year Nine geography.

Lauren: I'm googling weddings abroad.

Lauren: I've invited you to edit my new Pinterest board.

Lauren: Actually, forget a beach, I've found the most amazing Jimmy Choo white shoes – can't have sand anywhere near these babies.

Lauren: I've set up a Twitter and Instagram account. Follow me @

BestWeddingEverCharlieLovesLauren

Lauren: Do you think I should have a harpist? If it's a church wedding, we might need a harpist. That's the vibe I want.

Lauren: I've just emailed you some pics of owls who LITERALLY DELIVER THE RINGS UP THE AISLE!!!! I must have one! I can't decide which breed is cutest? Check your emails.

Lauren: I've sent you some links to dresses they make in China. What do you think? They look amazing and they're so cheap!

Lauren: I've ordered two. Wedding diet starts here!

Lauren: I know I always said a summer wedding, but what about a December date? What do you think?? We can have mistletoe centrepieces. Would need to be next year though I guess.

Lauren: Could get Dad to give me away dressed as Father Christmas. Lol.

Lauren: Should I order long sleeve gloves? Are they back in yet?

Lauren: I just spoke to Joely – she's already trying to make this all about her. Said she wants a plus one, even though there's no way she'll have a boyfriend. She's not bringing yet another ugly reality star to one of our parties.

Lauren: Charlie says he wants anal on the wedding night, haha. Haven't done that since 2008. Will my haemorrhoids survive the trauma? RHOID RAGE! Lol.

Lauren: How much do you think a Ferris wheel in the garden would cost?

Lauren: VEGAS HEN DO?????!!!!!

Lauren: There would be about 25–30 of us. Shall we do a week in Vegas? Or is that too much?

Lauren: Did I actually tell you that you're my maid of honour? YOU'RE MY MAID OF HONOUR!! You're going to be the best MoH that ever lived.

Lauren: We're going to have so much fun organising this hen and wedding together.

Lauren: We can have weekly wedding meetings! I've told Charlie he's
    not invited, ha.
Lauren: Clear your schedule for the next 18 months, lol lol!! JK.
Lauren: For real though.

I drop my phone.
Fucking hell.

2

Lauren is standing on a chair and is waving her arms about like she's conducting an orchestra. A really irritated-looking orchestra holding pints of Guinness.

'I'M GETTING MARRIED!' she shrieks again, beaming around the room at the other patrons, who are definitely not here for this on any level. Not one to be outdone, Joely clambers up on her own chair, shouting towards the bar that she's a 'badass motherfucking bridesmaid' and the 'deputy maid of honour'! Which isn't a thing, but who am I to question her enthusiasm? I make eye contact across the table with the frightened-looking fourth member of our group, Simone, and briefly wonder if I should climb up too? It seems a bit excessive and the loud tuts around us are getting really rather threatening, but I don't want to miss out on being part of the story.

We're in the fanciest bar our local area permits, and I've just bought us the second nicest prosecco on the menu – it cost £46.50! – to celebrate Lauren's engagement. It's Monday night and I'm still so unbelievably hungover from the weekend's hen do. I'm also surviving on about ten hours of sleep across four days and haven't even had time to unpack or do my washing. I'm literally wearing my red halter bikini as underwear. It's really digging into the skin of my neck, but let she who has never worn a swimsuit as underwear on laundry day cast the first stone.

There was no question of staying in tonight to recover

or sort out my life. I had to go straight out to meet Lauren the moment I got back from the dreadful hen do. There was much screaming and hugging and – oh yes – more screaming to be done, and much as I could've done with a night in, as The Official Best Friend, I wasn't really given a choice.

Just as the table next to us prepares to throw their beer over our entire group, a panicked barmaid rushes over, waving a stained tea towel at us.

'Get down from there,' she hisses, and Lauren does so, looking a little shamefaced. Joely sits back down too, but very slowly, all the while making sarcastic eye contact with the barmaid. I smile at the woman nicely, trying to catch her eye so I can give her a meaningful nod towards the expensive fizz. I feel like spending a lot on alcohol in a place like this means it's probably OK to be loud and annoying. I bet they let footballers jump on the chairs.

The barmaid gives us one last scowl and the four of us giggle like schoolgirls as she stomps off. Usually I'd be embarrassed, but I'm way too thrilled for Lauren. She's wanted this engagement for ages and it feels like it's been a pretty long time coming. She and Charlie visited a ring shop together a year ago – 'Just in case' – and since then, every time they've taken a holiday or celebrated any kind of anniversary (FYI, five years since their first blowjob is *not* an anniversary), everyone's aggressively checked her hand and demanded to know if she 'has anything to tell us'. There was a really awkward moment at Christmas when Charlie got down on one knee in front of her whole family – her mum started crying – but it turned out he'd just stubbed his toe.

'KILLJOYS!' Joely shouts at the hostile room and Lauren shushes her frantically. The pair of them glare at each other for a few seconds.

Joely is Lauren's cousin. They were born just days apart, so they've been pretty much treated as sisters – twins, even – since birth. They're really close, as you'd expect, but they're also fiercely competitive and bicker like you cannot even imagine. And it's over everything and anything. I've honestly seen them get into a shouting match over a salt and pepper shaker before. But it was one of those combo contraptions, and they are really very confusing, so I get it.

The third bridesmaid of the group is Simone. She's Charlie's little sister – Lauren's soon-to-be sister-in-law – and a total duty pick. She seems really sweet, though, hovering now on the outskirts of all the inane shrieking. She's only nineteen and I think she's a bit overwhelmed by all this noise. Even though we've only just met, I can tell with some certainty that she finds strangers screaming and climbing on the furniture in a public place quite intimidating. Which is understandable. But I'm afraid she really will have to get used to it if she's going to be part of this #TeamBridesmaid thing.

I top up everyone's glasses, wondering how to make the point that I spent more than our usual £5.50 on the bottle, without sounding like I'm making that point. I can't think of anything, so instead I raise my glass.

'To the bride!' I say, grinning.

Lauren giggles and shouts back, 'TO ME!' while Joely cackles. The nearby tutters tut some more as Simone cheers quietly too, glancing self-consciously over her shoulder to gauge how close we are to being thrown out. I would hazard: very close.

I push down a feeling like I want to hug Simone and tell her things will be OK. I remember being nineteen and worrying all the time about what strangers thought of me. It's much better being twenty-eight and only caring what

22

my friends, family, work colleagues, acquaintances and every single follower I have on social media thinks of me. Much, much better.

I take another sip of my fizz, feeling its warmth spread through me. I've never seen Lauren look this happy; she's absolutely glowing. She's the type of person who is always running around, taking charge, getting shit done, looking after me. It's gratifying to see her stop and enjoy this moment. Even if it is just for a moment, this needs marking.

'Hold on,' I say suddenly, feeling all emotional. 'I want to make a proper toast.'

Lauren puts down her drink and we stare at each other, grinning for a long second, silently communicating like we always do. I briefly consider climbing up on the chair but catch the barmaid's eye and decide against it.

'Lauren,' I start, my voice wobbling a bit. 'You've been my very best friend since I was twelve. I remember the first day back at school after the Easter holidays, seeing you that first time. You were standing over in the corner with the cool kids on the basketball court, looking so grown-up. I was impressed by your super awesome Nike cap, and the crimped orange-y yellow hair sticking out from under it. I never thought I'd be cool enough to hang out with you. And then you came over and asked me about the pink streak in my hair and I realised you were nice, too. I told you all about my obsession with the singer P!nk and then you listened for a good ten minutes while I tried to justify the exclamation mark in her name, even though there is no justification. Then we screamed the words to 'You Make Me Sick' at each other and you laughed so hard you spilled Apple Tango all over yourself.'

Lauren sniffs, her eyes wet, and Joely snorts. Simone looks

confused. I understand these must be strange, foreign words to her. Does Apple Tango even still exist?

I clear my throat and continue, 'You could've used your popularity powers for evil at school, but you didn't. You were so kind and generous. You lent me all your *Sweet Valley High* books, one by one, and we read them together and called ourselves The Unicorn Club. I was the loser new kid no one liked, and you took me under your wing. You're still that person, always looking out for me and making me feel like somebody special and important. Protecting me whenever you can. We've seen each other through the best and the worst of life. You helped me recover from my first big heartbreak, when Ben Gage dumped me in front of everyone at the freshers' ball in week two of uni. You were there when my parents split up.' I pause to swallow. 'And you encouraged me to apply for my dream job and made my CV look all shiny. You're always rooting for me, and you make me a better person, Lauren.'

Joely grins at us, while Simone still looks confused.

I keep going. 'Lauren, back at school, I thought you were the most beautiful, cool and funny girl I'd ever met, and 16 years later, I still think that. I feel very lucky to call you my friend and even luckier to be your maid of honour.' I pause, thoughtfully. 'I'm so happy for you and Charlie. He is an excellent choice and we all adore him. Much, much better than 2011's bed-wetter, Gary. But let it be noted that he is very lucky indeed to have you and he better be worthy of you. I can't wait to help you plan this wedding, Lauren, and I will really try not to let you down.' I break off and Joely bursts into applause.

Lauren leaps up to give me a hug, shouting, 'That was so beautiful, Lilah, I love you so much and I hate you for making me cry. You have to make a toast at the wedding! But don't mention that Nike cap. I wore it for three months straight and Charlie would call the whole thing off if he found out.'

We start giggling again, and next to us Simone suddenly starts loudly sobbing. 'I don't have any friends as nice as you lot,' she wails, and Lauren, Joely and I all look at each other a bit awkwardly. Simone continues, speaking in her cut-glass accent through tears. 'I moved to London last year and all my school friends stayed at home to have babies. I'll never find a boyfriend and I'll never have children. It's so unfair. I've got no money and I *so* wanted to prove to Dad and Charlie that I could make it on my own and stand on my own two feet, so I put my whole trust fund into this "Toblerone scheme" a boy on Tinder told me about. I thought I was going to make a huge pile of money – he said I was.' She looks around at us, tearfully. 'How was I supposed to know it was a pyramid scheme and they'd just re-branded the shape? I thought I was going to get rich and eat mounds of free chocolate.' She trails off into muffled incoherency, as the rest of us look at each other bewildered.

I pat her kindly. Poor little thing. Being young is hard.

Simone suddenly points accusingly at Joely's generous bosom. 'And you are so pretty and have *huge* boobs, which totally isn't fair. No boy will ever like me because I don't have any boobs. I'm basically just nipples.' She cries harder, waving at her childish figure.

I search for consolation and find none.

'Of course you have boobs!' Lauren says warmly, putting her arm around her new sister. 'Those are definitely boobs. All you need are nipples, anyway. Nipples are the basic ingredients of boobs.'

Simone looks flummoxed. 'I have the . . . basic ingredients

for boobs?' she says slowly, and I nod encouragingly as Lauren gives me a helpless look.

Joely chimes in loudly. 'You're lucky,' she says, patting her own chest, which jiggles happily in response. 'Without a bra, these are already somewhere around my vulva. I have to push them aside when I'm having sex. And it's only going to get more and more inconvenient as I get older. At some point I'll need to have them up in stirrups for intercourse.'

Simone looks a little cheered and I pick up my glass. 'Let's get back to the celebration,' I say, clinking her drink and smiling nicely.

'Yes,' shouts Joely, adding, 'it's a Monday night, so let's drink ourselves to death!'

Simone's face falls again and she stutters, 'Actually, my cousin drank himself to death . . .'

Joely cuts her off. 'OK, that's enough about you for now.' Simone flinches as Joely continues, 'We're here for *my* cousin, Lauren; we don't want to gossip about your weird family right now.'

Joely doesn't care what Simone or anyone thinks, and that's probably what I like most about her. We all grew up in the same area, outside Manchester, and we knew each other as teenagers, but Joely went to a different school. It wasn't until after uni when we all moved into Manchester city and shared a flat that the three of us got to be best friends. Living together has a way of cementing a friendship – or cracking it wide open – and honestly, we could've gone either way. It was great for the most part – bonding over drunken takeaways, bonding over drunken film nights, bonding over drunken My Single Friend dates (yes, there was a lot of drinking and a lot of bonding) – but Lauren did almost murder Joely on a weekly basis over the bins. And also the washing up. And the hair in the drain. Oh, and also the hoovering. Basically, we wouldn't be where we are today if we hadn't eventually agreed to pitch in for a cleaner.

Joely is a plus-size model and actually kind of famous now. It is the weirdest thing when someone you know – someone who has peeled you unconscious out of a plate of garlic dough balls – becomes a Famous Person. She started blogging about clothes and beauty stuff five years ago, and last year she realised she was doing so well, she could quit her job as a fashion PR to be a full-time 'social media influencer'. I was so worried about her doing that, because I couldn't believe that was a real job that would pay her very real rent. But she has 2.3 fucking million followers on Instagram and one of those blue 'verified' ticks! She makes way more money than any of us now, and, whenever we're out, young girls are constantly coming over to fawn and ask for a Snapchat-filtered selfie with her. Actually, I'm surprised Simone hasn't said anything yet, because she looks just like every one of Joely's other fans – young, posh, fashionable and scared. You wouldn't believe the stuff she gets sent for free, too. Designer bags, posh make-up, clothes that never fit (why send a plus-size Insta-grammer size-eight clothes?!). She gets offered free luxury holidays just about every day, and all they ask for in return is some Instagram comment saying it's great. I told her she can't take the holidays because it wouldn't be ethical – and also mostly because they won't let her take us – but we've all agreed designer bags are absolutely fine.

The whole fame thing is confusing. But looking back now, it seems like it was always pretty much inevitable for Joely. She's had that star quality people talk about, right from day one. But probably much, much more important and relevant is just how extremely, ridiculously good-looking she is. She looks like that model, Ashley Graham, but hotter, taller and larger. Everything about her is big and luminous. As long as we've been friends, people have always turned and stared at her longingly when we enter a room. And unlike me – worrying that it's because everyone is judging me – Joely firmly believes and knows it's because she looks gooooood. She's always been my most terrifyingly confident friend, and it totally works for her.

She dominates every conversation, drawing in all the attention, and taking control in situations where I cower. All of which, I know, makes me sound like I'm a jealous bitch, and oh God I *so* am.

I'm really jealous of her effect on men, too. In case you haven't guessed, they are obsessed with her. They fall at her surprisingly in-proportion size-nine feet. It's weird because, if you scroll through some of the thousands of social media comments she gets on every post, you'd assume men hated her. The amount of male 'fans' telling her she's too fat to live and that she deserves to be raped to death is just . . . well, I guess, actually not that surprising with social media these days, but it's still awful. And yet, put her in front of a group of blokes in a bar and it's like they're hypnotised. On any one night out, at least three or four guys will come over to ask her out, or send over drinks. Joely loves the attention – which is handy given what she does for a living – and can give as good as she gets. If there's a man she fancies across the room, she'll just go over and ask him out, without any fear. Obviously, she's really offensive, like, all the time, and I wouldn't want to piss people off like she does, but I do wish I had the bravery to stand up for myself more and be honest like her.

Basically, I am somewhere between wanting to be Joely, and wanting to have sex with her.

Lauren squeezes Simone reassuringly, as Joely continues excitedly, 'Come on, then, Lozza, what are you thinking about for this wedding? Summer? Winter? What's the plan?'

Lauren looks sheepish, waving her hand dismissively. 'Oh, we don't have to get into all that tonight,' she says hurriedly. 'Let's just drink and chat. I don't want to be a boring bride who takes a notepad around with her everywhere she goes. Let's talk about you guys. Lilah, how's work? How's Will? How many cups of tea did you have to fetch for Rex today?'

I shake my head. 'Don't be silly, we want to talk about this!' I cock my head at her. 'Lauren, you're engaged! This is your big day!'

She takes a deep breath and makes eye contact with each of us around the table. 'OK, I don't want to freak anyone out, but Charlie and I have talked about it. And we've officially decided on Saturday ninth of December for the wedding.' She pauses and Joely looks at me, confused.

'*This* year?' I say, alarmed.

Lauren grimaces. 'Yes. And I know that's only six months away, but we don't want to waste the next two years obsessively planning this. I've seen enough mates go off the deep end planning their wedding. And Charlie really wants to do it sooner rather than later. He's worried about his grandparents not being alive much longer, and it's not going to be an over the top wedding abroad or anything . . .'

Joely shushes her furiously, leaning over the table towards her cousin. 'December?' she says, looking horrified. 'It can't be done, Lauren! What the hell are you thinking? People don't plan weddings like this in six months! You're going to have an atrocious fuckbag of a to-do list, Loz. It's impossible! The dress alone usually takes at least three or four months to be ordered and fitted.'

Lauren's eyes widen and she swallows hard.

I try a little more tact. 'It does sound like it might be a bit of a rush,' I say carefully. 'Are you sure you can't wait a little bit longer? Don't you want to enjoy being engaged for a while? And I thought you always wanted a summer wedding with a strapless dress? Are you sure a December wedding is what you want?'

Lauren takes a deep breath. 'I know all that. I know it's a big ask, but it's do-able,' she says, giving herself a determined shake. 'We're going to have the ceremony and reception at Charlie's dad's place, right, Simone? So the venue is already sorted. We just need to sort out the smaller stuff – a marquee, flowers, decorations, table plans, guest list, invitations ... Oh, and I've already ordered some cheap – non-strapless – dresses from abroad, which are possible wedding dresses, so they might be OK. And I know you'll help me, won't you?' She looks at me beseechingly before continuing. 'I think we can get most of what we need at, like, a couple of wedding fairs, right? So I just need to make speedy decisions and be prepared for a few compromises. But we can totally make this happen in six months ... can't we?' She pauses, swallowing hard, and I can see the cogs in her brain whirring.

'You're insane,' Joely pronounces, throwing her hands in the air. 'You don't realise all that's involved with wedding planning. Tell Charlie you don't care about his dying grandparents – soz, Simone – and that you want to do it next summer, earliest.'

Simone looks a bit hurt again but doesn't say anything. Lauren bites her thumbnail and I can see she's processing the magnitude of what's ahead. I feel myself breathing heavily, because she's not the only one. This is going to be a mammoth job.

Lauren looks at me, seeing my fear, and her lip trembles. She reaches for me, searching my face for reassurance. And I do the only thing I can and offer it.

'Don't worry, Lauren, we've got this,' I say firmly. And then I take her sweaty, quivering hand and I squeeze the hell out of it.

Wedding Number Two: Charlotte and Eamonn, Town Hall, Greater Manchester

Theme: Cheapness. It's on a Wednesday, which should tell you everything you need to know. Also, everyone keeps talking, misty-eyed, about 'finding love second time around', as if it's some kind of miracle, just because the bride and groom are in their fifties.

Menu: Smoked salmon starter, followed by chicken and a meringue dessert. Veggie option: stuffed red pepper with goat's cheese.

Gift: Joint membership to the National Trust with benefits @ £135.

Gossip: Despite being in her later life, the bride went pole dancing for her hen do, where she predictably slipped and broke her nose. She has two black eyes and spent her wedding day following the photographer around, telling him to please please Photoshop the pictures.

My bank balance: £305

3

Tom's lip trembles as he opens the door and sees me standing there. Bless my little brother, he does find things difficult. He pulls himself together as he notices the two figures standing with me and says with enthusiasm, 'Oh, hiya, reinforcements!' There is relief in his voice.

I've got Lauren here with me – she insisted on coming. She said I shouldn't have to 'deal with those arseholes' on my own. I pointed out that Will would be coming along to support me, and she just waved her hand dismissively. 'Your boyfriend is a sweetheart, Lilah,' she told me, graciously, 'but he's too nice in these situations, too diplomatic. I've known these idiots for half my life; I know how to handle them. I've got your back, I'll look after you.'

I fucking love Lauren.

On that subject, Tom very much loves Lauren too, but in a less platonic way, and he hugs her for a second too long after ushering me and my bodyguards inside. 'Thank God you've arrived,' Tom says to me when he eventually lets go of Lauren, pulling me in and whispering ominously in my ear, '*They're both here.*'

I pull away and place my hand on his shoulder, making square eye contact like I'm an army captain, reassuring my troops as we head over the trenches and into a hopeless battle. Which isn't even really an analogy – it's basically exactly what is happening.

'Don't worry, we can handle this,' I say determinedly. 'Are

they on opposite sides of the room pretending not to see each other, like usual?'

Tom nods, wide-eyed. 'They are,' he confirms. 'But they also each keep beckoning me over to their corner to slag the other one off. I've tried pretending I can't see them, but it's not working. You have to save me. Dad says he's going to slash Mum's tyres when she next goes to the loo.'

Let's get this out of the way right now: my parents are the worst. I love them because they're my mum and dad, but yeah, they're fucking awful. They divorced a few years ago and since then, it's like they can't see anything else. Their hatred of each other is all they care about and it's all that gets them through the day. And yet they still insist on being in a room together for events like this one – my brother's 25th birthday – in their quest to prove who is the bigger person. When I called each of them this week to discuss Tom's birthday, the conversation with both went something like this:

Me: Yes, I know it's his twenty-fifth, but he really, really doesn't want a fuss. He says he'd happily just go for lunch with all of us separately.

Mum/Dad: Why doesn't he want a fuss? Is this your father/ mother's doing? Because if he/she thinks I can't cope with an evening in the same room as him/her celebrating my only son's birthday, then he/she can go fuck him/herself. This is grossly unfair. I am an extremely, extremely mature adult – far more mature than him/her – and I am more than capable of being civil for the evening. He/ she may not be over our divorce, but I *certainly* am. I've moved on. I'm fine. I don't give a tiny shit about him/her.

Me: No, really, Mum/Dad, it's not that, he/she hasn't said a word, I promise. It's just that Tom doesn't want to do a big thing this year, and y'know, it's probably better for you both if you two aren't forced into a room together . . .

Mum/Dad: What do you mean by that? Has your father/ mother said something? Tell me what he/she said? Tell me EXACTLY.

Me: Oh, no no no, nothing, I promise. It's just—

Mum/Dad: I am an adult and even if he/she can't be civil, I can be pleasant. I'm *always* pleasant. Even though he/she is a bag of dogshit with a garbage mouth.

Me: OK, fantastic, I'll see you on Friday evening then. Can't wait.

They are both determined to prove they're winning the divorce. And it makes them super selfish. Anger does that to people, I think. It makes them only see their own problems. When I speak to my parents, it's all we talk about: their raging, burning fury about where their life has gone. Even at her cousin's wedding the other day, all Mum talked about was what a shit-for-brains my dad was. Sometimes it's funny, but mostly it's just tedious and embarrassing.

Which is how we find ourselves all here today, waiting on tenterhooks for an explosion as Tom's friends stare, completely absorbed, while the two sixty-year-olds glower at each other across the room like babies. But in a totally grown-up, civilised manner, of course.

Will takes my hand and squeezes it as we head into the large, open-plan living room. Tom lives in what he likes to call an 'urban commune'. Try not to roll your eyes – he's a sweet guy, really. It's essentially a big house with lots of housemates, who come and go fairly freely. Tom's a bit of a drifter and says he hasn't 'found his calling' yet. Which, I think, really just means he doesn't want to work for a living. He's currently earning his pocket money as an 'apprentice caricaturist', which, yes, is exactly what you think it is: someone who's learning to draw caricatures of tourists. You know the guy – he's always in your way on a busy pavement and he's always got a bad drawing of Jack Nicholson pinned up. And when you do let him draw you that one time because you feel sorry for him, he gives you a fucking huge nose that makes you go home crying and googling Harley Street surgeons.

'Gogetadrinkgladyou'rehere,' Tom says in one long breath, as we survey the room. He pats me awkwardly, gives Lauren a lingering, longing look, and then turns on his heel, scuttling off in the direction of the stairs. He gestures hurriedly to one of his greasy-haired friends, who runs after him. I know where they're going: they're off to hide in Tom's bedroom with a videogame, never to return. Leaving me to deal with all this. I can't believe my brother's twenty-five; I swear he's still fifteen.

I feel Mum and Dad's eagle eyes watching me as I cross the room. They're waiting to see which of them I will greet first. I will get so much passive-aggression based on this decision. Thank God we foresaw this eventuality – we totally have a plan.

'You ready?' Will whispers, grinning at me. I nod determinedly as he adds in my ear, 'After this, let's you and me go get a burger and we'll eat it in our pants on the sofa at home and then have bloated sex. We're really great at sex – even fat, burger sex – don't you think?' I giggle and he goes on. 'And hey, if you're *really* good, Lilah, I'll even go through your phone and delete all the pending news podcasts you have stacking up. I know you feel guilty for not listening to them, but we both know you only really want to listen to the gruesome murder-y podcasts.'

Will knows me too well.

I totally listen to the headlines of the news though!

Sometimes.

'Right, break!' Will hisses, as he and Lauren peel off in formation. Lauren to my mum, Will to my dad. Distract and conquer – this is the plan and precisely why I brought body-guards with me. I breathe a sigh of relief and head for the kitchen. I will most definitely need a drink for this.

When I return with a plastic pint cup full of wine, Will joins me, looking shifty. He is in full secret-service mode. He tried to get us to use codenames and a password earlier, but Lauren told him to stop being a dope.

He leans in excitedly. 'I told your dad there were old copies of *Loaded* mag in the upstairs bedroom,' he says in a hushed voice. 'He's gone to have a quick look. Now's your chance – go say hi to Alice. Hurry, though, he won't be gone for long.' I give him a grateful smile and stand on my tiptoes for a kiss. He immediately goes red – kissing in public is very much not Will's bag, particularly around in-laws – but he gives me a quick peck, and then his trademark goofy side grin. When he's feeling bashful, only one side of his mouth goes up. It's one of my favourite things about him.

Right, OK, if you promise not to judge, I will tell you how Will and I met.

You ready for this? No judging, remember?

It was in a free clinic about a year and a half ago, where we were both waiting for STD checks.

Just routine! Just routine, I swear.

Kind of routine.

I mean, I was probably due a test anyway. But OK, the week before, I had done 'the sex' with some guy from Tinder, and even though we used a condom, I worry about the stuff that gets up the sides, y'know? And also, after we'd finished, he took it off but then there was some more . . . touching. And I kept thinking, what if there was jizz on his hands and it got on my vagina? I didn't pay that much attention in sex education to all the euphemistic bananas, but the impression I got from the shouty PE teacher taking the lessons was that everything to do with genitals gives you hepatitis.

Anyway, I was in the waiting area, rehearsing what I'd say when I got into the tiny room and the nurse asked me if I'd ever had anal sex. ('Hmm, maybe once? By accident? It was just to impress this one lad because he used to go out with a glamour model.') I didn't realise I was pulling faces until the boy across from me, soon to be known as 'Will Hunt', started giggling. He awkwardly waved hello from his plastic chair and we smiled at each other. Me, full-on I-fancy-you-and-will-let-you-get-stuff-up-the-sides-any-day smile. Him, the first of many goofy side-smiles. I came out of the room a few minutes later and he was waiting awkwardly by the door to ask me out. We went for a drink and talked for hours about our lives and his work in the charity sector, as well as my fairly new job at the time – as an assistant producer on a daytime quiz show.

And when we both got the all-clear via a text eight days later, we celebrated with unprotected sex because I am just the absolute worst.

Condoms are over, STDs are in. Tell your friends.

That story isn't exactly wedding-speech material, so I just tell people we met on a dating app like everyone else.

'Oh Lauren, my pet, how wonderful,' Mum is saying coolly, examining her ring with a hint of disapproval as I join them. 'I'm sure you'll be very happy together. It's about time Charlie proposed. How long have you been together now?

Five years?' She doesn't wait for an answer before continuing dramatically. 'I had a chance to be happy once, but your father –' she shoots me a look – 'ruined all that. The fat twat.'

I ignore her, leaning in for a hug and a kiss on the cheek. 'Hey, Mum, nice to see you,' I say as she pats me distractedly.

'It hasn't put me off marriage, though,' she goes on, tittering prettily. 'If anything, it's made me more sure about getting re-married one day. After all, any man I meet now is going to seem absolutely fantastic after my previous experience. He will seem kind, loving, generous, and – at the very least – not a disgusting degenerate.' She glances nonchalantly over at the stairs, where my dad is re-emerging empty-handed and looking bereft. No luck with *Loaded* then.

Mum clears her throat and adds in a loud stage whisper, 'And whoever I date next is bound to have a much, much BIGGER PENIS.'

I take a long, slow, resigned breath. I don't need to look over at Dad to know he can hear. As can all of my brother's agog friends, who have fallen silent.

Mum opens her mouth to go again and Lauren takes a small, decisive step forward.

'That's enough now, Alice,' she says firmly. 'You don't need to say things like that in front of your daughter. Or, indeed, the whole room. No one needs to hear about Harry's willy, especially when Harry is their father. Not under any circumstance, really.' Lauren puts a protective arm around me and I feel a rush of gratitude – and a rush of fear that Mum will kick off.

'Oh, but I barely mentioned his TINY WILLY,' Mum starts, and Lauren gives her another hard stare. She harrumphs and blusters, 'I'm just saying that marriage is a wonderful thing and you're very lucky to be able to experience it with a man who isn't a dumpster fire of a human being.' She looks at me penetratingly before continuing. 'And make sure when you have children with him, Lauren, that you firmly agree on a name *before* you go into labour.'

Ah, yes. Thanks for that one, Dad.

So yes, my full name is Delilah Mary Fox. Which, yeah, I know, sounds like a character from *The Animals of Farthing Wood*. Or maybe porn. Depends where your brain's at.

My dad, Harry, is an obsessive Tom Jones fan and my mum was still high on gas and air when they registered the birth. She didn't realise what was going on until about a week later. Same thing happened with my little brother, who is even less subtly called Tom Jones Fox.

I don't want to be ungrateful, but I am really incredibly ungrateful. I hate it. My name draws attention and laughter wherever I go, and I've spent my life trying to convince people to call me Lilah instead of Delilah – or worse still, *Delly*. That was what the idiot boys at school always called me and I fucking hate it. Sometimes they would get even more creative and call me Delly the Belly, if they felt like maybe I'd temporarily forgotten that I was fat and needed a reminder.

But that was obviously all ages ago, and is very much long-forgotten history. I'm totally not holding on to a hundred different grudges that I can never fully avenge. ABSOLUTELY NOT.

At least Facebook lets me see how terribly their lives are all going now.

Lauren shakes her head. 'Alice . . .' she says warningly to my mum. She's heard all these speeches before, as have I.

Mum tuts. 'There's no need to be snappy, Lauren. I'm not even talking about Lilah's father necessarily, just . . .' She pauses, noting my friend's unchanged steely expression.

40

'Congratulations on your engagement. I hope you'll be very happy.'

Lauren smiles broadly and starts talking about veils, as across the room, I make eye contact with Will. We are barely twenty minutes in and he already looks defeated, grimacing as my dad talks animatedly, hands gesticulating wildly. I don't need to be able to hear the conversation to know my dad is currently justifying the size of his penis to my boyfriend. Poor Will. We share a little helpless shrug and I try to silently communicate that I will make it up to him later by going on top. Usually I can't be bothered – who has the energy for that, especially post-burger binge? – but he's earned it. Will nods, perking up like he gets it, and I turn back to my mum, who is telling Lauren about her own veil – which she set ablaze in a symbolic bonfire when she got her decree absolute.

Hmm, maybe the penis chat across the room would be better . . .

4

'I'm afraid we really do need someone here right away, if at all possible. It's an emergency.'

I'm using my nicest, most professional phone voice, and wishing I could muster more authority, but I don't think I have it in me.

'Yeah, see, I dunno if it's poss, though,' says the girl on the line, who clearly has me on loudspeaker in her office, and is simultaneously texting on her mobile while I plead. I can hear the clicking of the phone's keyboard noises she hasn't bothered to turn off.

'Did I mention I'm calling for Rex Powers? From *Quiz Monsters*?' I try again but she doesn't seem impressed. 'He says you usually do this for him at his home and are often able to accommodate his last-minute requests?'

More text clicking.

'Is there someone else I can talk to, maybe?' I say, trying to be strong, but wimping out of saying the dreaded 'your manager'.

'Nah,' she says, and it's barely a word, more of a noise. 'The others are all the way downstairs, so I can't ask them, and I'm not going down there to get 'em. I could do Rex at his place on Thursday?'

I lay my head on the desk in front of me, the phone hot on my ear. I can feel the cancer waves creeping into my brain.

'You see, the trouble is,' I say, my voice muffled by the wood

42

on my face, 'we're going on set in an hour and a half, and Rex says he really needs his chest done before the cameras can go on. He says you guys know exactly how to wax and style it to perfectly accentuate his man cleavage. Those are his words – I don't know what they mean.'

She's silent for another long moment. 'Yeah, we do do that,' she says. 'Loads of men love that one. But my boyfriend usually drives me to outside appointments and he's at the football.'

'Please,' I say again, and I hate the desperation in my voice. 'We'll get you a car. A posh car. We'll pay you twice your normal fee. Please. You don't understand, Rex won't let us start filming until his chest is done, and the producer will blame me if we're stuck here all night yet again.'

She sighs.

I try one more sympathy tactic. 'I might get fired.'

The phone clicking stops momentarily. 'OK, fine, where am I going?'

I've already told her three times, but I explain again, keeping the impatient scream firmly inside my head.

As I hang up, Rex thunders into the room. 'Is she coming?' he booms in his infamous quiz-host voice. His shirt is hanging open, showing off the aforementioned unruly and hideously un-contoured chest hair.

'Yep,' I say cheerfully, giving him a thumbs up, like it was no trouble.

'Well, tell her to hurry fucking up,' he says impatiently. 'Every minute that goes by, these blasted chest pubes get longer.' He gestures at himself and my eyes accidentally look at his body hair. I swallow some bile.

'You don't know how hard it is for me, darling, having

43

such thick, luxuriant hair,' he tells me dramatically, slumping down on the sofa in the corner. 'You're so lucky to have thin, unimportant hair that the public don't care about.' He lays a flannel across his face. 'Get me some hot water, will you?' he says. 'I'll do my pores while I wait.'

I want to tell him we have runners and interns for this kind of thing. I want to point out there's a sink literally next to his stupid head. I want to tell him to fuck off. But I don't. I just go over and fill up the bowl.

You wouldn't believe it, but I am not actually Rex's PA. Unfortunately, I made the mistake of *not* making any mistakes early on in our working relationship and now he thinks I am the only one he can trust to do anything. He says the runners are 'a bag of burning poop' who 'cock everything up'. Which is true, but it's still not my fucking job.

When I started here nearly two years ago, I was so sure it was going to be the dream role. I'd done my time as a runner at a production company, then as researcher somewhere else, then as researcher again. Getting bumped up to AP was a big deal. And not just any old AP – I'm the assistant producer at one of the highest-rated daytime quiz shows on BBC9! I've always been obsessed with quizzes. When I was growing up, Franny and I used to watch *Who Wants to Be a Millionaire* every day, and our joint life aim was to be someone's phone a friend. For a long time, as a teenager, I thought Chris Tarrant was my ideal man, until I realised he doesn't actually know the answers to any of the questions, he just reads them out. I can't tell you how many Sunday pub quizzes I've dragged Lauren and Joely along to. Franny's the best teammate, though – she's the smartest person I've ever met. She was in Mensa when she was younger! She has one of those photographic memories, and an IQ of

156, which is incredibly handy in those seventies pop trivia rounds.

Anyway, working on *Quiz Monsters* seemed like it would be the most brilliant, fun job in the universe, and I was so sure those Facebook fuckers with their eight kids and nappy posts would die of jealousy. But it's never quite what you think it will be, is it? Everyone told me the host was 'difficult' – they warned me – but I thought I could handle it. I mean, I'm great with difficult people! I can nice-person anyone into submission! But it feels like all I've done with my two years here is turn myself into Rex Powers' lackey. And I'm still not totally sure he even knows my name. He calls me 'darling' a suspicious amount.

I step out of the office and flag Sam down. She's the only runner who isn't a total moron, and I'm her official 'mentor' here.

I really like her, actually. She's great. She's straight out of school, couldn't afford to go to university (because who the hell can these days?) but still wanted desperately to work in telly, so has been doing work experience like a demon for two years, while simultaneously working night shifts at a bar to pay her way. She's a grafter and proper northern, so of course she thinks all the other rich interns and rich everyones are idiots. Actually, I picked her CV out of the pile just to annoy Rex and my producer, but she's been a godsend.

'Can you get me an urgent car?' I say, handing her the address. 'Tell them it's genuinely life or death.'

'Ooh, is it for someone famous?' she says excitedly and I grin. If you work in telly you're not supposed to get starstruck, but Sam loves a famous person. We have guest stars on the show sometimes and she can barely keep a lid on it.

She is so excited about this massive end-of-series live celebrity special we're currently planning. I'm excited too, but it is also the bane of my existence. You have no idea the egos I'm dealing with. It's funny because the very few A-listers I've dealt with have always been absolutely dreamy. They are professional and friendly and get on with whatever you've asked them to do. But anyone D-list or below? You cannot imagine the levels of dreadful. I think it's because the lower down the celeb scale you are, the less prepared you are for the unscrupulous yes-men who descend on you when you find fame. These people will say absolutely anything to get in with you. They will climb up inside your rectum and nestle there, taking the free drinks and the free drugs, encouraging your ego to spiral out of control, until you truly believe you're the most beloved A-list celeb to ever leave *Love Island*.

Actually, shh, but I think maybe I'm kind of starting to see a bit of this in Joely.

And you should see the fees these people are commanding! Not to mention their dressing-room rider demands. There's an ex-Hollyoaks actor I won't name who has genuinely requested 'three women' be provided in his room 'upon arrival'. I am tempted to call his mum and sisters and have them be there.

But I'm hoping it'll be worth it. Live TV is always the most exciting kind of TV, and it's great for my CV that I'm heading this up.

'Sadly no famouses this time,' I tell Sam, shaking my head. 'Oh, but Davina McCall's recording in the other studio next week,' I say in hushed tones, checking no one can hear us gushing.

'Ooooh, I love her!' Sam says and I laugh. Duh, everyone

46

loves Davina. She's a glorious, shimmering goddess, and when Rex gets crushed to death by his own inflated ego one day, I pray Davina will come take over as host of this show.

Sam runs off, already on her phone, sorting the taxi.

I pull out my to-do list, stretching my arms to the ceiling as I do. I'm going to yoga later and I can't wait to sweat the day off. It's full-on when we're mid-series like this. Eighty episodes, recording every weekday for months – it doesn't stop. The latest group auditions don't start until next week, though, and Aslan – my fellow AP and work husband – is babysitting today's contestants. I might just have time to grab some food from the canteen before filming starts.

My phone vibrates in my back pocket. I keep it there because it feels nice on my bum cheek and I'm not ashamed to say it.

Six messages are waiting patiently from Lauren: three asking for my thoughts on prawn cocktail starters (I have no thoughts on prawn cocktail starters) and the others listing agenda points for our next wedding meeting later this week. It feels a lot to me like items we've already talked about. Many times. In fact, I am fairly certain, barely a few weeks into this engagement, we've already exhausted every possible element of wedding chat. But every time I think a decision has been made, something else comes up. So much for Lauren's promise to make quick decisions. I breathe out, feeling a tiny bit overwhelmed. Work is too busy for prawn cocktails. Sliding my phone back in my pocket without replying, I head for the studio canteen. I need a coffee, some cake and a Franny chat.

Franny is my grandma. Granny Franny is her name, which – I know! – is hilarious, isn't it! But she's not just *my*

47

grandma; she's the communal grandma around here. She got the job of tea lady/canteen supervisor just after I became AP. The impression I get from the rest of the catering staff is that she just sort of turned up one day and told them she was having a job. It's ridiculous, given how competitive TV is, but Granny Franny is a force of nature. She barrels in, announces to the world what she wants, and won't take no for an answer. And because she's literally ninety years old, I think everyone felt too awkward to say no. She threatens to die on you if you say no to her, so it's probably better they didn't try.

I really love having her so close to me. I want her around as much as I'm allowed, at all times. Because even though she's more alive than anyone you've ever met, I still know there is a ... *time limit* on this relationship. I hate even thinking that because she is my favourite person in the entire universe, but I have to be somewhat realistic – she is a nonagenarian, after all. Granny Franny is like a mum and a best friend, as well as being a brilliant grandma. My parents had quite a volatile marriage from day one, and Franny only lived two streets away, so I spent most of my childhood over at her house doing our quizzes, and listening to her recite whole chapters from books she'd memorised for my bedtime stories.

Much as I love my parents, I think of Franny as being the one who really raised me – all the good parts of me, anyway – and our daily lunches together mean a lot.

In the steamy cooking area, Franny looks as fake-busy as ever. Her role is mostly supervisory, because she doesn't actually really know how to cook, but she definitely likes to boss people about. Her 'experience' is deeply appreciated, by which I mean, the rest of the kitchen staff are afraid of her. As I walk over, Franny is waving her walking stick in the air. She doesn't really need it, but she says it makes her look 'grand, like Maggie Smith'. She says she's the dowager of the canteen, which is 'way better than Downton fucking Abbey'. The subject of the stick-waving is poor Andrea. Andrea is Franny's closest friend and also Franny's worst enemy; she gets a lot of stick, literally and figuratively. Right now, Franny is shouting at her about the chip fat needing more fat. Her cooking advice is almost always 'more fat'.

As she spots me across the kitchen, her lovely creased face lights up. Andrea gives me a relieved nod hello and shuffles away as I join my grandma, resting my head on her shoulder.

'I've only got ten minutes, while Rex gets his chest waxed,' I say conversationally, as I help myself to a tuna sandwich from the counter and hand her the usual egg mayo.

'Can I watch?' she asks as we sit down at a table around the back. She fancies Rex.

I roll my eyes as Franny narrows her eyes at the sandwich.

'This looks fucking disgusting,' she mutters resentfully.

I snort. 'Your girls made it, didn't they?'

She shrugs and all the loose skin around her face rearranges itself into an expression of disapproval.

'You can't get the staff these days,' she says, peeling back the cling film before taking a large, happy bite of the wilting bread. Mouth full, she continues, 'I would put my last shilling on Andrea having made this one – it tastes like Andrea. It has that metallic tang of cheap French perfume and sad, abandoned wife.' She cackles evilly and I have a sudden memory of her reading me Roald Dahl's *The Witches* when I was little. She was so good at the scary voices.

Franny takes another bite before continuing – she always prefers to have a mouthful of food when she's talking. 'So how is my darling Rexy today?' she says, through smooshed egg. 'I'm glad to hear he takes care of himself, although personally I do prefer a full chest.' This is true to the extreme. Franny's usual type is very small, very hairy men. Her last husband, Husband Number Four, was the spit of Danny Devito.

'He's a nightmare, as usual,' I say, and she reaches out to stroke my hand soothingly. It's nice but now I have egg on my hand.

'You should put him in his place occasionally. It would be good for him' she says, gently scolding, and I laugh out loud.

'I'd lose my job, Franny. He likes his assistants silent.'

She cocks her head at me. 'He doesn't treat your friend Aslan like that, though, does he? And he's the same work level as you, isn't he?'

'Yes,' I say, swallowing a bite of my sandwich. 'But he's a man. He's less experienced than me, he started this job after me, and bless him, he's not as good as me – but obviously he's on more money and gets more respect. It's the way the world works. You should see the way the contestants all ignore me when he's there, or treat me like I'm the tea lady.'

Franny puffs out her chest, sitting up straighter. 'Nothing wrong with being a tea lady, Delilah,' she says huffily.

'Oh no, no, I know,' I say quickly. 'I only mean that it's not my job. I'm meant to be the assistant producer – I report to the actual producer of the show! – and yet I always seem to be the one fetching and carrying. And Rex is the worst of them all. He's always openly telling everyone how he likes his women submissive – he even says it on the telly. It's his *brand*. He thinks women should be in heels and lipstick at all times.' I sigh.

'You need to stand up for yourself more,' she says, thumping her stick on the ground. 'You let people run you ragged and take advantage. Your boss, your colleagues, even your family. Has that brother of yours paid back that money yet?'

I blush. It's been a few weeks since I lent Tom another £100, and of course he never pays it back. I can hardly get him to answer the phone, never mind transfer money into my bank account.

I shake my head and Franny sighs, changing the subject. 'How are things with Will?'

I smile at this, thinking about our lovely, quiet weekend together. We went to the cinema to see a shit horror film on Sunday, and then did our traditional race home. He got an Uber and I got the bus, and even though he beat me, we agreed that I was the true winner because I didn't have to deal with the social awkwardness of chatting to the Uber driver.

'He's fine,' I say simply. 'Work want him to take on some extra projects this summer, so he's going to be busy, but if he does well, it could mean a big promotion for him.'

Franny nods. 'Well, tell him he still has to come see me some time, even when he's a big-shot charity mogul. The last time I saw him, he promised me we could get drunk on sherry. Maybe he could even join us one Thursday night, Lilah? He owes me, you tell him that.'

'I shall indeed,' I say, standing up. I better go check how Rex's chest contouring is progressing.

'Oh, your dad rang me earlier,' she says suddenly. 'He says you haven't returned his calls from the other day and he wants you to know that your mother is a witch. He says his penis used to be a perfectly good size, but they did something to him during the vasectomy – it wouldn't stop bleeding afterwards – and now it's not as big as it used to be but it's still better than average.'

I shriek and cover my ears. 'Oh my God, Franny, why would you tell me this? About your own son, too?!'

She throws her head back, cackling. 'I just thought it was funny. I'll say anything if I think it's funny.'

Wedding Number Three: Harriet and Jamie, Trunch Hall, Liverpool

Theme: Red and gold. The bride's side were all in gold, while the alcoholics on the groom's side were glowing bright red.

Menu: Smoked salmon starter, followed by chicken and a meringue dessert. Veggie option: stuffed red pepper with goat's cheese.

Gift: A personalised Moet magnum @ £120.

Gossip: Groom's dad surprised everyone at the reception with a performance he'd been practising for weeks. He sang 'Blurred Lines' by Robin Thicke. Yes, that song basically about rape. What is your point?

My bank balance: £232.56

5

I. Am. Broken.

It's Sunday night and I've spent a long weekend with Lauren and Joely at a wedding show fair thingy. Which means I've had forty-eight hours of being shoved out of the way by intense-looking women with unwashed hair in a bun and crazy eyes. There was this one particularly feral lady, who I think might haunt my dreams. She was trying to rip a bouquet in half to prove some kind of a point to a florist, and when security literally carried her away, she screamed that we were 'cum for brains' and that every single one of us would be 'butt-fucked in hell'. The florist didn't seem that bothered, she said it happens to a lot of her brides, and that the woman who'd been taken away – Marie – was usually a 'really nice lady who works in HR.' And yes, she'd still be providing her with the tulip and lily arrangements they'd agreed on in saner moments. Lauren was impressed with her professionalism – she says she's going to hire her.

It was really full-on, and oh God, I'm worried about Lauren turning into one of those screaming ladies. I'm already seeing hints of it. There was definitely a moment earlier when I thought she was going to go full bridezilla over the type of chocolate they use in the chocolate fountain. It was like when Bruce Banner started his transformation into the Incredible Hulk but instead of gamma radiation, Lauren's trigger is Lindt. Obviously I love her, but she's always been a, er, high-octane human. Planning a giant wedding in

54

less than six months is going to be the most stressful thing imaginable.

I got back from the event a couple of hours ago, drained and broken, to find Will already in bed, reading. He bounced up, pleased to see me, proudly presenting some fridge left-overs for my dinner. We watched an episode of *Game of Thrones* together, then had guilty sex, knowing full well it was inspired by the sexy incest. That show has really done a lot for the image of incest, hasn't it? The producers should bill counsellors for all the hours of therapy we need now.

Lying in bed, I told Will about my day, and he listened intently as I told him how Lauren had settled 'definitely this time' on another gown. This will be her – hold on, let me count – seventh choice of wedding dress. She hated all the internet dresses she'd ordered (who saw that coming?) and we've been scouring bridal shops ever since for alternatives. Now all I see when I close my eyes is an endless sea of white silk. But Lauren says the dress is the most important part. She says that even if Charlie stands her up at the altar, so long as she has an incredible dress to wear, she 'won't care'. She started talking about how she'd be like Carrie Bradshaw, running after Big in her perfect dress. Forget the groom or the vows, Lauren says any decent wedding is only about the dress and the attention. Joely agreed very noisily with Lauren, so I did too.

Beside me, Will shifts into the big spoon and I can feel he is tensing to say something.

'Lilah?' he says sleepily into my neck. 'Will you marry me?'

I sit bolt upright in bed. What the fuck?

'Are you serious?' I squeak, my heart suddenly beating too fast as a wave of sickness washes over me.

He opens one eye, squinting at me. 'What?'

I turn to face him properly. He's smirking. I fight the urge to shake him.

'Will, I'm not kidding, I need to know if you're being serious.'

'Yeah, go on, marry me,' he says, but his tone is still light.

'You're proposing to me like that? Are you really, seriously proposing to me like that? Is this a joke?' I poke him and I can feel my palms are clammy. 'Will? Will?'

He closes the eye again and smiles lazily, rolling over in the bed and away from me.

'I'll take that as an enthusiastic yes then,' he says.

I stare down at him, my heart still thumping. Was it a joke? The tightness in my chest and shallow breathing indicates that my body, at least, thinks not. It's not the first time he's mentioned maybe becoming a Mr and Mrs, but it was always in a big ONE DAY kind of way. He's made several references to it – casually talking about a misty, unrecognisable future together in the countryside wearing wellies. I would always smile and nod, without giving it much thought. And there's certainly never been an actual proposal before – jokey or otherwise. Also, now I'm thinking about it, this is exactly the type of proposal Will would do: something laid back and post-coitus. He's a low-key person, and doesn't like drama and attention. He doesn't have it in him to do something elaborate or public. He cringes at those viral flash-mob proposals that end up on YouTube and won't even read Buzzfeed for fear of a dancing in-law.

Maybe this is . . .

No, no, come on, he's joking, he must be. We've only been together about twenty months, and I still feel too young at twenty-eight to be thinking about marriage, even if everyone else is. But then, every age I've been has felt too young for anything grown-up. I'm still not sure I'm ready to lose my virginity, even though that ship sailed when I was fifteen, thanks to my summer holiday boyfriend, Jim.

Side note: Jim still sends me regular inappropriate Snapchats about taking my 'cherry'. He got really excited by that cherry-themed filter recently.

Also, if I'm being completely honest, I'm not sure getting married is what I want anyway. I've never been that fussed about the idea. I wasn't one of those kids dreaming about my Big Day or marching elaborately dressed Barbies up the aisle in my bedroom. I was usually too busy making my Barbies have sex with each other to worry about whether it was sanctioned in the eyes of the Lord. Marriage never really seemed like an important thing. I've talked about it a bit before with Lauren and Joely – and even Tom, actually – and they all said I would change my mind. I thought I probably would too, but actually, the more of my life I spend at these endless weddings and hen dos, the more sure I feel that it's not for me. The expense, the showiness, the stress and the expectation raining down on you – none of it feels like it will ever appeal to me.

Plus, of course, my biggest marriage example isn't exactly a glowing endorsement of the institution. My parents racked up a good twenty-five years of mutual loathing before their divorce. Would I really want to take the chance of ending up in something like that? I never want to hate someone as much as my parents hate each other. I know that isn't the fault of marriage, exactly, but maybe they wouldn't have stayed together for so long if they hadn't signed a pointless piece of paper and made vows to a God they don't even believe in.

Silence fills the room and I can feel Will is waiting beside me, his shoulders tense, but my throat is too tight to say anything.

I stare at a spot on his back and fight the urge to pop it. He hates it when I do that. Although it would probably resolve this maybe wanting-to-marry-me thing. He very nearly ended things during our fourth date, when we were meant to be watching the latest Marvel movie at his place, and I got obsessed with an ingrown hair on his leg. I ended up using my tweezers on it and he hid in the loo for half an hour until I swore I'd never do it again. But I was lying. Will says I'm a weird mixture of being too over-familiar and too private and hard to read. But he says it nicely, like he thinks it's a good thing.

Right, enough now. God, even if a proposal was something I was waiting desperately for, getting engaged this year is completely out of the question. I've been to three weddings already in the last couple of months and I'm still reeling from Harriet's last weekend. Maid of honour Nina and the other bridesmaids did a rap and Will hid in the loo for ninety per cent of the day. And we still have so many others to get through this year. Plus, of course, the ever-increasingly mammoth task of being maid of honour for Lauren. She keeps telling me in a jokey voice that I 'better' be there for her and how she needs my 'absolute commitment' as her maid of honour. I keep telling her I'm up for it and it'll be fine, but I'm starting to really shit myself. There's still so much to do, and Lauren keeps changing her mind about everything.

But what else can I say? I can't say no now, just because it's starting to look like this is going to require the most insane amount of time and effort – not to mention money – in human history. My overdraft is starting to creak and I've just applied for a third credit card to keep me going through this Year of a Million Weddings.

Lauren would also be completely livid if I got engaged ten

seconds after her. Like I was copying her or trying to steal her thunder. We're not at school anymore, with me trailing around behind cool, popular, beautiful Lauren. We've finally escaped that friendship dynamic – and I'm not about to start it up again.

Will knows all this. He knows I'm a total people pleaser and he knows getting engaged right now wouldn't be allowed. That's even if we were actually ready for something like that. Which we're absolutely not.

The silence has gone on for too long now, but this isn't some throwaway conversation I can just ignore. I have to say something, respond properly, talk it through. I can't escape by pretending I've fallen asleep or something.

The silence stretches out.

I pretend to be asleep.

Breathing heavily into his neck, I take a moment to enjoy how nice and peaceful – serene, even – this feels, just lying here in the . . .

OK, yeah, I'm still thinking about the proposal.

Was it a proposal? There wasn't a ring. He didn't go down on one knee. That's the stuff we're supposed to expect and want, isn't it? Honestly, I should be cross he tried to propose in a pool of his own semen. Is that the story I'm meant to tell my family? 'Oh, Mummy dearest, Will popped the question half asleep while his balls were resting on my leg.' I wait quietly in the semi darkness, his body heat warming me through.

Why am I not just saying yes? Will and I get on so well. We have so much fun and so much in common. And he's sexy in a way. Lots of ways. Very sexy! He's quite tall – tall enough for me anyway, since I'm only five foot three – with dark features and sweet grey eyes. And, oh, he is so, so nice. Really nice. I know that doesn't sound particularly exciting, but it's a big plus point in the together-forever column. And personally, I think nice gets a bad rap. You always see people screwing up their nose disdainfully when they call someone 'nice' – like it's a terrible, lame flaw. I don't get that. Like, my parents' relationship – that wasn't nice. They revelled in torturing each other – they still do. They enjoy the drama of being unhappy and fighting constantly. Hating each other seems to be their 'thing'. Which I guess is fine, except I wish they wouldn't drag me into it so much.

So yeah, nice is nice. It's easy and straightforward and there's no fighting.

OK, look, the only tiny problem with nice is that it's hard to criticise someone for anything when you know their intentions are so good. I really struggle to tell Will when he's upset me, because I know he would never *mean* to hurt me. Telling him off would be like kicking an adorable, innocent puppy, and I couldn't do that to a puppy. Not that he's a puppy. My boyfriend is not a puppy. He's lovely. And even if he were a puppy, puppies are BRILLIANT. But he's not one. Don't tell him I called him a puppy.

The heat of his body is suddenly too much and I roll away from him, my mind drifting into a weird white future. And when I fall asleep, I dream vividly about a screaming woman in a florist, ripping the heads off puppies.

6

Rex barrels into the meeting room, sending interns scattering like bowling pins as he goes. Grabbing a chair at the head of the table, he spins it backwards, kicking a researcher in the crotch as he mounts it. The guy howls but Rex takes no notice.

'Are these trousers too tight?' he barks, and the whole room's eye level drops to the bulge on display, straddling the open back of his chair.

Aslan, sitting across from me, is the first to recover.

'Absolutely not, Rex,' he says authoritatively. 'In fact, I've been meaning to tell you all morning how bloody fantastic your *silhouette* looks today.' He makes deliberate eye contact with me and I have to turn away, pretending to look for a notebook. He will not make me laugh in a meeting again. Not this time.

Rex looks suspicious. 'Are you sure? Do you think maybe I should go even tighter then?'

Aslan pretends to think about this hard. 'Look, Rex, I'm going to level with you.' He leans in across the table. '*Yes, I think you should go tighter.*'

Rex nods very seriously and my boss, the series producer, clears his throat.

'Maybe we could chat about this in wardrobe after today's meeting, Rex?' he says firmly. 'We have a lot to go through.'

Rex looks bored, but listens as we talk through the latest batch of questions and go through any updates on the live

61

celeb special. That's my area, and I list off who we've got tentative yesses from so far. Then I tell them about the ex-*Hollyoaks* actor and his rider request. Everyone laughs except Rex.

'Can we do that then? Can we request hookers? Why didn't I know about that?' he says to me, completely straight-faced.

I swallow my feminist outrage at the word 'hookers' and pretend to think about it, hoping my producer will save me. He's meant to be my manager; surely this is inappropriate work conduct? Have we learned nothing from Harvey Weinstein?

After an awkward silence, Aslan clears his throat and dives in. 'Actually, Rex, rumour on the A-list grapevine has it that sex workers are totally passé these days.' He gives Rex a jovial bro (brovial) slap on the back and laughingly adds, 'And you can't fool us, Rex! We know you don't need to pay someone to take care of your needs – you have hordes of women clamouring to date you! Especially in those trousers, I bet. Look, you can't walk into a room without people falling at your feet.' He gestures at the researcher on the ground, still holding his kicked penis. 'You're just trying to make us all feel better about having to be close to someone so attractive and intimidating, aren't you, Rex?' He finishes his speech with a wink.

Rex takes the bait and nods self-importantly. 'You got me, Aslan. Never mind, Lilah.'

The producer clears his throat and returns to the agenda.

Aslan grins at me across the table. I smile gratefully.

I'm so jealous of Aslan. He's got the Rex-pandering absolutely nailed – he always knows exactly what to say to get the host to do exactly what he wants. Obviously, I'm a massive suck-up too, but in a wimpy, passive way. Aslan knows how to manipulate people with his sycophancy. I just cower and let them take what they need.

I suppress a yawn, wishing the room was cooler. The meeting rooms are always so hot, it's infuriating. The company policy is that it's not worth installing air conditioning given we usually have exactly one day of summer in Manchester per year. But these rooms somehow magnify the sun's rays, so that it feels like a sauna, night and day. And with most of the production team all crammed in together – and Rex's crotch stretched out and bulging across the back of that chair, giving off waves of heat (I swear there's practically steam wafting off his groin) – there's no escaping it.

But it's not just the temperature making me sleepy. I was out at Lauren's again until fairly late last night. This week's obsession is with her wedding Instagram account @BestWeddingEverCharlieLovesLauren. She's put me in charge of it (password: AllOtherWeddingsSuck) and says I need to get everyone to follow the account now, before the wedding, so we can keep everyone updated on plans and new developments. She also asked me if I could get everyone I work with to follow the account – to 'get the numbers up'. So far, only Aslan has obliged.

On the bright side, though, it's been pretty nice spending so much time with her and Joely on a regular basis. I realised the other day that's been the thing I like least about being a grown-up: how life and work gets in the way of sitting around, all day and all night, with your best friends. It feels like we've been able to recapture a little bit of that, seeing each other so much. Simone's been too busy with her latest career strategy to come to the meetings or help much with anything else. She bought a timeshare a couple of weeks ago, which will definitely work out just fine I am saying nothing it's none of my business. But a bit of distance is probably a good thing since she was clearly so frightened of us. Joely says we're better off without her helping because it would be like having a 'moron on work experience' around. She says Simone is a 'walking ellipses', and when I asked her what that means, she told me that Simone's whole personality is 'an unfinished sentence trailing off'. And I know that's mean, but you have to admit it's also fairly poetic.

By the time I get out of the meeting and over to the canteen, Franny is already halfway through her egg sandwich. She has a little bit of dried yolk on her cheek and I smile to myself, watching her eat for a long moment before I sit down. A rush of warm affection fills me for my messy grandma.

I'm going to tell her what happened with Will. I don't know why I haven't already. I usually tell her everything, but a long week has gone by and every time I opened my mouth to explain, the words wouldn't come. I think I just wanted to pretend it wasn't real. Because it probably wasn't! I still don't even know if it was a genuine proposal. He hasn't said anything else about it since.

'Um, Franny? Will sort of, kind of, semi . . . asked me to marry him,' I say and I sit down heavily.

She swallows and looks me dead in the eye. 'I hope you said no?'

I feel a pang in my stomach.

'I thought you liked Will?' I say, a bit worried. Franny's always said the right things about my boyfriend – I thought they got on well – and it really matters to me. If Franny didn't like the Significant Someone in my life, that would be a deal-breaker. Not only is she super smart (Mensa, don't forget!) and a good judge of character, but she's the most important human in my life.

She's already waving her weathered hands dismissively, before the words are out of my mouth, bits of her egg sandwich hitting the table next to us. Three assistants on their lunch break stare over.

'I do like him, I do,' she says impatiently. 'Especially when he brings me sherry. He's a sweet boy. Very sweet. Like a puppy.'

I glance over my shoulder guiltily, like he might hear. He's not a puppy, I promise he's not.

She goes on. 'But, my darling, sweet, wonderful girl, you're not ready to get married.'

I study the crumbs on the table and say casually, 'Everyone else is doing it.'

'If everyone else jumped off a cliff,' she twinkles at me, 'you should be climbing up the rock face instead.'

I give over to the cheesy moment and smile broadly at her. Franny's always been a fan of doing the very opposite of whatever you're meant to.

She pauses and looks hard at me again. 'Do you want to get married, Delilah?'

I open my mouth to reply, and instead I feel myself start to well up.

Oh God. Tears? Now? Really? I glance over at the nearby assistants but they're caught up in their own conversation.

I shake my head, trying to dismiss the sudden emotions, feeling annoyed at my unnecessary reaction. I don't even know why I'm crying.

Shit, I wish I had more control over myself! I'm such a stupid, stupid, stupid dickhead. I don't cry like a normal person, I never have. The moments when crying would be a perfectly reasonable, acceptable reaction – that's when I clam up and get all dead inside. But any level of unnecessary kindness and I lose it entirely. Last week I went to the GP to get a repeat prescription for the pill and the nurse asked me if there was anything else I wanted to talk about. I fully burst into tears. I didn't have anything to talk about, I just couldn't help it. It's like a trained response. Especially when I'm hormonal and tired. I will cry over kindness, unkindness, margarine adverts, Jennifer Aniston never reuniting with Brad Pitt, the abstract concept of death, a really nice door. Anything.

Except I'm not even hormonal, so that's not it.

'Oh, my darling girl, what is it?' Franny says, reaching for me and pulling me in for a cuddle. I sag into her and let the tears roll down my face for a minute.

'I don't know, actually. I'm sorry,' I say a little weakly, trying to get myself together. 'I think I'm just really tired. I was out again last night with Lauren and I've been working too hard lately. I have such a huge to-do list. I have so much to think about with all these weddings and hen dos – plus it's costing me a fortune – and I'm worried I haven't been spending enough time with Will. I keep cancelling our date plans – twice in the last couple of weeks – and he's been so nice about it, but he wouldn't tell me if he was annoyed anyway. And I'm scared things are weird between us because of this non-proposal. Oh, and, of course, I've been running about after Lauren so much . . .'

Franny tuts. 'How is that bridezilla of yours?'

I try not to smile. 'Don't be mean, Franny. Lauren's not that bad.'

Franny narrows her eyes and mutters, 'Yet.'

I ignore her, sitting back up and dabbing my eyes before continuing. 'And it's normal that she wants everything to be so completely perfect. You only get one wedding, after all.'

Franny cackles. 'You can have as many weddings as you bloody well want,' she says. Franny has been divorced three times and outlived her last husband, Geoffrey. He was a farmer she met online – the one who looked like Danny Devito – and they had a long-distance relationship because he lived in Somerset. Franny said it was 'mostly just about sex, anyway'.

I know, I know, try not to think about it too much.

When Geoffrey died two years ago, Franny and I started spending even more time together. As well as seeing her here all the time, we also have our Fuddy-Duddies United club every Thursday evening, over at the local youth club. It's us and around fourteen hot mess old women just like my granny. Franny and I started the club a few years ago as a place to practise our pub trivia and talk about the latest sudoku app updates. We knew it was essentially a bad rip-off of the WI, and I did suggest we join the actual WI, but Franny said they're 'too cool' now, because 'the jam-making isn't the priority it once was'. So we asked the council if we could use the space every Thursday night. They said yes, and we've converted it for our needs. Since then, we've expanded a bit and turned into something more than just a trivia club. We started being more proactive in the community. We do fundraisers and charity walks for the homeless, and visit local schools to life coach kids who hate us. It's great fun!

It keeps everyone active, and I don't want to sound like one of *those* people, but it makes me feel good on the inside. We, like, *help* people. And for a while, loads of new people wanted to join. We had women of all ages coming along on a Thursday night – even Lauren and Joely turned up to one meeting. But one of the original old-lady members – Molly – hated that. She said she didn't want all these 'young people' and their 'modern world ways' intruding on her club. So she used her old lady powers to drive them away by being racist and – even worse – judgy. And the younger members did not like it. Old people being weird about the Chinese is one thing, but when they won't stop calling your new unicorn jumper 'hideous, cheap polyester shit', that will drive anyone away. So now it's just the old ladies and me again.

Actually, it's probably my favourite night of the week. It's hard to explain how awesome it is speaking to these incredibly clever women about their lives. And plus, they always have the BEST gossip about the woman who lives across the road, above the souvenir shop. The latest is that she's apparently having an affair with the dog walker! He's only 22!

Franny is still speaking. 'But that's another reason I assume you'll say no to Will – your best friend would never forgive you if you got engaged while she's engaged. Not that I think Lauren's diva tantrums should stop you if you actually wanted to do it.'

'Oh, I know,' I say hastily. 'I wouldn't do that to her. I wouldn't want to steal her limelight. Trust me, I'm more than happy for Lauren to have her moment. And it's irrelevant because I really think Will was only joking anyway. It was just a joke. He is such a joker.' I laugh but it's hollow, and Franny cocks an arched, quizzical eyebrow at me. It conveys so much, that left eyebrow of hers. Arching one brow is a skill I have always wanted to master. I practised for months when I was little, but these face-slugs I have won't do anything but sit there looking cross. They're very straight and dark, like a child has taken a whiteboard pen to my face. And I specifically say *child*, because they're also entirely unsymmetrical. It is very sad. As if that wasn't bad enough, the right one has a big bald patch in the centre, from when Lauren gave me a 'makeover' aged fourteen. I ended up with green hair, purple sparkly eyeshadow and extremely over-enthusiastically tweezed brows. A bit of one never grew back properly so I have to colour the patch in every day.

'I said no to him, so I'm not sure why I'm even still talking about it. It's not a big deal.'

Franny side-eyes me as she licks her fingers and dabs at the crumbs on her plate. 'Good girl,' she says agreeably.

'Anyway, yes, Lauren is great, thanks for asking.' I quickly change the subject back. 'I'm meeting her and Joely for our weekly wedding meeting on Friday. This one is about making a final decision on the hen do over a glass of fizz. It's very important.'

Franny tuts. 'Hen dos these days.' She rolls her eyes exaggeratedly. 'It used to be that going for a glass of fizz *was* the hen do. Never mind pre-hen dos to plan the sodding hen dos. It's all so excessive. Everyone wants to out-do and one-up everyone else. You're not going abroad, are you?'

I look sheepish. We are definitely, a million per cent going abroad. In fact, I'm still trying to subtly talk Lauren down from a week in Vegas. It would be logistically impossible with the amount of people she wants to invite and with only a few months to plan it. I also really, really can't afford it. Not with all the other weddings and hen dos I'm doing this year. I keep being seized with panic when I think about my outgoings and the increasingly terrible financial situation I'm in. So I don't think about it. That is the healthy way I deal with my problems.

'Er, nothing's set in stone just yet,' I hedge.

She narrows her eyes at me. 'Are you going to get an actual holiday for you and Will this year?'

I laugh. 'Oh God no. As well as Lauren's, I have a ton of

other hen dos and weddings this year. That means loads of trips away, not to mention the actual nuptials themselves.'

I mentally start making a checklist for myself to crack on with tonight. I urgently need to book train tickets and a hotel for my friend Emily's Devon wedding in a couple of weeks. I need to find the log-in for her wedding website – God knows where I put it – so I can find the link to their Debenhams gift registry and pick out a present for the happy couple. There's also another overnight hen party coming up in London for a work friend, so I need to get a tutu for that and some presents for the eighteen goody bags I've been asked to sort out. I'll worry about the rest of the weddings – and everything on the Lauren to-do list – after I've sorted those.

I feel the weight of everything all of a sudden, and out loud I add, 'And I need to mass order some wedding outfits from Asos.'

Franny looks bemused. 'Can't you just wear the same frock to them all?'

'Oh Jesus no!' I am mock-horrified. 'Think of the Instagram scandal, Franny! Everyone from my school days follows me on there. You can't be seen in the same clothes more than once or twice when social media is *watching*.' I laugh.

Now Franny looks really aghast. 'Bloody hell, you lot. We don't need the government or Big Brother secretly watching us anymore, do we? We're all volunteering our every move and action on Tweeter, or whatever the hell it is now. And what is this nonsense about your school friends? Most of them were horrible to you anyway. What do you care what they think?'

I don't know how to explain why it matters, because it probably doesn't really, so I fall silent.

She continues loudly, 'This is because you used to be fat, my darling.'

Oh bloody hell, the fat thing again.

She starts waving at Andrea, who scurries straight over with two slices of lemon drizzle cake. She drops the plates in front of us with a clatter and runs back to the kitchen before Franny can comment on the state of the dessert.

'You were fat,' Franny goes on, wiping her fork on her dress and ignoring my sigh. 'And you listened to those stupid little fuckheads in your year about not being worth anything. You believed it, and even now you're still trying to prove something to them – and maybe to yourself. But you don't have to. You didn't then and you don't need to now, either, my darling girl. You are worth ten times any of them.'

I look around the room, desperate for some kind of distraction. I don't want to be talking about this. It's boring and not even true.

Franny goes on: 'I thought when you met that friend of yours – what's her name? It's something modern and ridiculous?'

'Joely,' I confirm.

'Julie, that's it, darling. The really fat one. I thought when you got close to her, you might take a leaf out of her book. Get a bit of confidence and start liking yourself a bit more. Instead –' she gestures at my body – 'you got thin. Which is fine, I suppose. And you'll always be beautiful, whatever size you are, Delilah, but now you run around trying to prove things to people who don't warrant a second thought from you.'

I sigh. She's got it all wrong. It wasn't like that.

Franny smiles nicely, sensing my irritation. 'My wonderful girl, I just want you to realise that you can say no to people occasionally. You know that, don't you? You don't have to go to all these silly things. Send your best wishes and love, then make room for your own life and things you want to do. You have a wonderful life waiting for you here; don't waste your time living out other people's dreams. And what about Will? You have to make room for him and stop sidelining him in your life if you want it to work between you. Maybe this proposal of his was about trying to get your attention, stop the pair of you drifting apart. If you want to be with him, you should be listening to what the two of you need.'

I sit up straighter, determinedly brightening to show her I'm fine. 'OK, I hear you, Franny,' I say, 'but you really don't need to worry about any of this. This year is going to be really busy, yes, but I don't have any other option. These are my friends, and their weddings are important. It's really, totally fine. I'm excited.'

It sounds a bit hollow but never mind.

I know Franny means well but she doesn't get it. I don't have a choice in this. I have to do everything that's expected of me. Once the weddings start, it's like an endless parade. You say yes to one girl you only knew a little bit at university and suddenly you can't say no to the other university friend you only knew a little bit. And when you've helped arrange one friend's hen do, your other friends expect you to do it for them when it's their turn too. Once you've spent a fortune on someone's big weekend in Ibiza, why wouldn't you do the same for everyone else? It's wedding politics and it's a very delicate balance; an endless white treadmill covered in fresh flowers. Franny doesn't have a clue about any of that. She's lucky she missed this generation's obsession with showing off. It's only started happening in the last few years. I blame

America. It's usually their fault when we do things, isn't it? We copy everything they do.

And, really, it's not just about it being a duty, it's also that I don't want to miss out on anything. There's so much happening around me, everyone is moving so fast. Marriage, houses, babies. I would feel miserable and so lonely watching it all play out on Facebook and Instagram without me. I'm ashamed to say I need to feel included. I'm afraid of being forgotten by my friends. It's that fear of missing out – FOMO – thing the internet talked about constantly in, like, 2014. Being invited to the most important day in someone's life means I count. I matter to them. It's a weird friendship yardstick, proving I'm liked. And just because I know that's silly and pathetic – and that I'm a trivial, shallow person for feeling like that – it doesn't mean these feelings aren't real. They still affect me.

I smile playfully at Franny. 'Anyway, I don't have anything else happening in my life. What else am I going to spend my money on, if not weddings?'

It's a rhetorical question but Franny looks at me a little sadly as she says quietly, 'Yourself?'

I get up, rolling my eyes as I turn away. I love Franny but this isn't helpful. I have to get back to work.

Wedding Number Four: Piers and Emily, Tilsbury Park, Devon

Theme: Traditional as fuck. Morning coats and tails as far as the eye can see. Which is not actually very far because there are millions of fascinators blocking my view.

Menu: Smoked salmon starter, followed by chicken and a meringue dessert. Veggie option: stuffed red pepper with goat's cheese.

Gift: A plush-looking toaster off the Debenhams wedding list @ £105.

Gossip: Bride found in tears just after ceremony because her 'wedding hashtag' wasn't trending. She'd been asking guests to 'build traction' with #SheepyMarriesLamby on their social media for the previous eight months.

My bank balance: £54

7

When I arrive at the bar, Joely is telling a man in a kindly voice to 'get back to your Lidl swamp'. She screams excitedly when she sees me and leaps out of her chair, almost whacking the hapless Lidl guy in the face as she does so. He slinks away, looking sulky in his fancy suit, back to his laughing friends.

'Lilah!' she says happily, encasing me in a big, soft hug. Joely gives the best hugs. OK, yes, partly it's because she's physically so large and cuddly, but it's also because she does this folding you in thing. She takes your whole person into her bosom, and never does that back pat everyone else seems to lead with. You know the patting I mean? Like they're so desperate to let you know they want the touching over as soon as possible. It's like they're tapping you out of a wrestling match. Really, I don't think Joely would ever willingly be the first to exit a cuddle.

She presses my face into her incredible chest and I let it happen, thinking about nothing and just enjoying the lovely feeling. So comforting and warm. Like sinking into a giant set of bottomless pillows filled with the softest feath— Hold on, I can't breathe.

I pull away, gasping for air, and grin at my beautiful friend. We've been getting closer lately, bonding over Lauren's madness, and it's been fun. She's nuts, of course, but she's also very wise. She has a way of seeing through to a problem, slicing through the bullshit. The other day I almost told her about Will's pseudo proposal. But I feel disloyal telling her and not Lauren. Really, I should tell them both, but it never feels like the right time and Lauren has so much on her plate – she doesn't want to hear about my dumb stuff right now.

We sit down, chatting excitedly about our week as she pours wine into my glass. Lauren is running late, like always, and Joely immediately starts complaining about her beloved cousin.

'Do you think we really have to keep coming to these meetings every week?' she says, exasperated. 'Haven't we talked about all this? Surely the endless WhatsApp chat is enough? Why is Lauren being such a demanding nightmare? We have lives too! I have an extra video to edit for my blog this week, and Calum Best has been pestering my agent for a date again, so I need to get that sorted so I can get back on the *Daily Mail* homepage.'

I nod. I get it.

Not the Calum Best part – I don't get that at all, what is she talking about? Is he even still a thing?

But I get her frustrations with Lauren. Her dramatic side has really kicked into gear in the last week or so. The texts start early and basically never end. Like, I went to bed at 1 a.m. last night, after an already long day of wedding texts, and woke up to this:

You have 17 new WhatsApp notifications
Lauren: Are you still awake? [1.07 a.m.]
Lauren: Is your phone on silent? [1.11 a.m.]
Lauren: Damn, I thought that would wake you up. [1.12 a.m.]
Lauren: Lilaaaaaaaaah, I'm worried. I think I hate my shoes. [1.22 a.m.]

Lauren: I don't know what I like anymore. What do I like? Do I like things? What if I hate everything? [1.28 a.m.]

Lauren: What if I dyed the shoes red?! That would be so edgy and cool, right? And perfect for a Christmas/December wedding! [1.45 a.m.]

Lauren: No, it's too Father Christmas, isn't it? [1.57 a.m.]

Lauren: Shall I dye them?!!!! I think I'm going to do it! [2.10 a.m.]

Lauren: I have some material dye in the garage from Charlie's tie-dye phase last year. [2.21 a.m.]

Lauren: I think I should do it. [2.22 a.m.]

Lauren: OMG SHALL I DO IT? [2.25 a.m.]

Lauren: Sorry, I know I'm being silly. It's 2.30, I have work in the morning, I can't start dyeing Jimmy Choo shoes in the middle of the night. What was I thinking????!!!! [2.39 a.m.]

Lauren: LOL, ridiculous, sorry. Haha, can't believe I was seriously considering doing that. Night babe. [2.50 a.m.]

Lauren: OK, I did it. Looks really, really terrible. These shoes cost £400. Charlie's going to kill me. [3.43 a.m.]

Lauren: Have also dyed my hands. [4.10 a.m.]

Lauren: Morning! You awake yet? Have emailed you links to possible new wedding shoes. [6.45 a.m.]

Joely: Hey, just a heads-up, I'm going to murder Lauren. [7.15 a.m.]

My phone is on constant high alert. And when Lauren's not texting me her wedding shit, Joely's texting to complain about the wedding shit.

I'm still trying to look on the positive side, though. The constant stream of messages is making me feel dead popular. Everyone at work thinks I'm so in demand! And it *is* brilliant to see Lauren so passionate about a project. I haven't seen her like this in ages.

She works in commercial advertising, coming up with

ideas and liaising with clients. She's really good at it from what I can tell – she's won awards and that – but she really hates everyone in her office (all men), as well as the work itself, which mostly seems to be centred around adverts for sanitary towels. The rest of her team (to reiterate – all men) don't want anything to do with that 'women stuff' so she gets stuck with all the feminine hygiene products, which apparently makes up seventy per cent of their revenue. She says she's trying to move away from the patronising shit – like, why is Mother Nature chasing you around in fucking pearls? And how can a sanitary towel be shaped 'especially for me', when I'm shaped like a pebbly Brighton beach down there? But that faux-feminist, faux-empowering stuff is all the clients ever want. So this wedding has been a great distraction from blue water and silky packaging. It's nice to see Lauren focusing and channelling her creative talents into something she genuinely cares about.

But still, she's being annoying.

'What happened to that one out of JLS you were meant to be seeing?' I say, moving the subject towards safer territory. 'I thought you were going on a few dates with him?'

Joely shakes her head. 'He's started going out with someone from last year's *X Factor* final. She has a single coming out, so his agent said she is more "right now" for his solo career.'

I nod sagely, like I understand. I do that a lot. These insights into the celebrity world are completely fascinating and completely perplexing.

'At this rate I'm going to have to leak some topless pics from my phone just to get some media attention,' she says, giggling. 'My agent said I could claim I've been hacked. He said hacking is really cool at the moment and my follow rates have dipped a little this month.' She throws back her head and laughs, and I join in. She wipes her eyes and goes on. 'Sorry, I know my life is utterly ridiculous these days. Who would've thought a couple of years ago that I'd find myself debating nude selfies?'

I snort. 'I'm pretty sure you were doing that three years ago. Weren't you dating that awful teacher back then? The one who prided himself on having catchphrases?'

'I've farted so I'll finish!' Joely shouts triumphantly and we both fall apart.

'Speaking of dreadful men with great hair,' she says, still giggling, 'how's your boss? How's work, how's life? Tell me everything, Lilah. And if you mention weddings, I will smash this bottle across your face.'

My mouth falls open and for a moment I'm at a loss for a response. It feels like ages since someone properly asked me how I am, without it coming back to someone's wedding or hen do. It's been all wedding, all the time lately. How even am I? Usually it would be Lauren checking in on my life, but she's been so preoccupied lately, it seems strange to be sharing this moment alone with Joely.

'I'm OK . . .' I start, hesitating.

Right, this is the time to tell her about Will's non-proposal and how awkward it's been between us since. It's now or never. Can I trust her not to say anything to Lauren? Is it a betrayal to tell one of them and not the other? Joely is looking at me quizzically, waiting for an answer.

Thankfully I am saved from myself by a commotion towards the front of the bar. Lauren has arrived and it looks like she's dropped an enormous pile of bridal magazines all over the floor. A group of women are on their hands and knees helping her pick them up. Lauren is bright red, her long blonde hair messy over her face, telling everyone she's sorry, sorry, sorry. Joely and I run over to help, collecting up copies of *Weddings*, *You and Your Wedding*, *Perfect Wedding*, *Elle Wedding*, *Brides*, *Bride Magazine*, and a whole host of other gleaming white publications. Lauren is still saying sorry, so we start saying sorry too, and then the women who've helped pick the mags up also start apologising. There's nothing more British than excessive, unnecessary apologising – apart from maybe getting angry at other people having too much fun.

We eventually sit back down to our drinks and, for a moment, I think we will pick up the conversation about me again. It feels like the right time to talk to them both about Will and I realise suddenly how much I need their advice.

'Guys . . .' I start and Lauren shoves a magazine in my face.

'It's wedding meeting time,' she says curtly. 'You two can finish your pointless bitching later. We don't have time for silly stuff.' She barks out a laugh to show she's joking, even though she's not.

Oh.

Feeling a bit stung, I dutifully study the pages, and half-heartedly listen as Lauren tells us about researching table stands. She cheerfully details how she and Charlie had a screaming row about marquees this morning and how she's changed florists. Again.

Around about bottle three, Joely starts getting twitchy. It's obvious she's bored, flicking table crumbs at an oblivious Lauren, who is still chattering away. Joely's even started vaguely making eyes at the Lidl suit guy, who's still hovering nearby, looking wounded by the earlier dismissal, but rallying his ego to make another attempt. They always come back. Men rarely take no for an answer when it comes to Joely – and not because she's so beautiful – but because she's fat. I've seen it over and over. Guys think she should be grateful that they're interested, and it won't compute when she says she's not. You'd be surprised how often a man approaches with a flirty smile, is rebutted and then gets nasty and angry. Which is when the horrible comments about her weight come out – those usually only found online where the literal wankers can hide behind their keyboards.

'Do you think you and Will might get married?' Joely says out of nowhere, turning her attention back towards us and interrupting a Lauren monologue about wedding make-up rehearsals. Lauren looks alarmed for a moment, and then rearranges her face into a neutral, polite smile. I feel the flush creeping up my neck and face, wondering for half a second whether Joely and Franny have been texting. They do that sometimes – they like to gossip about me.

I shrug. 'Maybe one day. But I'm not that bothered either way,' I say carefully.

Joely nods thoughtfully. 'Yeah, well, I guess your parents killed off some of the romance of marriage for you.'

All four of the Bolts – both Joely and Lauren's sets of parents – are happily married. To each other, I mean. Not in some interesting four-way group marriage set-up. Lauren's mum and dad have been together thirty-two years, they told me recently, while Joely's folks will soon be celebrating their fortieth anniversary. They're having a big party. Franny's coming as my date because she says she wants to have a look at these 'freaks' up close.

'Hey, don't make me out to be the odd one out here,' I exclaim, laughing. 'You two are the weird ones. I'm pretty sure nearly everyone's parents hate each other these days. Yours are the weirdos for still being in love. And yes, I know my mum and dad are particularly dysfunctional, but I don't think their unhappy relationship has got anything to do with how I feel about marriage. I've just never really thought much about it. I like the idea of a big party, but I'm not sure the rest of it – marriage – would make me particularly happy.'

Lauren snorts, 'Married or not, I can't imagine Alice and Harry ever actually being happy. They love the drama too much.'

Joely shifts her chair an inch closer to mine. 'What's the latest Jeremy Kyle shit going on with them? Please can you read us their most recent texts to you?'

I happily pick up my phone and scroll through, summarising for my friends as I go. Lauren looks a little impatient at the change in subject, but I ignore it.

'Last week Dad claimed he'd left an old signed Tom Jones album in Mum's attic that he urgently needed back. He said it has an enormous amount of sentimental and monetary value, so he wanted it immediately. Mum says he's a liar – that he never would've left any of his Tom Jones memorabilia with her – and if he really has, then she's going to eBay it. She says it's just an excuse to come over and steal her stuff. Dad's now saying he'll break in and she's threatening to call the police on him if he does. It's pretty good stuff. Look –' I hold up my phone to show my dad's text to me from the night before – 'he says Mum is a "garbage trash whore" in this one. I think he got that insult from *The Hills*.'

Joely shakes her head. 'How do they still get so angry with each other? They've been broken up for years now. It takes so much energy to be that furious for this long.'

I throw my hands in the air, used to it and only caring a little. 'Who knows?' I shrug. 'I still hold out a little hope that they might both meet someone else – someone nice – one day. I always thought they would move on at some point, but the one time Mum had a fling with Jack, that gardener – do you remember? – it made them both even worse. Dad kept calling her Lady Chatterley and Mum retaliated by sending him graphic descriptions of their sex life, just to infuriate him. Then Jack the gardener and Dad had a fight in a Homebase, throwing compost at each other and both got a lifetime ban—'

Joely interrupts me, crowing, 'Yes, I remember! Jack dumped your mum after that because he said he really needed access to Homebase for work purposes.'

Lauren jumps in, laughing. 'And then your mum keyed your dad's car and he called the police, who told him they'd arrest him if he didn't stop ringing them.'

We all giggle and I roll my eyes at my ludicrous parents. Most of the time it doesn't bother me. Being around them is like being a featured extra in some low-budget soap opera. But still, I feel a little weird talking to Lauren and Joely about them. I know they mean well when they ask about the situation, but they also read too much into everything. They think I'm damaged by my 'broken home' because they have a whole one. They can't see how it's possible not to be disturbed by warring parents, because their own parents love each other so much. Sometimes it does upset me, and I wish my brother was more communicative so I could rant to him occasionally. Actually, I tried to text him after this latest round of texts, but he never replied. He loves me, I know he does, but he would always rather hide his head in the sand. I try really hard to believe in the idea that people are just people. They are, aren't they? We can't expect mums and dads, or even little brothers, to be any better or grown-up than the rest of us. Having issues because my parents split up is like having issues if two close friends split up. You can be sad for people without making it your problem.

I sway a little on my chair, realising I am fairly drunk, as Lauren slightly impatiently steers the topic back again to weddings. She's talking about the 'tacky' big day our friend Catherine has planned for next month. Apparently Cath's going for a '2005 Jordan and Peter Andre vibe', and I shouldn't be surprised if the wedding dress is hot pink. Lauren is appalled and Joely thinks it's hilarious. I secretly think it's quite cool. Jordan and Peter Andre were awesome in their day, and if hot pink dresses and white horses pulling a fairytale carriage is Catherine's bag, then I think that's brilliant. It's brave. And at the very least, it should be more interesting than those 'classy', elegant weddings where you feel like you can't even get drunk without someone pulling you to one side and hissing that you need to pull yourself together. It always feels like you're not allowed to even speak to the bride at those weddings – like she's the queen or an A-lister on a red carpet – and any speaking at all has to be in hushed, reverent tones. Actually, I think that's the kind of wedding vibe Lauren's hoping for. But, y'know, that'll be lovely too.

Lauren is in the middle of a detailed explanation of the tradition behind veils, and Joely takes a long, bored swig from her glass. She is holding back, I can see she is, and I sincerely appreciate it. I need her here with me. Much as I am struggling with all this wedding stuff, I know it would be a lot tougher without her help. Especially with Simone gone timeshare AWOL.

As I'm watching Joely anxiously, Lauren pauses mid-sentence and looks at both of us in turn. She sighs and stops talking, looking down at her hands.

'I'm sorry, guys,' she says quietly, in an uncharacteristic moment of self-awareness. 'I know I'm getting carried away. I know some brides get obsessed with their weddings and don't talk about anything else. I don't want to turn into one of those boring mad bridezillas!'

Joely mouthes 'Turn *into*?' at me and I carefully ignore her.

Lauren continues: 'I know it's a lot to help me with and listen to, but I really need you guys to be my sounding board. I told Charlie to leave it all to me but I didn't realise how much it would involve. It'll be worth it, though! It's going to be the most amazing day of my life, and I want you two right there with me. And, of course, I'll do it for you when your turns come around!'

I smirk at this. So many of us do things for people because we want them to return the favour when the time comes. And I've never seen this more so than in the wedding universe. We go on expensive hen dos, we buy extravagant presents, all in the knowledge that they'll have to pay out for yours one day. It's classic friendship quid pro quo.

Lauren's still talking. '. . . It has to be perfect, but I really do want you to enjoy this process just as much as I am! It's cool, isn't it? You don't mind, you're having fun with all this, right?' She doesn't wait for any confirmation from us before adding, 'Now, Lilah, did you get those costings for hiring a Ferris wheel? We probably won't do it, but you spoke to them, right? What's their availability like for the December date?'

Wedding Number Five: Sophia and Khoi, Union Chapel, London

Theme: Unofficial but very real *hats* theme. Hats everywhere. Ratio of hat to mother-in-law would shame even Jamiroquai.

Menu: Smoked salmon starter, followed by chicken and a meringue dessert. Veggie option: stuffed red pepper with goat's cheese.

Gift: Crystal vase @ £85.

Gossip: One of the groomsmen brought a Tinder date as his plus one, so she was in all the pictures. He spent the rest of the night hiding in the loo until she left.

My bank balance: -£189 (Turning off text alerts from Lloyds.)

8

Will is in the shower when I get home from work. I wait by the bathroom door, desperate for a wee and thinking melodramatically that I have forgotten what he looks like. We have been missing each other a bit these last few weeks and I feel like I'm only seeing his sleepy nighttime self at the moment. Admittedly, that is one of his more adorable selves, but I miss the other Wills too. I miss seeing him in the daytime, I miss talking to him all evening while he's trying to watch telly. I miss him trying to eat with his mouth shut at mealtimes, while I loudly comment on his table manners. I miss laughing with him.

It's been a busy few weeks.

'Dude, I hate to rush you,' I say, knocking urgently, 'but I am going to leave a massive wet patch on this floor if you don't get out here right now.' I squat down on the floor to compress the wee and then immediately bounce back up because obviously that made the need worse.

The lock clicks and the door opens. Steam frames Will as he strolls naked out of the bathroom.

'Too good for towels?' I say, amused. He side-smiles and I suddenly forget my bladder as I look at him.

Oh no, there it is. I run, slamming the door behind me as I go.

When I come back out, my body singing with relief, he's in the living room, folding washing. He's put some pyjama bottoms on and his hair is combed through and slicked back.

I sink into the sofa, my eyes closing, fully exhausted and thinking how that seems to be my constant state of being lately. I feel him pass close by me, leaning down to peck me on the head, and I murmur a quiet 'hi' at him.

'Nice week?' he says gruffly. The smell of aftershave reaches me where I sit. He smells good.

'Hmm,' I half answer as my phone vibrates in my pocket.

It's Lauren, reminding me to get the hen emails sent out tonight. Oh man, I'm so tired. Does it have to be tonight? I've had such a long week at work. Rex told a contestant yesterday that she had nice tits and she – quite rightly – stormed off the set. We had to spend a frantic half day looking for someone else to replace her at the last minute. But even when we'd found someone, it still meant shooting ran late for the rest of the week. Oh, and I also got stuck with talking to the woman's lawyer. Aslan was supposed to sort it, but he explained that I'm 'just better at that stuff'. It's convenient that I'm so much better at the things he doesn't want to have to do.

It's been a very long week and Will deserves some of my time too. Surely the hen emails aren't all that urgent? I can totally just have an evening to myself with my boyfriend, can't I?

I realise Will's been talking while I think, and I open my eyes properly, trying to focus on what he's saying through my haze of exhaustion.

'. . . Do you fancy that? It could be really fun. And nice to spend some time together, don't you think? We could race there and back since it's not far.'

I have no idea what he's talking about. I give him a thumbs up and hope that's enough. 'Yeah, um, send me an email with the details and I'll put it in my diary,' I say and he nods. I drift away again as Will keeps talking.

'. . . And she's acting like I don't know what I'm doing – it's very frustrating. We had a chat the other day and it was like she had no faith in me at all. I just don't know how to handle it.'

Er, work problem? Must be a work problem.

'That sounds so . . .' I reach for the right adjective. 'Frustrating?' I try.

He looks at me oddly. 'That's what I said,' he says, but he's smiling. 'Anyway, it doesn't matter all that much. She's only on secondment with us for another few months. I just need to get through this period and then she'll be back in the US. It would be nice if I could prove myself to her in that time but it's not the end of the world and then I can . . .'

He's walked through to the kitchen to get a glass of water and I pounce on the chance to close my eyes again. The hen emails can definitely wait until morning.

I work my weekend out in my head. If I go to bed now, I can get up early to do them before I go out to meet Franny for breakfast. I have some work to do before Monday, but it can probably wait until Sunday. That's it, then – decided. I'll send them out in the morning. I've already looked through the Excel document Lauren gave me with everyone's contact details. The idea is that I can keep track of everyone once they've confirmed attendance and made payments, but the reality is that I'm going to have to transfer it all into a Word document because I don't have the first idea how to use Excel. I tried to copy and paste something earlier and it turned it into a mathematical formula. Fuck you, Excel. Oh – a thought occurs to me – but if I hold off sending them, there's a chance Lauren might check up on me. She's got such a tight, specific schedule and she's being a bit funny about things not being done the very moment she's asked.

I pause to consider how wrong it is that I'm scared of my best friend. But hey, who *isn't* terrified of brides?

I start to count up how many hours of sleep I'll get if I go to bed now. Really, I should stay up a bit longer and listen to Will's story. Sympathise about this ... work ... person? Must be a human person he's complaining about – he said *she*, didn't he? We really need to get some quality time in together. Catch up. I really do miss him and he must be getting annoyed with me being so busy all the ti ...

When I next open my eyes, Will is silently carrying me up to bed wrapped up in a blanket.

From: DelilahMFox@gmail.com
To: 30+ contacts in your address book
Date: 1 July

Hey lovely ladies,

Hope you're having a great week and enjoying all this, er, rain.

Most of you probably don't know me, so HELLO, I'm Lauren Bolt's maid of honour, Lilah. Does this call for a yay? I think it might do: YAY.

Hopefully you already knew she was engaged and I'm not ruining the surprise for any of you!

So anyway, Lauren's keen for me to get you guys all booked in for her hen do. I was supposed to send this email out yesterday, so please don't tell on me. We're only just at the beginning of making arrangements for it, and I will be coming back to you with a lot more details later in the year, but here's what we know so far!

- It'll be in Marbella.
- We'll fly out Thursday or Friday 5/6 October and return on Sunday 8 October.
- We're roughly estimating it's going to cost around £400/£500 each.

So, what I need from you guys right now is a firm yes or no if you can make it. I know it's a lot of money and only a few months away, so we (and Lauren) totally understand if you can't make it. But we really do need a definite yes or no now so we can confirm numbers. We need to make inquiries and preliminary bookings and figure out exactly how it's all going to work and exactly how much it's going to cost as soon as possible.

Once I've got exact numbers from you all, I'll be in touch later down the line about deposits and with more details on the various funzzz we'll be having.

Oh, and can you also only reply to me, save everyone getting annoyed by an endless group email!

Thanks so much. Can't wait to meet you all!
Lilah xx

From: RebekahSS31@hotmail.com
To: You
Cc: 30+

Hi,

Where will the hen do be? Will it be abroad?

From: Katie.Jacks@barclays.com
To: You
Cc: 30+

Hey Lilah

Katie Jacks here!!!! Nice to E-MEET YOU! Lol lol lol.

Thanks for the email, how exciting!!! I'd soooo love to come, just checking what dates you reckon the hen will be????

Thank you soooooooo much, can't wait!!!!!
Katie xxxxxxxx

From: Fiona89Mansfield@yahoo.co.uk
To: You
Cc: 30+

Morning Delilah,

Nice to hear from you!

I'll have to let you know later in the year whether I can do this. Put me down as a maybe.

Ta,
Fi

From: SimoneSweets1999@gmail.com
To: You
Cc: 30+

Hello again fellow bridesmaid, and hi everyone else!

I'm the groom's little sister (emphasis on little, lol) (my brother's a fat cheapskate) (just kidding, don't tell him I said that) (he won't lend me money) (Lauren's too good for him lol!)

Anyway, I'm hoping I can make this, just need to find the money, still haven't told Dad about the trust fund being gone. Do you want to use my new timeshare for the hen do???????

Simone x

From: Katie.Jacks@barclays.com
To: You
Cc: 30+

Hey Lilah,

Katie Jacks here!!!! Nice to E-MEET YOU! Lol lol lol.

Thanks for the email, how exciting!!! I'd soooo love to come, just checking what dates you reckon the hen will be????

Thank you soooooooo much, can't wait!!!!!
Katie xxxxxxxx

From: Katie.Jacks@barclays.com
To: You
Cc: 30+

Hey Lilah,

Katie Jacks here!!!! Nice to E-MEET YOU! Lol lol lol.

Thanks for the email, how exciting!!! I'd soooo love to come, just checking what dates you reckon the hen will be????

Thank you soooooooo much, can't wait!!!!!
Katie xxxxxxxx

From: NicolaBucan@carphonewarehouse.com
To: You
Cc: 30+

I'm in!
Thanks x

From: Katie.Jacks@barclays.com
To: You
Cc: 30+

Hey Lilah,

Katie Jacks here!!!! Nice to E-MEET YOU! Lol lol lol.

Thanks for the email, how exciting!!! I'd soooo love to come, just checking what dates you reckon the hen will be????

Thank you soooooooo much, can't wait!!!!!
Katie xxxxxxxx

From: Katie.Jacks@barclays.com
To: You
Cc: 30+

Hey Lilah!!

I keep trying to email you back but I don't think it's working!!!! Just wanted to check on the dates for the hen do??????

Katie xxxxxx

From: CarlieAnneHodkins@gmail.com
To: You
Cc: 30+

You have the wrong person. Can you take me off this group message.

From: NicolaBucan@carphonewarehouse.com
To: You
Cc: 30+

Katie, stop sending the same email over and over. We heard you the first time, babe!! And the dates were in Lilah's email anyway.

From: Joely.Bolt@FatJoely.com
To: You
Cc: 30+

Hey everyone,

LOL, Lilah. I can't believe Lauren's got you on such a tight schedule. I'm going to tell her you waited a full day before obeying her!

But yeah, I'm in, obvs. Can't wait.

Katie, STOP SENDING THE SAME EMAIL OVER AND OVER.

Joely x

From: JessMarsh@snappysnaps.co.uk
To: You
Cc: 30+

Hey Delilah,

Thanks for this. How much do you think it's going to cost, round about?

Also, can everyone stop cc'ing everyone else into their replies? My work email is getting overloaded.

Thanks guys,
Jess

From: CarlieAnneHodkins@gmail.com
To: You
Cc: 30+

Seriously, take me off this group message.

From: SofiaMathes@clintonscards.com
To: You
Cc: 30+

Hi there,

I'm out of the office this week. I'll be back in on Monday 13 October 2008.

I'll get back to you then.
Sofia

9

So it turns out a Jordan and Peter Andre style wedding is truly a thing to behold. There are hair extensions and tiaras everywhere I look, and everything from the dresses to the tablecloths are decorated using some variation of pink taffeta. IT IS AMAZING. Lauren is in her absolute element, hissing at every tiny detail and loudly stage whispering to me and Joely about it all being 'disgusting' and why it's the exact opposite of what she's planning for her big day. I keep trying to pretend I can't hear her because we're sitting on a table with all the bride's aunts and uncles, who look a bit put out.

Joely's having a much harder time of it. As the token single girl at every wedding we go to these days – and this is already number six this year alone – she's barely been allowed to sit down because everyone has someone she 'simply must meet'. She's been dragged around and around the room over and over again to be presented to the very few single guys present. Literally ANY single man. She's so far been pointedly introduced to a 62-year-old widower called Leonard, who wanted to talk to her about the Stephen King novel *Gerald's Game* to see if 'that kind of roleplay was her cup of tea'. She also met another man in his forties called Bernard, who is 'still technically living with his wife', but only because they 'can't afford to split up just at the minute'. Oh, and – my favourite – Catherine's second cousin, Brett, who has just done 'really well' on his A-levels and is turning eighteen 'any day now'.

There was also a really awful few minutes where she was forced to dance alone in the middle of the room to Beyonce's 'Single Ladies'.

Bernard tried to dance with her at the end.

Joely's trying to make the best of it, and keeps repeating the mantra: 'Any attention is good attention' and that everyone here – especially the awful men she's met – are all potential followers and subscribers. But she's really starting to look a bit dead behind the eyes, and has been in the loo quite a bit more than usual.

On the plus side, she reckons the teenager is quite fit, so she gave him her number. I think she's going to his birthday party in a couple of weeks. She said she can shag him and then he'll sell his story to the *Sun* and she can go on *Loose Women* to talk about age-gap romance.

I look around the room at all this love and goodwill, and think: seriously, fuck all of you.

No, just kidding. It's nice, I guess.

The whole day – service and reception – has been held in a remote Scottish hotel, and you can tell the couple have been really involved with every aspect of the day. They'd written their own vows, which went on for sooo long. I had to stop Joely throwing something, and at one point she did this really exaggerated, loud yawn – which the groom totally saw. He still didn't wrap shit up, though, and carried on talking for another twenty-five minutes or so. The speeches are up next, and they're bound to be even longer, so we're totally ditching. Joely has stolen two bottles of champagne and Will and I are trying to persuade Lauren to come hide in the catering tent with us. But she won't – she says she needs to stay and take notes.

I feel a bit torn. I don't want to abandon Lauren, but I'm

so sick of talking to people from school who I hated and never wanted to see again. Many of whom called me Delly the Belly back then, and definitely not in an affectionate way.

Crap. In fact, here comes another girl from school, who I haven't seen in ten years. She's in a white dress, which seems like a brave choice at a wedding, and is flapping her hands in our direction, squealing.

'Oh my GOD, hi, Lauren! I can't believe you're here! It's been forever!' she shouts at our whole table, before turning to Joely. 'And Josie, right? I remember you – you used to come to our school discos and snog all the boys in our year! Ooh, remember what happened with Dean Clark? That was totes hilar. It's so good to see you guys! How long has it been since we saw each other? Lauren, you never make it to the reunions, you naughty girl! We miss you! What's been going on in the last ten years? Tell me everything about your life! Are you married? Have you found your special someone to complete you yet? I got married last year, so yeah, my life is truly amazing. He's a lawyer, so . . .' She stops and smiles smugly around the table, waiting for everyone to acknowledge her enormous accomplishment in bagging a rich human.

Her name is Petra Mooney and I don't want to be mean, but she has this really whiny voice that hasn't changed since Year Nine. There was a stray dog that used to hang around the school playground and, I swear to God, whenever Petra talked at lunchtime, that dog would start to howl and wouldn't stop until she stopped speaking. It happened every single time, I'm really not even exaggerating.

Lauren smiles disinterestedly at Petra, while Joely barely nods an acknowledgement. Petra doesn't seem to notice the lack of enthusiasm from the group and takes a seat beside Lauren – recently vacated by an uncle with bladder issues (that's not a guess – he told us all about it over the main course).

Hopefully he leaked.

Petra pauses, scanning the uncomfortable middle-aged occupants of our table before landing on me and narrowing her eyes.

'Delly?' she says, unsure. 'Delly Fox? Delly the Belly? Oh my God, is that you?'

I nod, smiling as genuinely as I can. 'Hiya, Petra, how are you?'

Her jaw goes slack. 'Oh-em-gee, Delly! You look so different. You're so thin. What the hell. You've lost so much weight.' She stops briefly, plasters a fake smile over her shock and adds, sugar sweetly, 'Ooh, well done you, Delly! You look, like, sooo much better. I can't believe how different you look from school. You were so fat back then, haha! Sooo fat, do you remember? Do you remember how we all called you Delly the Belly? Haha. And now you're totally thin! I can't believe it. You've dyed your hair red too, right? It looks sooo cute. I love how ... *bright* it is. So, yeah, how much weight have you lost? Like, two stone? Three stone? Four stone? You're so much better-looking now! Spill, gurl – what's your secret?'

I half smile, then shrug uncomfortably. I really, really, really hate being told how much 'better' I look now I've lost weight. I hear it all the time. Every time I'm with someone who hasn't seen me in a couple of years, I have to sit there while they tell me that I'm 'acceptable' to them now. Actually, that's mostly why I'm finding seeing people here a bit uncomfortable. This is about the sixth encounter I've had just like this, with an acquaintance I haven't seen for years loudly bringing up my body like it's public property. I think it's completely weird the way we act like weight loss is some kind of miracle and praise people without knowing anything about their situation. Because the thing is, none of us know what's going on underneath the surface. You have no idea what's happening in someone's life. It could be an illness, it could be an eating disorder, or it could be that someone's just had a really shitty breakup and is too sad to eat. That was my situation, by the way. The guy before Will, who dumped me brutally for a girl he met on Tinder. I was heartbroken and too miserable to eat and the weight fell off me. Yoga has mostly kept it off but it wasn't some big, positive, happy thing. My eating was incredibly disordered and I lost three stone in three months. It wasn't healthy on any level. My nails all broke, my hair fell out, my skin was terrible – and all I heard was how great I looked because I was emaciated. Personally, I've never known anyone to lose weight except through misery. Joely's the happiest, most content person I know – which is why I don't think she'll ever be slim.

I also can't stand this assumption that I must've hated myself back then. Like, I must be sooo relieved not to be that person anymore. Yes, sure, I hated the way people *treated me* when I was bigger, but I didn't hate my body. I don't understand how people like Petra think fat-shaming my previous self – the person I lived as for about twenty-six years – will make me feel good. It just makes me feel humiliated and sad to hear how much they didn't like my previous body. How much more they prefer *this* version of me. It makes me look at my life before in a different way, like I was wrong and broken. And now that I've 'rectified' myself, I will be finally be allowed out into mixed society.

102

And I hate knowing that I'll carry this knowledge with me if I put the weight back on. Which is, y'know, statistically pretty likely.

I don't know what to say, so I half nod and glance over at Will beside me. I think I was hoping for support, or at least a distraction, but he's staring down at his plate. He's not having a good time and it looks like our escape window before the speeches has closed. He's been in a tiny bit of a mood with me for a few days now. He says he isn't, but I can tell he is. He's doing that thing where he doesn't properly look at me when we talk, and staring anywhere else. I keep trying to cheer him up today, hoping he'll snap out of it, but it's not working.

To be fair to him, I get it. I know he's been feeling neglected lately. What with everything that's been going on with Lauren, and all the hen do and wedding stuff, it's taking up a lot of my time. I know it must seem to him like we can't even get through an evening without some mini crises cropping up that Lauren needs my help with – and no, it can never wait until tomorrow. And now it's not even just Lauren bothering me at all hours. Will and I haven't had a single conversation lately without my phone beeping with yet another message from a confused hen who doesn't know how to apply for a new passport and thinks I'm supposed to sort that kind of thing out for her since I'm the maid of honour. And what with work, Franny and Fuddy-Duddies United, I guess I've not really been home much lately at all. This is the most we've been together in weeks and all I've done today is talk to other guests. And then yet another wedding invitation arrived yesterday from one of his cousins, who's marrying his boyfriend after eight years together. It's so romantic, they're getting hitched in a castle on New Year's Eve!

But when I went to RSVP yes online, I could tell Will really wanted to say something. I asked if he was OK and he looked a bit weird.

'It's fine,' he said in a small voice. 'It's just . . . it's just that I was hoping we could do something special on New Year's Eve. Something just the two of us. I thought we could go away together maybe . . .'

And then he'd stopped as he spotted the panicked look on my face, thinking about the money something 'special' would entail. He immediately backtracked and said we should definitely go to the wedding, and then he laughed like he was being silly.

I feel really bad, and I know we've committed to an unbelievable number of weddings in the space of a year, but it's not like we have a choice! It's his family. And it'll look homophobic if this is the one wedding we can't make it to! We have to go. I can't say no without a reason, can I?

Thankfully, across the table, Petra has already lost interest in my new look and is grilling Lauren about her wedding plans. They're currently talking themes and Petra is boasting competitively about her own wedding, where they had a 1920s vibe with a *Bugsy Malone*-inspired first dance. Lauren is making approving noises but is pulling the face she pulled when we arrived at the hotel earlier today and saw all the pink taffeta. She shows Petra a venue on her phone that she made us all visit last weekend. She and Charlie were supposed to be absolutely decided on her father-in-law's place for the wedding but this other place had a cancellation and Lauren said she 'just wants options'. This venue specialises in 'country' weddings and has actual peacocks who attend your big day with you. The peacocks will – upon request – walk you down the aisle. It's really cool. Or fucking ridiculous, I'm not sure which. Lauren's dad is apparently in a huff about this part and says he can walk her down the aisle wearing 'stupid feathers sticking out of his arse' if that's what she wants.

'Do you know about the giant wedding fair in London next week?' Petra suddenly says self-importantly, gripping Lauren by the shoulders. 'It's going to be massive and vital for any bride. You simply must go. All brides that really *care* about making their wedding day special should go. If only to be *seen* there, yars? All the top florists and designers and planners will be there. You *must* go.'

Joely and I exchange a panicked glance. We've already been to approximately 9,500 wedding fairs. We've surely seen everything weddings have to offer at this point. And if we have to go to this one, does that mean Petra's coming too? We've already got enough cooks in this boiling-hot wedding kitchen and we definitely don't need another voice on the bustling WhatsApp group.

'Of course I've heard of it,' Lauren says huffily, but she's bluffing. 'I'm on the list, obviously, but, er, I'm not sure I need it, to be honest. I have already spoken to all the, er, top wedding ... people in the ... country.' She shoots us a look that says to keep quiet and that we might have to cancel any plans we had next week for a trip to London.

Oh God.

Petra nods approvingly. 'Well, darling, let me know if you are and I'll come along. Might be handy for when Richard and I renew our vows, right?' she tinkers.

'Would you really renew your vows?' Lauren says, looking

shocked. 'But all that work and expense . . . Are people really renewing vows now?'

She looks upset and I search her face for something. Is she still having fun with this? All this competitive wedding fair talk feels very forced and unlike Lauren.

'Are you finding the planning a bit much?' I say softly across the table, and she looks at me like I've slapped her.

'Of course not!' she snaps. 'It's wonderful and I'm on top of it all. I told you six months was plenty of time. I'm fine, it's fine,' she falters before speedily adding, 'I'm just imagining my parents' face if I said I wanted to do all this over again in a year. They've given us so much money, and they're using it as leverage, demanding we invite some distant cousins to my wedding.' She tuts and adds loudly – just as the bladder-problem uncle returns from the loos – 'I've barely even met these dick pricks.'

He looks perturbed by the language, turning on his heel and walking off again. Maybe he just needed another wee. Those infections get you like that.

Lauren continues, unabashed, 'I don't see why they have to be there. Why would they even want to come? Mum says I have to invite them because I went to theirs when I was, like, seven. I hardly remember it, except that the whole day was totally gross. They had a buffet, ugh, and I had to wear a purple flower-girl dress that didn't even fit me. Everyone kept patting me like I was a dumb dog.'

Joely snorts. 'I had to wear the same thing. It wasn't that bad. And I got petted way more than you because I looked much cuter in purple.'

They glare affectionately at each other for a second, and then Petra – realising she is no longer the centre of attention

– starts screaming about dancing, jumping out of her seat and knocking over the pink taffeta centrepiece.

'Come on,' she says, ignoring the mess and grabbing Lauren's hand. 'Let's get this party started.'

I'm panting embarrassingly as I arrive at the Fuddy-Duddies United meeting. Two whole minutes of running and look at me. Sweat is pouring down my face and my knees are threatening to buckle – completely pathetic. Forget the sissy yoga, I need to start doing more of those aerobics classes.

I'm late and I sneak in at the back, knowing I will get told off by at least eight different Category-A grandmas.

There are three types of old lady who attend the FU (why yes, I do enjoy saying FU every time, thank you for asking). There's the aforementioned Category A – the really grumpy, angry-at-everything women, who want to tell you specifically and furiously about how many fields this whole area used to be made up of and how everything has been ruined by their disappearance. Category B is a smaller group, comprised of ladies who act bewildered and afraid of everything you say. But they will definitely still ask you about Facebook. Over and over. And it doesn't matter how many times you explain it to them, they still don't get it, and will never get it, so stop spending half your evening every single week going through it. And definitely don't let them look at it on your phone because they will totally 'like' photos of your bastard ex-boyfriend from 2010.

NB: This is more advice for myself.

Oh, and they also want to talk about the fields this building used to sit on.

Then there's Category C: the mischievous grandmas.

These women are totally on Snapchat, and like to wind the other two categories up with the tales they bring back from the frontline of 'young people' and their 'filters'. Although, if pressed, Category C do also enjoy talking to you about fields that are long since gone.

I'm going out on a limb right now and saying fields are a big thing for old ladies.

Franny rules them all, as a Category A-, B- and C-type grandma, and the smartest of them all.

Today she is clearly in C – Mischievous Grandma – mode as she smiles widely at my sneaky entrance, pronouncing loudly, 'Ah, Delilah, you're here at last! Tell the group about that mad wedding you went to at the weekend.'

I freeze in the act of sitting quietly down at the back. Catherine's wedding. She wants me to tell everyone about the wedding. Of course she does. Oh God.

Obviously, Franny's already heard about it during our lunches together this week, but these ladies have not. We stare at each other now for a full ten seconds. She knows this story will infuriate and confuse the group – that's why she wants me to tell it.

They all turn in their chairs towards me, knitting paused mid-stitch around the room.

I clear my throat and make eye contact with 84-year-old Molly's always-watering right eye. She's a Category A.

A for Angry.

'Oh, Franny,' I hedge. 'They don't want to hear about yet another one of my weddings! We have much better things to talk about. We have to start preparations for our breast cancer tea party next month. And I haven't downloaded the sudoku update yet, but I hear really great things.' I nod encouragingly at the room, waiting for someone to chime in.

Franny takes a step towards me, menacingly. 'Tell. Them. About. The. Wedding,' she repeats, that damned left eyebrow going again. There will be no more debate.

I swallow. Dammit, this is meant to be my respite from wedding nonsense.

'Right! Well, yes, the wedding. It was lovely . . .' I say. 'The bride wore pink, and so did the groom.'

Molly's right eye starts watering angrily.

Franny's smile gets wider, more wicked. 'And then later?'

I hang my head, defeated. 'Later on, things . . . things got out of hand. It was meant to be a cash bar, but the groom was so drunk by five o'clock that he volunteered his credit card to buy everyone's drinks for the rest of the night. He then bought seventeen separate rounds of Jägerbombs for the entire room. And for some reason, he insisted that every glass came topped with whipped cream. There was whipped cream everywhere – on the floor, on the walls of the marquee, on the ceiling. Then one of the cousins broke his ankle slipping in the cream and got taken away by ambulance.'

The group is silent, staring at me.

'Then?' says Franny merrily.

I sigh. 'Then the groomsmen all got into a fight and they knocked down one whole end of the marquee. Unfortunately it was the section where all the parents and grandparents were hiding. The groom tried to help his new mother-in-law out from underneath the tenting and she thought he was attacking her, so she punched him in the groin, which then made him throw up all over her.' I take a deep breath. 'So it was around then that the management started going crazy and shouting that the bar bill had hit fifteen thousand pounds and that they'd also have to pay for all the damage. The bride started crying and screaming hysterically, and said the money

110

was meant to be the deposit for their new house. She said she wanted a divorce and then the groom – who was still being sick – also wet himself.'

There is a long, heavy silence as the ladies in the group process what I've said. Franny looks the happiest I've seen her in a long time as she surveys the room and waits for reactions from its occupants.

At last, Molly speaks. She is *livid*. Her left eye has now joined the right in the angry watering.

'A . . . a . . .' She can't even get the words out. She is spitting with the effort. 'A . . . PINK DRESS?'

The room erupts in delighted gossip about new fashions and what's-wrong-with-tradition comments and, of course, some stuff about fields that used to be here.

Oh God, I wish we didn't have to talk about this. The FU is meant to be my one escape from wedding chat. I'm here to feel better about my life and hit them with my latest quiz questions. They're my practice audience and they always get every single question right. They're amazing.

One of the Category-C ladies, Annabel, shuffles closer to me. She can barely contain her excitement. 'Do you have any pictures of these pink wedding outfits?' she says in a low, conspiratorial voice. She wants to see it first so she can lord it over the others while they're distracted. I pull out my phone for her to review Facebook. She flicks expertly but disinterestedly past the carnage shots – kindly uploaded by the best man, who has tagged the mother-in-law in an action shot, dripping with Jägerbomb puke.

'Are you not interested in the boozy, fighty stuff too?' I ask curiously, as Annabel shrieks with happiness at shots of the pink ceremony.

'Ha!' she huffs, not looking up. 'You think we didn't get up to that kind of nonsense when we were young too? Getting drunk and being sick on each other hasn't changed much in centuries. That's not shocking at all, love, but wearing a pink wedding dress . . . now *that's* exciting. Look at this poor, silly child!' She jabs a gnarled finger at my phone screen. 'She looks like a walking blob of candy floss! Can you even imagine what my mother would've said about this? She would've sent me to live in a convent just for suggesting such a thing.' She sighs, adding dreamily, 'Isn't the new world we live in just wonderful? What I wouldn't give to be young now.'

I give her arm a squeeze. 'Believe me when I say, Annabel, that it is mostly pretty shit.'

A furious Molly interrupts (her eyes are both streaming heavily now). 'And you, Delilah, *you*. I expected better from you! Attending a wedding where the bride wears pink? It's unthinkable. You shouldn't be associating with such nonsense. And isn't this the sixth wedding you've been to this year? It's only March, young lady. Can't you save it for the summer, like we used to?'

'It's July, you stupid old bint,' snaps Franny, always protecting me, even at twenty-eight.

'How are you affording all this, anyway?' Molly adds, ignoring Franny and narrowing her eyes at me suspiciously. 'I expect that stupid job of yours pays stupid money, doesn't it? I don't pay my license fee just so you can go off to pink weddings all the time.'

'Actually, Molly, I make very little mon—' I start but she's not interested in any facts.

'It's not like in my day when you had to actually do proper work – intense manual labour – to earn a crust. You lot swan about with your internet and your touch screens, and expect everything to be handed to you on a plate.'

'How much did you pay for your house, Molly?' Franny says sweetly. 'About two thousand pounds, was it?'

Molly shuts up.

Just then, one of our more recent additions to the group, Ethel, comes running in. She looks distraught and I can see the gleam of her balding head through white, thinning hair as she passes under the light.

'Ethel, what's wrong?' I ask, standing up, a little relieved for the distraction. She shakes her head, confused and frightened (Category B). Maybe she accidentally caught a few minutes of *Ex on the Beach* again. That took three long months to explain.

'I was trying to use the computer in the office . . .' she begins, stuttering. 'My grandson keeps sending me emails and I was trying to print them out so I could read them. But the phone in there kept ringing, so I answered it and it was this chap with a foreign-sounding name – I think it was Mussolini . . .'

I feel confident it was not Mussolini. This feels very racist.

Ethel keeps going. 'And he kept talking about the youth club and had we got his messages.' She shakes her head. 'I didn't know what he was talking about and then he said this building has been earmarked for closure. They're knocking it down. We're being evicted! No more Fuddy-Duddies United! He said we're on notice and they're giving us a couple more months to make alternative arrangements but then they're shutting down the building either way!'

Ethel bursts into tears as she finishes her speech and Molly screams at the rest of us, 'WHAT DID SHE SAY?!' I don't know if it's shock or she really couldn't hear – Molly only wears her hearing aid about twenty per cent of the time because she says she likes the freedom of not being able to hear people when it suits her.

113

I replay Ethel's words in my head. Evicted? How can that be? Shit. This is awful news. Alternative arrangements? What does that mean? This group has been coming here for years. It's a second home for many of the ladies. We've even converted the loos to be old-lady friendly and there's nothing else like this anywhere nearby. We can't afford to rent anything. Alternative arrangements? There is no alternative. For a few of these women, it's the only time they leave their house. It's brought the community together. They need this.

Ethel is still sobbing and starts talking again through her tears. 'He didn't even make small talk when I answered the phone. He just asked me who I was, and then started shouting at me. He was horrible. He didn't mention how sunny it's been either. What kind of gentleman doesn't mention the weather when it's been so very warm? It's like he didn't even care. Do you think it's my fault this is happening? It's not my fault, is it?'

Franny puts an arm around her, shushing her kindly. Ethel buries her face in Franny's shoulder and quietens.

I look around the room at the shell-shocked faces. No one says anything. Everyone is just looking at each other. Franny and I make eye contact and I see fear.

Right. No. No, I'm not having that. I'm not having my grandma scared. I'm not letting my grandma and all her friends be thrown out on the street. No, I have to do something to stop this. We need this building, they can't just knock it down. I'm sure it's a misunderstanding or maybe a mistake – who knows with Ethel. It might seem like a silly little women's group to outsiders, but it's much, much more than that from the inside. It matters.

I feel adrenaline pumping through me and a renewed sense of purpose takes hold.

I'm not going to let this happen. I'm going to ring this bastard council man and talk some sense into him. They can't do this. I'm going to find a way to make all this go away so these ladies can stay in the place where they feel safe and happy. I'm going to fix this.

Wedding Number Seven: Lindy and George, Gregor House, Lancashire

Theme: Harry Potter – THAT'S RIGHT. All four groomsmen wore different house colours. Bride's dad grew a Hagrid beard especially. Awful jokes in the best man's speech about the bride's 'wizard sleeve'.

Menu: Smoked salmon starter, followed by chicken and a meringue dessert. Veggie option: stuffed red pepper with goat's cheese.

Gift: J.K. Rowling-signed framed pic and photo book with all their Potter convention pictures @ £72.50.

Gossip: Groom had attempted last-minute platinum hair dye, to look like bride's fave character Draco Malfoy. Somehow looked exactly like Myra Hindley.

My bank balance: -£347.12

11

'And was the pig related at all to the queen?' Will asks, deadly serious, looking the waiter straight in the eye and holding the menu up. Neither of them blink.

'Aah, I don't belieeeeve so, sir,' the man replies at last, carefully. 'Because . . . it's a . . . pig. But I do know it was hand-reared by monks off the coast of a Scottish island and fed exclusively plum tomatoes. It is the most tender, beloved pig meat you'll ever know. It simply melts in your mouth.'

Will looks disapproving. 'I'm not sure I want a melting pig in my mouth. I'm not David Cameron.'

The waiter looks panicked. 'It's just a saying, sir. I mean it's delicious.'

Will nods excessively. 'I see, I see. But you're saying it's unlikely the pig has any royal connections whatsoever?'

The waiter pauses. He cannot tell if Will is an inbred moron – like so many of the other guests I can see around us in the room – or if he is being played.

I take a long sip of my wine to stop me laughing.

'As far as I know, the pig *is* of noble breeding,' he says slowly, like he's talking to a rich, spoilt child. 'But not, er, royalty.'

Will tuts loudly, and the waiter adds hastily, 'But I will double check on that for you.'

Will nods again and closes his menu. 'We'll both have the fifteen-course disgusting menu please.'

'Um . . .' The waiter pauses. 'Do you mean the degustation menu?'

117

I can't help it, I snort, immediately covering my mouth with my napkin and pretending it was a cough.

'That's the one, my good man,' Will says jovially. 'And more wine, if you please.'

He grins at me and I feel all warm inside. Sure, it might be the wine, or it might be what a great time we're having, and how much-needed this time away together really, really was.

We're in one of those hotel restaurants where you pay an insane amount of money to have a million tiny courses of nonsense food hand-crafted personally by a Michelin-starred chef, and then it comes out and it all basically tastes like watercress. You know the one.

We decided yesterday – spur of the moment – that we were going to ignore everything and run away for the night to a super posh hotel, thirty minutes away. Will suggested it. He said we both needed a break and that it would be good to finally get some time alone together. There was the tiniest hint of a passive-aggressive tone to his voice, but I chose not to acknowledge it, and immediately went upstairs to pack my one black lacy, frilly thing.

But then I unpacked it because I was worried Will might take it as a sign that I wanted to have loads and loads of sex, when actually the one time would be perfectly sufficient, and then I mostly wanted to sleep, eat and lie down in the hotel spa.

I can't say enough how much Will and I really needed this. We haven't had a break in ages, and all our money seems to go on family and friend commitments instead of each other. We've always talked about travelling together one day, but Mr Barclays and Mr Natwest might have something to say about me deep-diving further into their credit system.

Genuinely, at this point, I feel like I could singlehandedly bring about another financial crash. Hmm, I wonder if they'd consider giving me a government bailout?

Don't think about it. Denial ain't just a river in the world somewhere (should've paid more attention in Year Nine geography lessons).

Luckily Will insisted on paying for this, and I was so excited, I let him. I even called in sick to work so I could go get my hair done to look nice for the trip. It really needed doing properly anyway – I haven't been for ages. I was too traumatised after my last visit in January, when this new hairdresser kept touching my hair way too erotically and making noises that seemed inappropriate. Then, when I asked for a trim, he insisted I 'trust him' with a 'funky look' he wanted to try out on me. I weakly protested and told him I'm too old – or possibly too young – for 'funky', but he didn't listen. I sat there watching the situation in the mirror get increasingly dire and not being brave enough to stop him. I mean, gawd, going to the hairdresser is such a horribly stressful experience as it is, having to stare at your own stupid damned face under yellow lighting for hours on end, and then trying to work out if you're allowed to accept their compliments on your hair, or whether you have to go, 'Well YOU did it'.

It's all totally ugh. So I definitely didn't need a fucking rogue hairdresser turning me into Rod Stewart.

After three hellish hours he got the tiny ta-dah mirror out to show me the back, and I told him it looked 'really great'. I thanked him profusely, tipped him generously – and then went to the loo to cry at my reflection. Lauren picked me up for lunch afterwards, and was so nice when she saw how upset I was. Firstly, she told me it didn't look that bad at all and that Rod Stewart is actually a pretty big inspiration for the autumn/winter catwalks, and then she went into full-on

Lauren Bolt Rage Mode, insisting on storming back into the hairdressers and screaming legal words she'd heard on *Ally McBeal*, while I hid around the corner. She got my money back and a big fat voucher that I've obviously been way too scared to cash in. But still. She was truly amazing.

I feel a bit sad, suddenly, at how far away all that feels.

I didn't even tell Lauren I was going to the hairdresser today and I haven't mentioned this spontaneous mini-break either. I used to tell her every minutiae of my life, and now I'm too scared she'll get cross with me for taking a night away from her to-do list.

The waiter returns with our first plate, which looks like a blob of dead jellyfish and tastes like – yes – watercress. I thank him, resisting the urge to put on a Russian accent. In posh hotels like this, I'm always desperate to *Pretty Woman* the shit out of the situation. Try to somehow convey to everyone around us that Will is my rich client and I'm here to do his bidding.

Ooh, maybe I should buy a blonde wig.

I turn to ask Will if he's up for doing the sexy stranger thing in the bar later and find him staring misty-eyed across the restaurant. A stressed-out-looking family are hissing at each other in low voices a few tables away, telling their two kids to 'shut the fuck up and sit the hell down' as they run in a circle around the table, trying to stab each other with butter knives.

'Cute, huh?' he says and smiles at me dopily.

'Hmm,' I say, as vaguely as I can, taking a mouthful of watercress jellyfish and feeling fear creeping up my spine. First a non-proposal, now . . . what even is this? Is Will getting broody? Children are basically aliens to me. They're so far off my radar that the other day on my train platform, I thought it was a group of dwarves waiting a few feet away. My brain went to that place long before it reassessed them as school kids.

'Hey, after this,' I say, trying to distract him, 'shall we order in McDonalds to our room? You know they do deliveries now, right?'

He smirks. 'Are you not excited about the purple caterpillar dish that's coming up next?' he says and we both laugh. We laugh a lot, and it's not at the joke, but relief at being here together and having fun.

He reaches over and takes my hand. 'I've missed you so much,' he says suddenly and I feel the weight of the last couple of months lifting.

'Me too,' I say.

12

I stretch my hands out towards the long mirror covering the length of the wall, feeling everything else in my life melt away. The eviction notice for Fuddy-Duddies United, Lauren's increasingly crazy eyes whenever I see her, and my multi-coloured bank statements – it all floats away.

I'm in my early morning yoga class and it's totally wonderful. This is my – and I know this is a lame word but I'm going to use it anyway – sanctuary. I've been coming to yoga for the last couple of years, at least twice a week, and more when I have time. Which I don't lately.

It's like having a brain colonic, washing out all the nonsense and flushing the mess away, at least for the hour I'm in here. For that time I'm in the room, nothing really counts except my limited limbs and the sweat circling my face and down into my mouth, which, yes I know, is gross.

But it feels amazing.

Not that I'm good at it. I'm the most inflexible person who ever existed. Really, Will has to do all the work in the bedroom. But I've definitely seen improvements since I started. I feel taller and leaner and fitter. And so much clearer.

I reach into a downward dog, feeling my spine creak with happiness. Ooh, it's good.

Around the room are several familiar faces moving into the regular poses, alongside the usual scattering of frightened-looking newbies, who look like they want to cry. I catch the eye of a lady who always comes to this Saturday class with her husband, and takes the same spot at the front. We've never actually spoken, but in my head they are the Wiggums from *The Simpsons*. They look exactly like Chief Clancy Wiggum and his wife Sarah Wiggum! Weirdly so. They even have a bit of a yellow glow in this dim lighting.

I consider again now how interesting it is when people date someone who looks just like them. I notice it happening more and more. My Facebook feed is full of them! Couples who are basically dating themselves, who fancy themselves. Because that's what you're saying when you date your clone – that you want to have sex with yourself. Isn't that funny? I think it's funny.

A few feet away, Chief Wiggum grunts loudly as the class changes position, and I try to redirect my focus back into my breathing. That's what you're supposed to do. It's all about the breathing, they tell us over and over.

But two years of classes later, I can officially, unilaterally confirm: it's fucking not.

Mate, breathing I can do *any time*, and much as I love yoga, I just can't get into the hippy-trippy side of it. I'm here to sweat and repeatedly fail to reach my toes; I don't want to hear about, I don't know, *monks* or my soul or the universe.

But even though I'm impatient with breathing and struggle through every class, I still find this to be sooo much better than the gym. I have never been a gym person, it's just not for me. There's one attached to this yoga studio and I slink through it every week, back against the wall, feeling inadequate. There are just so many taut, veiny people shouting at each other about squat thrusts and leg days. It genuinely scares me. I tried going along a couple of times a few years ago and I just wandered around feeling lost and lonely. I ended up speed-walking on the treadmill for twenty minutes and then I left.

The yoga instructor talks us through our final posture and then makes us lie down in the dark, in the disturbingly named 'dead body pose'. You're meant to lie here totally still for ages to 'centre' or something. The guy leading the class always says this is the hardest position, which is obviously horseshit, but I get what he means; it's because staying still is difficult for people like me, people who are always moving. The trouble is, if I lie still for more than thirty seconds I will . . .

Yep, I fell asleep and then immediately woke myself up with a loud snore. I try to loudly clear my throat to cover it, but everyone definitely heard. The almost-naked instructor comes over, wearing his Speedos. And by the way, it's not even that hot in here, this isn't Bikram yoga. He just wants to show off his body as he leans over, his bulge horrifyingly close to my face.

'You OK there, Lilah?' he says in what is meant to be a soothing whisper.

'Yes,' I squeak, getting the pitch totally wrong. Mr and Mrs Wiggum sigh across the room at me. I'm ruining their bliss. Oh no, I really hope they'll still be able to breathe OK after this.

'Just take deep, calming breaths there,' he tells me and I smile tightly. 'Let everything go. Lie still for at least another five minutes and then make sure you get a good night's sleep tonight, OK?'

I nod, hating him. I should get some sleep, should I? Great to know, thanks so much.

I give him and his big lumpy penis a thumbs up and try to keep still.

The thing is, there's just too much going on for stillness and bliss at the moment.

Lauren is full bridezilla now. She's basically having a nervous breakdown but will scream at anyone who points it out. Then I had my brother on the phone this morning, asking to borrow more money. He says he needs to move, because now Mum and Dad have been around to his urban commune, the 'vibe' is ruined. He says he'll give me his new address, but I'm not allowed to pass it on. And obviously I had to say no, because I'm utterly broke.

Things are hell at work too. Rex has started kicking off about the *Quiz Monsters: Live Celebrity Special*. He says all the celebs I've managed to line up for it are old news, and the whole thing has a been-there done-that feel to it. He wants me to come up with some extra element to make the format glitter a bit more. He told me I should stop relying on his 'dazzling abs and teeth to pull in ratings'. Which is so irritating. As if handling a dozen celebrities – their schedules and their egos – in a *live* setting isn't exciting enough?

I tried brainstorming yesterday with Sam and Aslan, which went something like this:

Me: So, guys, any ideas on how we can take this celeb special to the
    next level? Give Rex something to thrill his Twitter followers?
Aslan: That's a great outfit you've got on today, Lilah. You look
    fantastic.
Me: Um, thanks. So, ideas?
Aslan: I'm just saying, you've nailed your look.
Sam: What if we do the whole thing on a plane, and when one of the
    celebs gets a question wrong, we throw them out?
Aslan: With parachutes, you mean?

Sam: No.

Me: Right, OK, I really like your thinking, Sam. But I have a feeling that might be seen as too extreme – too far away from the original *Quiz Monsters* format. Anything in between? Aslan?

Aslan: Oh Lilah, you don't need my help on this one. You're great at all this. A natural with the ideas side of things. Don't be shy – tell us what you're thinking.

Sam: That's super unhelpful, dude, she knows what you're doing.

Me: She's right, Aslan. Please don't Rex-pander me. I need your help. You're meant to be working on this special with me.

Aslan: OK, yeah, sorry. I just don't have any ideas. It's a quiz show; we can't reinvent the wheel.

Sam: Oh, how about some kind of wheel?

Aslan: Yes! Great idea, Sam. Like the wheel of fortune?

Sam: Or, like, we could attach the celebrities to a large wheel and have Rex throw knives at them?

Me: Hmm, again, I think that might be too far away from the original quiz concept. And possibly a little bit un-insurable.

Aslan: You know Rex would love it, though. Especially if that one out of Take That's coming on – you know their feud goes way back.

Me: Since the thing with Lilo, yes, I know.

Sam: What's the thing with Lilo?

Aslan: Well, she . . .

Me: No, Aslan, we don't have time for the whole story. Google it, Sam. It was in all the papers. There was a high-speed car chase, drug cartels, they nearly killed each other, blah blah. Come on, guys. Anything else?

Sam: Death fight match?

It went on and on like that for an hour, and just when I thought it couldn't get any worse, I pulled a pen out of my bag to make some notes, and only realised it was actually a tampon when I tried to write with it.

Ah, sod bliss. I grab my towel and sweaty mat and head for the showers.

Wedding Number Eight: Daniel and Seiji, South Farm, Norfolk

Theme: Rustic. There were leopard-print rugs across every surface, and a big log fire that immediately went out but continued to smoke the whole afternoon, choking out an asthmatic great uncle.

Menu: Smoked salmon starter, followed by chicken and a meringue dessert. Veggie option: stuffed red pepper with goat's cheese.

Gift: Silver candlesticks @ £60.

Gossip: On the morning of the wedding, one of the wedding party announced she and her girlfriend had decided to have a civil ceremony *later the same day*. They took the best man and half the guests off with them as witnesses.

My bank balance: -£595.01 (plus one or two credit cards, but they don't count, right?)

13

We've been waiting for Lauren for thirty-five slow, tedious minutes and the woman behind the counter – who was already giving us the stink eye just for being alive – now absolutely, definitively hates us. The only reason she hasn't thrown us out is because Joely pulled a fairly dramatic DON'T YOU KNOW WHO I AM move on her when she started muttering about other appointments. Joely suggested Resting Bitch Face call the manager if she wanted to discuss the next lengthy blog post she'd be putting up about how 'up its own arse' this place is for her millions of followers. And then she sent the woman scurrying off to bring us two more glasses of champagne.

In case you couldn't guess by the level of unnecessary snobbery behind the counter, we're in a bridal shop. It's actually the sixth bridal shop we've visited around Greater Manchester over the last few months, in Lauren's quest for gown perfection. But right now, our bride – who is supposed to be here with us trying on an array of different types of white froth and lace, while we gasp appropriately – is instead stuck in traffic. She keeps sending us messages, ordering us not to leave, but I'm finding it increasingly difficult to cope with the shop assistant's dirty looks. I feel like Julia Roberts in *Pretty Woman* again, but it's not sexy this time and I don't feel the urge to wear a blonde wig. She quite quickly spotted that I am the weaker of the two and is now focusing her fury in my specific direction. And honestly, I'm not sure I can handle the pressure much longer. I'm going to run out screaming and crying any moment now.

My phone rings – maybe it's Lauren. Hopefully she's here!

But it's not, it's Dad. Should I answer? Can I deal with this? At least if I'm on the phone, it'd be harder for the woman to force us to leave.

'Hey, Dad,' I say, pressing my phone to my ear and making my way to the front of the store, away from Joely.

'What's new, pussycat?' he says, predictably.

'Not much. Busy as ever. I'm in a bridal boutique at the moment, waiting for Lau—'

'That's great, love,' he interrupts. 'Listen, have you spoken to your bitch mother?'

Immediately. Great. I roll my eyes.

'Please don't call her a bitch,' I try weakly.

'I would love to not call her a bitch, Delilah, I would absolutely love that,' he says enthusiastically. 'But she IS a bitch. She is behaving like a bitch and is a bitch down to her core, so what else can I do? Tell me what I should do, what word should I use, because it is the only word that describes her.'

'OK,' I sigh. 'No, I haven't heard from her.' But just as I say it, my phone lights up against my ear. A quick look confirms it's a text message from Mum. She wants me to know my dad is a garbage toilet. When I put my phone back to my face, Dad is mid rant.

'I really mean it, the woman should be tested for rabies. I'm not even saying that in a mean way. I'm actually worried for her health. I feel like she is going to fall into a rabies coma very soon – any moment now – and then it's going to be too late to save her. Like, I hate the bitch, but I don't want to see her dead, and she is clearly demonstrating all the symptoms of early-stage rabies. Foaming at the mouth, being insane, general uncalled for rage. It's really obvious that's what she has.'

'Has anything actually happened, Dad?' I say a tiny bit impatiently. This is not a new speech.

'Yeah, and I think this fact is going to blow your dick off, Delilah,' he says dramatically, using another phrase he's picked up from late night American telly. 'She's started seeing that turd, Jack, again. She sent me a cock picture and it looked a lot like the ones she sent me while they were together.'

'Dad, that's charming—' I start, but he's still going.

'So then I sent her a pair of tits I found on the internet and she came back immediately and said they were clearly Kim Kardashian's, and unless I was getting off with Kim Kardashian, then I was a pathetic loser.'

'That is very harsh—' I try again.

'And I tried to call your brother to talk to him about it, but he didn't answer, as usual. It's really ruined my day, Delilah. I was trying to watch old episodes of *The Voice*, the ones where Tom Jones performs, and your mother has completely ruined that experience for me. You need to talk to her, Delilah. Tell her she's a vile bitch. Use those words.'

'I can't do that, Dad,' I say, feeling tired. 'Listen, I have to go. I'm in the middle of stuff. But I'm sorry you've had another little falling out with Mum. I'm sure she didn't mean any of it.'

He scoffs as I quickly say bye and hang up.

My parents are the worst.

Across the room, Joely sighs with frustration as she takes another gulp of fizz. 'How long before we can leave, do you think?' she says, not waiting for an answer as I sit back down next to her. 'I have a date tonight and I want to go get my vagina steamed before the place closes.'

I give her a quizzical look and she nods – she's serious.

'Gwyneth Paltrow does it,' she explains. 'She's been going on about it for years, about how it has healing and rejuvenating properties. Plus, I'm assuming, it makes your fanny way clean.'

'What exactly needs healing and rejuvenating in your vagina?' I say, genuinely curious.

She shrugs. 'I dunno. I get a lot of compliments, but it has had a rough ride of it over the years. Some rougher than others. I expect it could do with a spring clean.' She laughs.

'Do you think mine needs a spring clean?' I say, worried.

Joely laughs again and this time it's more of a cackle. 'I shouldn't think so, babe. I imagine Will is very hygienic, isn't he? I bet he uses a Dettol wipe on his penis before and after.'

I giggle, but I feel a bit sad for Will. Even though I know Joely is only teasing, he would probably be upset. He can be sensitive. But the thing is, he *is* very clean. And I really like that about him! I can't be the only woman left traumatised in the past by a cheesy blowjob. Surely it's much better to taste Palmolive shower gel in your mouth than all-day sweaty pant odour?

Oh – it occurs to me in a rush – what if my bits taste like all-day sweaty pant odour? I am suddenly afraid. I am not flexible enough to check, so how would I ever really know? I need to do more yoga so I can get my head down there.

Or maybe less yoga, if that's making me sweatier. What is the right answer?

'Maybe I should get her steamed too, then?' I say, gesturing down there, and Joely looks horrified.

'Gross, gross, gross,' she shouts, clearly very upset. 'Please don't refer to your vagina as *her* or *she*. That is so offensive. Don't personify it like it's a little girl or something. What is wrong with you? I had no idea you were one of those kinds of people. Jesus, Lilah.'

I make a face, feeling ashamed. 'Sorry, Joe, I promise I'll never do it again.'

Her shoulders relax and she slouches further into her seat, checking the time again. 'Anyway, you can come with me to the beauty clinic if you like, but definitely don't get the vag steaming actually done. It's an absolute waste of money. All the experts say it's nonsense pseudo-science and, from everything I've read, it's actually probably quite bad for you. Your vagina is too precious to me to take any risks with, Lilah.' She giggles again, adding, 'But sod it. I'm going to write up the experience for my blog and it's going to get so many accidental hits from dirty old men using vagina-y search terms. I can't wait. Do you think I should include pictures or not? A before and after? Might be a bit much?'

Our phones both vibrate. It's another update from Lauren. She's still stuck on the road and is at least another twenty minutes away. Bugger.

A look suddenly crosses Joely's face. She looks over at me and smiles one of her huge, worrying smiles.

Uh-oh.

'What?' I whisper, a tiny bit scared. Her look reminds me of the time I told her I'd never shoplifted anything and so she took me into Superdrug where she forced an eyebrow pencil into my bag and then flashed the security guard so I could get out unnoticed. That was last year.

Joely doesn't answer me. Instead she jumps up and strides over to the furious-looking shop assistant, who stares at her, saying nothing and bristling with hostility.

'We've decided not to wait for our bridesmaid anymore,' she tells the woman loudly.

Um, bridesmaid?

'So we're just going to start trying dresses on already.'

WE?

The shop assistant pauses for a moment, the silence dripping with her disdain. I feel myself pale. What is Joely doing?

'Both of you?' she says at last, her tone carefully studied boredom.

Joely is nodding. 'Yes, sweetie. Lilah and I are marrying each other, so we're both going to be in wedding dresses for our big day this December. Is that OK with you or are you a filthy homophobe that needs exposing to my millions of followers?'

The women stiffens, sensing the potential publicity crisis.

'Fine,' she snaps. 'Pick a few dresses out.' She waves at the curtained area. 'You can both use the large changing room at the end.'

Joely turns back to me, her face glowing. She is trying not to burst with excitement.

'Come on then, *my darling fiancée*,' she crows. 'Let's choose a few dresses to try on.'

'You're going to get us in so much trouble,' I hiss. 'And you can't flash your tits to get out of this one.'

She ignores me, grabbing my hand and dragging me over to the first row of elaborate dresses. Row after row of white, cream and ivory is laid out before us. Lace, satin, twinkling beads and raw silk dazzles me. They're all so beautiful and expensive.

134

'We shouldn't be doing this!' I whisper, my voice full of fear, fingering a fitted bodice with a mermaid skirt.

'Shush.' Joely isn't listening. 'Don't be silly, this is going to be amazing. I've always wanted to try on a wedding dress. Haven't you?'

'No,' I say truthfully, but now I'm thinking about it, white is such a good colour. I look really nice in white.

We hang tags on several dresses at random and the shop assistant follows us around, picking them up passive-aggressively and escorting them reluctantly over to the changing area. Joely grabs my hand and I squeeze it as she leads me excitedly into the room, pulling the curtain across.

'Let me know if you need any help,' the woman says through gritted teeth, definitely not wanting to help.

'More champagne please!' Joely sings as she whips her top off in a single move with one hand. She's clearly used to doing that.

Oh, man, she gets naked with such ease. I am still plucking awkwardly at my t-shirt, wondering if I can subtly hide my boobs in the wide folds of the curtain somehow, meanwhile she is already taking her knickers off.

Hold on, she's what?

'You know you probably definitely don't need to take your knickers off, Joe,' I say, trying not to be too obvious about admiring her downstairs natural look.

'I know.' She nods. 'But they're so rank, I feel like they shouldn't be anywhere near this dress.' She stops to stroke the glorious white satin of the nearest gown before continuing. 'I'm hoping the steam cleaner place will steam my pants too. Like a two-for-one deal down there. They're yesterday's because I haven't been home yet – I had a Bumble date last night. I thought he was going to be a really cool, sexy hippie type, because he had long hair and his name was Rayn. But it turned out his name's Ryan and he just can't fucking spell. He was so dumb, he doesn't even know what bananas are. How do you not know what bananas are? He thought I meant bandanas, how weird is that? Anyway, his dumbness was just too cute – I had to sleep with him. I hadn't shaved my legs, though, so I didn't take my tights off during sex and just told him it was a medical condition.'

'How do you . . . Did you cut a hole . . . ?' I begin, but the mental image is too much, and I laugh instead.

She laughs too and her whole big, beautiful, naked body jiggles happily. 'What are you looking at?' she says merrily, because I was totally staring. 'Are you horrified by my left boob? I know it's much bigger than the right, but the nipple is so much nicer, isn't it?'

I laugh again and turn back to the dresses. 'Which one are you trying on?' I say, not wishing to engage in that nipple chat. Not again. She always wants to know which nipple is better looking and we've told her a thousand times it's the left one. Obviously. Duh.

We pick out dresses and help each other climb in. It's nothing like putting on any dress I've ever worn before. The closest comparison is like wrestling around inside a wet suit. Things have to be positioned and placed. My boobs have to be slotted into the right section. It feels like a filing system alphabetised with body parts. Joely is not even close to being able to get hers on properly, given they all come in a standard size 12–14, but the effect – at least from the front – is still dazzling. She's going to make a really gorgeous bride one day. Maybe even to Rayn/Ryan? We could serve bananas after dinner as, like, an inside joke.

136

My dress is an over-the-top meringue of a dress. I couldn't have chosen more of a costume. It's so not me, but it's wonderful and dramatic. It's too big for me and Joely pops her head out of the changing room to order the surly assistant to fetch some clamps that will hold it together at the back.

Ready at last, we draw back the curtain and walk side by side towards the giant wall mirror. And there we stare, silent and united, at our reflection.

'WE LOOK SO GOOD!' shouts Joely at last, and I catch the assistant in the mirror, sneering and rolling her eyes.

'We really do,' I agree, nodding at myself happily. Not even the other woman's obvious judgement can take away from how cool this is. I am fully in character now, swishing my enormous skirt around, feeling like Elizabeth Bennett, and enjoying the filmic feel and sound of it.

'Er, Lilah?' a nervous voice interrupts our giggling, and I turn around in slow-motion to see Will standing by the door, car keys in one hand.

It's Will. Will is here. Staring at me with an odd look on his face. Shit. I forgot I asked him to pick me up at five. I assumed we'd be done by now, and then I didn't let him know we were running late.

Will is here. And I am here. We are both here in a bridal boutique, where I am standing in a puffball white wedding dress staring at my suddenly very, very pale boyfriend.

'This is not what it looks like,' I say quickly, wondering what it looks like.

There's another moment of silence and then he goofily side-grins. 'You look phenomenal,' he says, and takes a step closer. He laughs as he circles me, admiring the dress from every angle. 'White is so your colour!'

(Told you.)

I laugh too, relieved that he's not freaked out.

Wait, why isn't he freaked out? He should definitely be freaked out.

'That dress is just . . . it's just . . .' He trails off, looking lost and wide-eyed, exactly like a puppy.

He's not a puppy, I remind myself.

'A silly meringue?' I finish for him.

'No, no, I love it!' he says, emphatic now. 'I think it's beautiful and you look so . . . well, Lilah, you look so beautiful.'

He looks misty-eyed at me and I suddenly really want to take the dress off and put my t-shirt back on. It's hot in here. Isn't it hot in here? Did they turn up the temperature? Why would they do that? Don't they know sweating in a wedding dress is unbecoming?

The shop assistant interrupts. 'Can I help you, sir?' she says, using that extra unhelpful tone she's a total expert in.

He sneaks a look at me and Joely, who winks at him.

'Er,' he says, thinking on his feet, 'no, thanks, I'm fine. I'm just the groom, having a sneaky peek at my bride's dress.'

Nope, wrong thing to say. Joely throws her hands up in the air, exasperated.

'The groom?' the woman says icily. 'I thought you two –' she jabs a long, thin finger at me and Joely in our wedding finery – 'were marrying each other?'

We exchange a look and my fake wife-to-be pipes up hotly, 'Do you have some kind of a problem with a three-way marriage? Because that is straight-up prejudice and my millions of followers—'

The woman interrupts. 'Get out'.

That's more than fair.

*

138

Back in our own clothes and in the car twenty minutes later, Joely asks to be dropped off at the steam-cleaning clinic. Will wisely asks no questions when the address doesn't turn out to be a launderette and the two of us sit in companionable silence on the drive home.

'You really did look amazing earlier,' he says suddenly, turning off the radio.

I feel myself blush beetroot. 'Thank you. Er, you look, er, amazing today too, Will,' I say awkwardly. It's all I can think to say, and Franny taught me to always return a compliment. Even if it is incredibly confusing to do so.

Will shakes his head, smiling. 'Did you love it? Wearing the big dress? Pretending to be a bride? Imagining being the star of the show?'

I look over at him but he's staring straight ahead at the road, his hands at ten and two on the steering wheel. Road safety matters to Will.

'It was quite fun,' I say carefully. I don't know where he's going with this. It's as close as we've come to discussing the non-proposal, and I don't know if I want it to get any closer.

He hesitates and then adds, 'Don't you want that for yourself?'

I clear my throat. 'Hmm, maybe one day,' I reply as nonchalantly as I can, thinking that playing dress-up today was probably enough for me. It was fun but didn't feel right. The idea of wearing one of those for real – in front of hundreds of people – seems so far away and alien. And not in an exciting way.

'But what about our future, Lilah?' he says, a little impatiently, and I shift uncomfortably, aware of my seatbelt digging into my neck.

I've never really heard Will be impatient before, certainly not with me. This is new.

He goes on: 'Don't you want us to have our own lives too, Lilah? We had all these plans we made last year. I thought we were going to travel together around the States? Hire a car, take a backpack and road trip across the Midwest. What happened to that? Are you still saving any money towards it? Because I am. In fact, I have the money. I'm ready to go. I want to go.'

Are we really so out of touch? Of course I'm not saving money. Everything I earn is going towards hen dos and travelling about to castles and new outfits and wedding presents. I'm barely covering my half of the rent, never mind saving anything. I am very much negative-saving. How has he not realised that?

He sighs and continues: 'If I'm being totally honest with you, Lilah, I feel very much second fiddle these days. Like our lives are on hold. I . . . I don't want to be one of those couples who *used* to have plans, you know? Who used to do things together and used to have fun. We had such a great time at the hotel a few weeks ago, but then it just immediately went back to us having no time together at all. I don't want to wait forever for our lives to move forward.'

I shake my head. 'It's not forever,' I say simply, adding silently, *It's just this year*. But I know that is too long for him to wait. I can't ask him to wait. I know I have to find more room in my life for him now.

'I'm sorry things have been so busy lately,' I say, feeling awful. 'It's just that with Lauren and her hen do, and all the other weddings we've got happening this year, I've been run off my feet. Plus all that's happening with Fuddy-Duddies United and the council now. Oh, and work as well, with the series finale approaching and the live celebrity special . . .' I trail off. He knows all this. He knows my excuses are legitimate. He knows the last couple of weeks have been me chasing my tail with the council, leaving messages, writing emails, speaking to the rest of FU about what we can do. And so far getting nowhere.

'But I promise I'm going to make more room for you,' I say earnestly. 'I still want to have adventures with you, Will, of course I do! Us travelling around the world might have to wait a little bit longer, because you're right, I haven't been putting much of my salary aside for it lately. But I will, and it will happen. I'm excited for that part of our lives. And I'll tell Lauren she has to back off a bit, OK? Maybe we can make the wedding meetings every other week, instead of every week. I'll ask her to stop sending me so many messages about everything and we'll have more time just the two of us to talk. OK, Will? I'm sorry, I know this hasn't been very fair on you. Don't be cross with me. I'm sorry.'

We pull into our driveway and he turns to me, smiling softly. 'Of course I'm not cross with you,' he says nicely, and then opens his mouth as if to say something more, but my phone vibrates, interrupting us. It's Lauren. Of course it's Lauren. He sees the name at the same time as I do, and climbs out of the car, striding for the door and heading straight inside, without looking back.

I sit there, feeling a little bit shaky.

Oh God. He seems really unhappy. He's never stormed off before – even if that was a really quite tame sort of storming off, and actually possibly more of a going-inside-off. Still, though, it wasn't good. But what else can I do? I've taken too much on, but I can't just drop any of it. It's all too important. Will just has to wait and be patient, it's the only option.

I sigh and open Lauren's message.

I'm here. Where are you guys? This shop assistant is a right smacked-arse-faced bitch.

14

Franny is glittering with excitement about something. She has been bursting to tell me all day about a kind of scheme or prank she's got going on. She loves a scheme or a prank. She kept dropping hints at lunch, but now it's the end of the day and she can wait no longer.

'I've humiliated the shit out of stupid Andrea!' she says, brimming with glee. We've been unloading one of the industrial dishwashers in the canteen kitchen together, and I pause in the act of shaking water off a colander.

'You've . . . you've humiliated the . . . shit out of Andrea?' I repeat slowly, waiting for the punchline.

She takes the colander out of my hand, dumps it still wet on the side, and leads me to a seat out the front, bouncing from foot to foot. As Franny would say, no job is finished until it's totally half-arsed and left undone. She sits down heavily at one of the tables and immediately lights up a cigarette.

'Franny!' I gasp dramatically. 'You're really, really not supposed to smoke indoors, you must know that – especially not in a TV studio—' I start, but she waves me away, smiling sweetly.

'They're not going to tell me what to do,' she says, puffing happily. 'It was fine back in my day and it's fine now. I can't be doing with all this worrying over everything. Everywhere I turn I'm being shouted at about yet another thing causing cancer. Chocolate causes cancer, chocolate saves you from cancer. Alcohol causes cancer, alcohol saves you from cancer.

Vegetables cause cancer, coffee causes cancer, walking to the loo causes cancer, going to the loo causes cancer, being alive causes cancer—'

'OK, yes,' I interrupt a list that didn't sound like it was going to end, 'that's true, but smoking definitely causes cancer. And other stuff.' I fan a hand in front of my face, the smoke giving me an instant head rush. 'Fine, but please put it out quickly if anyone comes in.'

'Course I will, Delilah, my darling. I'm not stupid,' she says, rolling her eyes at me affectionately. 'I always put it out and blame one of the interns when anyone asks about the smell. Ha!' she cackles, and I glance nervously over my shoulder at the canteen door. Her laugh really carries along these big echoey corridors.

'So, anyway,' I change the subject, watching her puff contently, 'what have you done to Andrea this time?' I am trying not to sound judgemental, but really, poor Andrea.

'Oh, that idiot,' she says happily, through a haze of smoke. 'I am so sick of her asking me to bloody sponsor her for everything! This morning she announced that she's planning on doing Dry September. Am I really going to sponsor her to not fucking drink for four weeks? Piss off am I!' She throws her hands up in the air, exasperated, and ash flicks into her lap, settling in a neat pile and smouldering through her canteen smock. I notice there are several small burn holes, and wonder if it's from the ovens or from a person regularly smoking indoors during work hours.

Let's not think about it.

'Firstly, Dry September is not a thing,' she shouts, leaning across the table towards me. 'Dry January isn't even *really* a thing, never mind Dry September. Unless you're talking about that one boring man-less month I had in 1973!' Franny

144

cackles again. 'And secondly, why should I give that moron my well-earned pension money to *not* do something? How is that difficult? You're just *not* doing it. It's easy. Unless she's a raging alcoholic, in which case she should stop anyway.' She pauses and looks thoughtful. 'That's a good idea, actually – I'm going to tell everyone Andrea's an alcoholic.'

I nod enthusiastically, mentally apologising to Andrea, who is a perfectly nice divorcee who always gives me extra chips when I am having a hard day.

'Anyway,' Franny goes on breezily, 'when she sent around this latest email talking some nonsense about raising money for Green Peace or some other shit, I decided to start my own JustGiving page. I'm asking people to sponsor me in telling Andrea she's a dickhead. I've already raised more money than her and I've only been going for half a day!' She throws back her head, wheezing at her own joke.

I wince. 'It's a little bit ruthless, Franny,' I try.

She looks outraged. 'It's not ruthless! If anything, it is ruth. I'm the most ruth person you could ever hope to meet. Call me Granny Ruth.'

I'm torn. I know I should tell Franny off. It's all very unkind, and she doesn't even do anything around here. But I am also sick to death of Andrea's constant emails about sponsoring her – I've had about eight in the last few months.

A stern voice from behind me interrupts us. 'What's going on here, then?'

I squeal, instinctively diving under the table. Once there, I realise it was possibly the wrong move. I'm afraid there is a chance it could come across as the *tiniest* bit childish and cowardly, and since I now recognise the stern voice as that of my runner, Sam, I have to say, I sincerely regret doing it.

I clear my throat, and from under the table, I say loudly

145

and casually, 'Oh, I found that earring you were looking for, Franny.'

I climb out, staring at the ceiling and hoping that might've worked. When I chance a quick look at Sam, she is looking at me very innocently.

'Well done on finding that earring, Lilah,' she says, her eyes wide. 'Franny is really lucky you were willing to get down there under the table so very quickly to look for it – and just as I came in and caught you guys smoking indoors.'

Franny cackles and slaps a hand on Sam's shoulder, forcing her into the chair between us. 'Have a seat, kid,' she says, and then adds conspiratorially, 'Do you want a cigarette?'

Before I have a chance to panic, Sam shakes her head. 'No thanks, Granny Franny, I don't smoke.'

Ah, phew.

Franny looks a little sulky that no one will smoke with her, but cheers up when Sam pulls a tub of M&S mini chocolate rolls out of her bag to offer around.

'You really shouldn't smoke, Granny Franny,' Sam says, shovelling chocolate into her mouth. 'Don't you want to live to be a ripe old age?' She snorts and Franny doubles over, hooting.

'You're great, you are,' she tells Sam, and I feel proud of them both, just as Franny adds, 'Do you want to sponsor me to annoy Andrea?'

'The other lady who works here?' Sam says, gesturing towards the kitchen, as if Andrea were still in there. 'I already did. Five quid. Everyone was talking about it at lunch today and I heartily agree with your proposal. Seriously, if I get another one of her forms shoved under my nose when I'm trying to get my lunchtime plate of chips, I will lose my shit.'

'You two . . .' I halfheartedly attempt the moral high

146

ground, but they both look at me with judgemental eyes that say: 'You hid under the table five minutes ago.'

My phone rings and I'm tempted to dive under there again when I see the number.

Franny leans across, clocking the caller ID. 'The scumbag!' she pronounces and I grimace.

It's the council man who spoke to Ethel. He's ringing me back at long, long last. I've left this guy four voicemails in the last couple of weeks and I can't believe it's taken him this long to get back to me. It's outrageous. I kept trying to talk to other people in his office about what's happening with the FU building, but they all said it was Mr Canid I needed and he would ring me back at his 'earliest convenience'.

And here he is.

'Hello?' I say, in my most grown-up phone voice.

'Mrs Fox?' says the man at the other end, who I have already decided is the worst person who ever lived.

'Speaking,' I say superciliously. 'But it's *Ms*, actually.'

'This is Mr Canid from Manchester council,' he says. 'I believe you've been trying to get hold of me.'

I sit up straighter, feeling powerful. He sounds like such a shit. I can tell from his voice that he's in his fifties or sixties, and I'm picturing a wide, ugly tie, on a wide, ugly man.

'I have, actually, yes. For a few weeks now,' I say, my voice a pitch higher than I would like.

'Apologies, I've been away. I only just got your message,' he says, but he doesn't sound the least bit apologetic.

Messages PLURAL, I don't say.

Sam leans over to Franny and asks in a loud whisper, 'What's going on?'

Franny elbows her and tells her to 'shut up' but then relents, whispering, 'They're trying to shut down the building where our Fuddy-Duddies United group meet. We don't have anywhere else to go, and my girl Delilah is going to stop them.'

We make eye contact across the table, and she gives me an encouraging nod. I stand up. It helps me feel in control.

'Fine, well, Mr Canid—'

'Canid,' he corrects me, petulantly, even though it sounds exactly like what I said.

'Canid,' I repeat, irritation creeping into my voice. He's already annoying me and I haven't even started.

'You're not pronouncing it right,' he interrupts me again.

'I'm pronouncing it exactly the same way you're pronouncing it,' I say.

'Canid,' he says again.

'CANID', I shout back.

He sighs, dissatisfied. 'Don't worry about it, Ms *Fax*. What do you need from me?'

OH, THIS MAN. He's so rude!

I am momentarily at a loss for words, furious at his brazenly unhelpful manner. And then all the lost words rush out at once.

'You had a phone conversation with a colleague of mine recently – Ethel Galding – about the closure of the youth club building we use for our weekly group meetings. I want to know exactly what you think you're doing and how the hell this has happened. We've had no notice, no warning. You had absolutely no right to blindside an elderly woman during a phone conversation like that. You knew full well you were dropping a bombshell and you deliberately did it to someone you obviously knew wouldn't fight back. How dare you do that? How dare you think it's OK to speak to her in the way that you did? How dare you act like it's acceptable to throw a group of elderly women out onto the street with nowhere to go? There are no other buildings in the area we can all get to, you're effectively shutting down our group. These are people's lives you're dealing with here. It's despicable and you should be ashamed of yourself. Well, Mr Canid, I'm here now and I'm not such an easy target. I won't be going down without a fight.'

There is silence at the other end of the phone and I feel amazing. I feel articulate and angry, and *adult*. A surge of electricity and power bounces through me. I haven't spoken to somebody like that in years. Maybe I never have. I know people see me as a pushover, but not now, not today. Oh no, sir! Today I am standing up for the weaker and the less fortunate. I am bringing down The Man. I feel strong and righteous and like I really can make this situation work out OK.

He clears his throat. 'It's *Canid*,' he says icily.

I nearly scream with fury. I nearly smash the phone on the floor. I nearly punch the wall beside me.

Wow, anger feels really good. How come nobody told me how great this feeling is before?

'Mr *Candice*,' I say sarcastically, my voice unrecognisable with all this amazing malice behind the words, 'I want you to tell me how we're going to fix this situation.'

He sighs. I can hear his disinterest. I picture him loosening his big, fat, ugly tie on his big, fat, ugly body.

'I'm afraid you can't fix it, Ms Fox. You're just going to have to find a way to live with it. I understand your passion, but it's misplaced. And unless you're willing to buy the build-ing from us yourself – and I should mention here that it's not for sale – then we're closing the place and knocking it down come October. Since you are clearly very upset about all this,

I offer the council's sincerest apologies for the inconvenience. But I will also flag up at this point that we did, in fact, sent multiple letters. Firstly about the proposal, then about the appeal process, and then about the decision itself. And they all went unanswered and unchallenged.'

Hold on, what?

'Excuse me,' I say, suddenly wrong-footed. 'You definitely didn't send any letters – that's not true. There have been no letters, I've never seen anything like that. Where did you send these so-called letters?'

On the other end of the line I hear him shuffling some papers, sighing again like he doesn't have time for all my silly, womanly *emotions*. 'They were addressed to a Ms Francine Fox,' he says, reading. 'That is the contact name we have. I assume she's a relation of yours?'

Fuck.

I look at Franny, sitting there looking forlorn. She widens her eyes at me questioningly.

'Hold on a second,' I mutter into the mouthpiece, clicking the dickhead on mute.

'Franny, did you get any letters from the council in the last few months?' I say hurriedly, my voice as even as I can make it. 'About the building? About evicting us?'

Franny scowls. 'Oh, maybe,' she says dismissively. 'Who keeps track of these things? If a letter's not addressed by hand, I know it's not going to be any fun, so I throw it away.'

'FRANNY!' I explode, and Sam, still sitting there quietly, looks awkward. Franny looks amused by my unexpectedly angry response and my frustration boils over. 'Franny, get that smirk off your face!' I say, my voice higher than usual. 'We could've done something to stop this. We could've lodged a protest months ago when the decision was being made. They probably had open meetings about this, where members of the public could put across their point of view or complain about the decision. No one protested and now we've missed it all. He's saying it's too late. We're out. The building will be gone by October. Why didn't you tell me about the letters? I could've read them for you. I could've sorted this out.'

For a second she looks a little contrite and guilt fills me. 'Sorry,' I say quickly. 'Look, this isn't your fault. Sorry I shouted. You're right, nobody really reads letters anymore. They should've emailed us or called sooner. And my name is on the administrative list too, there's no reason they should've sent everything to you.' I pause and add again, 'I'm really sorry for getting cross.'

She shrugs like it's OK but she still looks wounded. I sigh and take Mr *Cunt*id off hold.

'Hello?'

He's gone. Crap crap crap. It's probably going to take me weeks to get him back on the damned phone. We don't have time for this cat and mouse silliness. As if there's any point trying to speak to him again anyway – he was the very opposite of helpful just now. And what would I even say?

Shit. I feel like we've gone backwards. At least there was still hope before this call. It feels like that's been crushed now. I feel crushed. He sounded so sure, so certain there was nothing we could do.

And how was I pronouncing his stupid name wrong? I was saying it completely right! The guy is a lunatic. I bet he has no friends at all. I bet he had one friend one time, but then he kept correcting stuff that didn't even need correcting, just to be mean, and then that friend was like, 'OK, we're no longer friends because you're the worst and now you have

151

zero friends again.' And yet he still didn't learn his lesson. What a dickhead.

I look at Franny again. She's slowly chewing on a mini choc-olate roll from the tub and looking sad. Her yellow-stained fingers are fiddling absently with the lid and she suddenly looks really old.

I decide there and then that I'm not giving up. We can't just let this happen. They can't take this away from us. I can't let that moron on the phone win. The FU means too much to all those lovely women. And apart from all the other important reasons, I really don't think any other venue would let Franny bring along Geoffrey's ashes in an urn with her every week.

From: DelilahMFox@gmail.com
To: 15+ contacts in your address book
Date: 15 August

Hello lovely ladies,

It's me again, Lauren Bolt's maid of honour. I think I've now spoken to each and every one of you individually over email or WhatsApp? If not: hello! Hope you're having a really excellent week.

I just wanted to update you on our October Marbella plans for Lauren's hen do, as, after a bit of back and forth, I believe we do now have final confirmed numbers (phew!). Thanks everyone.

SO!

There will be 16 of us flying out to Puerto Banus on the evening of the 5 October, returning late afternoon on the Sunday, 8 October.

We'll be in a self-catering apartment, as it looks like we'll be out and about a fair bit, but the price below does include a few meals out.

For flights, accommodation and all the exciting hen-based activities we have planned, it's going to be £425 each. Really hope that's OK.

I've already paid the deposits on everything and need to pay for the flights in full this week, so would you guys all mind transferring the cash as soon as you can, ideally in the next few days?! So my fifth and favourite credit card doesn't die too painful a death!

Thanks so so so much in advance.

You'll find flight details and my bank details are highlighted in BIG RED LETTERS on the itinerary **attached**!!

We'll be sending around more info about things like the theme, and anything else you might need to bring along, in the next few weeks.

Hope that's OK.

So excited!
Lilah xx

PS. Sorry to sound like a total broken record, but would you mind just replying to me? Think a few people got annoyed last time about all the group messages!

From: RebekahSS31@hotmail.com
To: You
Cc: 15+

Hi, can you give me your bank details?

From: Katie.Jacks@barclays.com
To: You
Cc: 15+

Hey Lilah,

Katie Jacks here again!!!! Soooooo sorry again about allllll those emails you got last time! Lol!!! Hopefully my stupid email account won't do it again this time!!!! Let me know if it does!!!

Thanks for your lovely email, I'm soooo excited to meet you!!! So just let me know exactly how much you need from me and I will transfer this weekend!!!!

Thank you soooooooo much, can't wait!!!!!
Katie xxxxxxxx

From: Fiona89Mansfield@yahoo.co.uk
To: You
Cc: 15+

Morning Delilah,

Thanks for this!

Unforch I can't make it to this now. Didn't realise when I said yes that it meant definite yes.

Ta,
Fi

From: Katie.Jacks@barclays.com
To: You
Cc: 15+

Hey Lilah,

Katie Jacks here again!!!! Don't worry, my email isn't re-sending the message again this time!!!!! I just wanted to say I realised the amount – £425 – was in your email, lol!!! Sorry about that lol lol! So just let me know your bank details and will transfer this weekend. I will set a reminder, lol!!!

Katie xxxxxxxx

From: Katie.Jacks@barclays.com
To: You
Cc: 15+

Hey Lilah,

Katie Jacks here again!!!! Don't worry, my email isn't re-sending the message again this time!!!!! I just wanted to say I realised the amount – £425 – was in your email, lol!!! Sorry about that lol lol! So just let me know your bank details and will transfer this weekend. I will set a reminder, lol!!!

Katie xxxxxxxx

From: Katie.Jacks@barclays.com
To: You
Cc: 15+

Hey Lilah,

Katie Jacks here again!!!! Don't worry, my email isn't re-sending the message again this time!!!!! I just wanted to say I realised the amount – £425 – was in your email, lol!!! Sorry about that lol lol! So just let me know your bank details and will transfer this weekend. I will set a reminder, lol!!!

Katie xxxxxxxx

From: NicolaBucan@carphonewarehouse.com
To: You
Cc: 15+

Sounds great! Will send the money across in the next month or so. You'll defo have it before we fly in October.

Thanks x

From: Katie.Jacks@barclays.com
To: You
Cc: 15+

OMG SORRY!!!!! I think it did it again!!!! That's soooo weird?!!! Sorrrrrrrrrrry everyone!!! Lolllllll!!!

Katie xxxxxx

From: SofiaMathes@clintonscards.com
To: You
Cc: 15+

Hi Lilah,

Sorry, I can't make it anymore either.

Hope you have a good trip! Don't do anything I wouldn't do! See you at the wedding!

Sofia

From: CarlieAnneHodkins@gmail.com
To: You
Cc: 15+

WHY AM I STILL IN THIS EMAIL CHAIN? I TOLD YOU I AM
NOT THE RIGHT PERSON. I KNOW NONE OF YOU. I'M
NOT COMING TO MARBELLA WITH YOU. TAKE ME OFF THIS
GROUP.

From: NicolaBucan@carphonewarehouse.com
To: You
Cc: 15+

Oh, also, what's the theme going to be? And is it a hotel we're
staying at? x

From: Joely.Bolt@FatJoely.com
To: You
Cc: 15+

Hahahaha, guys, all the info is in Lilah's actual email and in the
itinerary attached. READ IT PROPERLY AND STOP GROUP
MESSAGING EVERYONE WITH DUMB QUESTIONS.

Have just transferred the moolah, L-dawg. Thanks for arranging all
this, you are a goddess.

Love y'all,
Joely x

From: JessMarsh@snappysnaps.co.uk
To: You
Cc: 15+

Guys, PLEASE stop cc'ing everyone into your replies! IT just rang me to tell me off about all the personal emails clogging up the server.

Thanks for sorting, Delilah, will transfer the money in a few weeks.

Thanks,
Jess

From: CarlieAnneHodkins@gmail.com
To: You
Cc: 15+

AUTOMATED MESSAGE: USER HAS BLOCKED THIS EMAIL ADDRESS.

15

'THIS IS FUCKING AMAZING,' says Joely, unnecessarily loudly.

'Shhh,' I say, panicked, but she's not listening.

'I CAN'T BELIEVE HOW INCREDIBLE THIS IS,' she adds, and I chance a furtive look around us to see which relatives are giving us dirty looks.

We're at a Hindu wedding for our friend Ravi, and Joely is being way too loud about it. But she's also dead right – it's absolutely amazing. A spectacle to end all spectacles. Dazzling, colourful and enormous. But the word enormous doesn't really cover it. It's more like huge, expansive and gigantic, all rolled into one weird hugexpansigantic word. I've been gaping like a fish from the moment we got here.

Proceedings were running quite late, but a few minutes ago the groom, along with his side of the family, all arrived at the temple, singing and dancing in the car park outside, before making their way in, to cheers from what must be about 800 people in one space. And because this is the world we live in now, everyone here is holding up their phone. It's a sea of black, white and novelty iPhone cases as far as the eye can see, with every single guest filming the procession. Within minutes, I know my Facebook timeline will be full of the same video, filmed from a slightly different angle. And I will watch every single one of them.

I've never seen anything like this and I feel very

sheltered all of a sudden. It's a good feeling, though, knowing I'm learning about other cultures and climbing out of my little white-person bubble. I'm seeing more of the world!

Oh maaaan – that sounded *really* sheltered, didn't it? Don't tell anyone I said that thing about seeing more of the world, that was lame.

The bride and groom are on stage now and we can't really hear what's being said. I don't want to entirely blame Joely for that, because we are quite far back, but it is also mostly her fault because she's being so noisily appreciative of everything around us.

'LOOK AT THEM.' She points now at the array of bridesmaids who are very many and all turn around to look at the woman who wants everyone to look at them.

'YOU SHOULD HAVE YOUR WEDDING JUST LIKE THIS, LAUREN,' Joely shouts down past me at her cousin, who gives her a withering, disapproving look.

'That would be completely inappropriate,' Lauren says haughtily, before adding, 'Stuff like that is called cultural appropriation, Joely. You need to get woke.'

'WHAT THE FUCK DID SHE JUST CALL ME?' Joely shouts in my ear, laughing, before leaning further over. 'YOU THINK YOU'RE BETTER THAN ME?'

Lauren rolls her eyes and Joely smirks.

'Jesus, are we saying woke now?' I murmur, but no one's listening to me. I wish for a second that Will was here with me, but he had to work.

When Joely turns back to me to talk again, I draw a line across my lips – the international sign for seriously shut the hell up or I will kill you where you sit.

As if there was any chance that would work.

'I went out with a south Asian guy last week,' she muses, but her voice is slightly lower, thank God. 'He was super sexy and we had a really good time, getting drunk and feeling each other up in a 'Spoons. But I think I ruined it when I got back to his house. I gave him a handjob in the living room and then wiped his *stuff* all over the sofa. He got annoyed, but – like I told him – it came out of him, it's his property, why should I have to hold it?'

I try not to giggle, but it bursts out of me. That image is too gross for words.

A middle-aged white woman the other side of Joely leans over. She has been listening intently for a while now and can apparently hold her opinions in no longer.

'If you keep giving away the milk, no one's going to buy the cow, dear,' she says primly.

Joely snorts and replies good-naturedly, 'Who are you calling a cow, lady? And whatever, everyone is more than welcome to my milk. It's free range, organic and pasteurised. Plus, I have plenty to share and it's not about to run out any time soon. Why shouldn't I give it away while I can?'

The lady looks shocked, but that only encourages Joely. There's nothing she likes more than being shocking.

'I'm a socialist, see?' she continues in her 'helpful' voice. 'I like to share what I have. I don't have much, but I do have milk.' She laughs raucously and the woman tuts, furious. She turns away pointedly, her nose in the air, and there is a moment of wonderful silence, before she turns back, this time looking directly at me.

'Your friend is very rude,' she says and I swallow hard. She is pretty rude, there's no denying that. Joely snorts again but doesn't comment.

The woman continues to peer at me over her glasses. 'Do you give your body away to all and sundry too, or are you married?'

I shake my head, fighting an urge to disassociate myself from Joely. It's bad enough that I feel this desperate need to please my friends, but wanting to impress mean strangers who slut-shame random women at weddings is taking it too far. I need to get a serious grip on myself.

'I . . . I am not married,' I say, stuttering and trailing off. I don't know how to answer the other part because sex with all and sundry – whatever that means? – actually sounds really fun and is a big part of why I'm so jealous of Joely.

The woman tuts again. 'But you're – what? – about thirty-five years old? Pray tell why you're not married yet?'

Ouch!

'I'm twenty-eight!' I say, trying not to sound too upset, even though I am really, really upset. Thirty-five? I don't look thirty-five, do I? Maybe it's all the stress lately.

She sniffs. 'You need to start using moisturiser, dear. I started at twenty and I've hardly aged a day,' she says as I politely avoid eye contact with her wrinkles. She keeps going. 'And either way, thirty-five or twenty-eight – it's all still too old to be this frivolous. I was married at twenty-one, back when young women were still ladies, and we did things properly. You better get a move-on because a wedding after thirty is terribly gauche.'

I cock my head. Gauche? What is that? Doesn't gauche mean left in French? Why is getting married after thirty left? What does she mean, like, left wing? Is this something to do with Joely's socialist comment?

'I have a boyfriend,' I squeak, hating myself for justifying

163

my life choices. Sitting between us, Joely tuts at me and crosses her arms. I know I'm betraying her by continuing to engage but I can't help it. I need to persuade this woman that I'm not a lost cause. Please don't ask me why, because I don't know.

The woman ignores Joely, nodding at me as she goes on. 'Ah, I see. But he won't get serious and pop the question? Unco-operative, is he? You need to lay down a few ground rules immediately. Men have to be led around by the nose, told what to do. They never get around to doing anything without being pushed into it. Tell this man friend of yours that you won't live with him until he proposes. And then stop giving *it* up so easily – I know what you girls are like. Give him a deadline of Christmas to get the proposal done, and then you can put out again once you're engaged, if you so wish.'

Christmas?!

'I already live with him,' I whisper, feeling silly and angry and defensive. And then more words come out of my mouth in a rush, and I immediately can't believe I've said it. 'And actually, he already asked me to marry him and I said no.'

Joely sits up straighter, as does Lauren on the other side of me.

'What?' they say at the same time.

Oh.

Shit.

Shit shit shit.

'Oh, well, I mean, not *really*,' I add hurriedly. 'It wasn't a proper proposal, just a throwaway comment, just a Will joke, you know? You know what he's like! He didn't mean it.'

Why did I say that? What was I trying to prove? This was not the way I wanted to tell them. And I didn't even tell *them* – I told a fucking nosy stranger. Dammit, that was so stupid.

Stupid stupid stupid.

He didn't even propose, not properly, it was just a laugh, designed to wind me up. He didn't really propose!! A picture flashes through my brain of Will's face when he saw me in that wedding dress. His excitement, and the hints afterwards, followed by the almost-row about wanting more from our future. If I'm being honest with myself, I know what that all meant. I know what he wants. But I don't want to face it. I'm not ready to face it.

This isn't the right time for us to be thinking about any of that anyway – and not just because I'm not ready, but because things aren't . . . they're not right between us. OK, it's more than that, they're actively bad. In fact, things have been getting dramatically worse since that day in the car. I was supposed to make it up to him the other day with tickets to the premiere of a new Marvel superhero film. He's been going on about it for ages and it seemed like kismet when Aslan offered me the tickets. Will was so adorably excited and seemed so happy, after weeks of being weird. I knew this mattered to him, I knew it was important, and I still messed it up. I got trapped in a wedding cake shop with Lauren and lost track of time. When I realised how late it was, I panicked. I tried to ring him but couldn't get any service so I dashed across town in an Uber I couldn't afford, running across a huge car park, only to find the cinema people wouldn't let me in, which was so unfair. Just because I was a sweaty, shrieky madwoman, covered in cake and demanding entrance to a film that started an hour before . . . It's outrageous and I will be writing to their head office.

I sat in the foyer, sad-eating popcorn until Will eventually emerged. And predictably, he was heartbreakingly nice about it.

I kept saying sorry and Will kept telling me not to worry, and because I'm not used to upsetting him, I didn't know how to handle it, so I just kept on apologising. I knew I was being annoying, but I couldn't stop. There was a point where I thought he was going to explode at me, and then my phone went and it was Lauren sending me pictures of alternative cakes. She was still in the bakery and she still hadn't made a decision.

But it was like that was my last chance with him. Everything's been different since then and I hardly recognise us as a couple right now. Not that we're arguing – we still can't even have a shitting argument – but we've moved into another type of relationship existence. One where we live in separate universes. We barely bump into each other at all and when we do, we're tip-toeing around. We've not spoken properly and we're only seeing each other when we climb into bed at night. And even that tends to be at different times. He's usually fast asleep by the time I get in after a long day of work, wedding chores, FU admin, complaining with Joely, and emotional maintenance with Lauren.

I don't know what to do, though. I know the problem is me and my schedule, but I'm still ignoring it. I keep telling myself that I just need to hold on a little bit longer, get through this busy patch, and then I can focus all my energies on him. We can spend all the time together in the world, fix things, do the travelling thing (what's another couple of credit cards?) and maybe even talk about this future he seems to have mapped out for us. Just another couple of months and then I swear I will make it up to him. I really will, and if you can somehow hear these thoughts, Will, know that I'm really, really sorry about all this.

And even sorrier that my apologies are mostly just happening inside my brain.

'When was this?' Lauren says sharply. 'When was this "joke" proposal?'

'Ohhh . . .' I wave my hand, as if to shoo away the conversation. 'Ages ago. Months ago. It wasn't a big deal, really. I didn't tell you because it wasn't real and it honestly didn't matter.'

She relaxes a fraction but I can tell she is angry. I can't tell if she's annoyed about her proposal toes being trodden on or about being kept in the dark about something so important. I'm not sure. It could be either or it could be both. Joely, though, looks delighted.

'What did he say exactly?' she crows, and I feel Lauren re-stiffen beside me. 'Tell me exactly the words he used!' She leans in even closer. 'How can it be a joke? You can't jokingly *propose* to someone! Will is mad about you, Lilah. I bet he meant it really! You know what they say – there's no such thing as a joke. What would you say if he asked you for real? Did you tell Franny? What did she say? I bet she told you not to do it, but you should totally say yes! Maybe you and Lauren could have a joint wedding!'

She definitely said that last thing deliberately to stir, and I shake my head decisively. I'm trying to read Lauren's expression out of the corner of my eye but she is blank-faced as I go on, as firmly as I can. 'There's nothing to say yes to! It's not a thing. I shouldn't have even mentioned it. And even if it was a thing, I don't want to get married now anyway. I'm not ready.'

'Well, you're a very stupid girl, if you ask me.' The woman is still listening and she sighs aggressively now. I wonder again what she's getting out of this conversation. She continues briskly: 'You should've bitten his hand off. Proposals don't come along every day, you know – especially for women *your* age. And that's nonsense about being *ready*. Why on earth wouldn't you want to get married? Every girl wants to get married. What else is there for you?'

Er, work? Friends? Family? Fun? LIFE? I don't say that, I just shrug helplessly.

'Her parents are divorced,' Joely interjects suddenly, apparently on the woman's side.

'It's not that!' I say, a little too loudly, and a few people in the rows in front turn around to glare at us.

I lower my voice to a whisper. 'It's not that! I just don't know if it's what I really want at all. Why do we get married anyway? I love weddings, and I understand that having a party for everyone you know and care about is wonderful, but I'm not sure I want one for myself. It seems like a huge amount of stress and expense. If I had that amount of money lying around, I'd rather buy a house, redecorate or go travelling. Do something that excites me. I don't believe in God, I don't believe in the sanctity of signing a bit of paper, and I think people and circumstances change too much to make a forever kind of promise like that. I don't know where I'll be or how I'll feel in a year, never mind fifty. I just don't *get* marriage. It's meaningless.' I feel Lauren shift uncomfortably next to me and I add quickly, 'I mean, that's what I think about marriage for me *personally*. I think it's a totally brilliant thing to do if you believe in it. I don't mean I'm against marriage altogether, I just mean . . .' I trail off as someone in front of us turns around and angrily shushes us. My cheeks flame as

I sink lower in my seat. Beside me, freezing cold vibes are coming off Lauren in waves.

The dancing is immense but I'm too distracted to truly enjoy it. I'm watching in a trance from the sidelines of the dance floor, as the array of beautiful colours fly in every direction. A few feet away, Joely is dancing like a madwoman with some guy, who leans in and whispers something in her ear. She shrieks with laughter and then shakes her head, striding away in my direction without another word.

She joins me and I say, 'He seems nice,' nodding at the forlorn-looking man she's abandoned.

'Oh, him?' she says. 'He's dreadful. He looks like a White Walker with a pinky ring. I am less than zero interested in him. Negative interested. Do you know what he just said to me? I asked him for dancing tips and he said, "I'll give you a tip, babe – my penis tip!"' She laughs and adds, 'Don't you think that's hilarious? I mean hilarious in a bad way. Men are just so interesting. Did he really think that would work? What was I going to say? "Sounds great – show me to the nearest floor space for the sex". And only his tip? What about the rest? Does he not know how sex works? His poor previous girlfriends. Or maybe he's never had any. I can't imagine many girls putting up with just a tip for very long.'

I laugh with her but I'm distracted. She takes my drink from out of my hand, taking a long sip through the straw, before handing it back. What's mine is hers full stop, and I like it.

'Where's Lauren?' I say, looking around a little anxiously. I'm worried about her. After the service, she shot off, muttering something about needing the loo and I haven't seen her since. The line can't be that long. Well, I mean, obviously it *can* be that long because it always is with the ladies, but I'm pretty sure there's more to it than that.

I can tell she's angry with me. I shouldn't have said that stuff about marriage – that was really dumb and insensitive. I shouldn't have said anything at all. She didn't need to know about Will's half proposal. Now she'll think I'm trying to steal her thunder, or her limelight, and it's very important no one steals any of those things from Lauren.

Joely sways to the music. 'Last time I saw her she was talking the bride's ear off about flower arrangements,' she says disinterestedly. 'She seemed fine, don't worry about her. Hopefully she stays over there, because I'm really at my shit-eating limit with her wedding babble. I really am.' She leans in for another sip from my straw, before continuing: 'Jesus, it started before we even got here today. She rang me at four this morning in a panic about whether she should let children come along to the day part of her ceremony. Like I give any kind of a shit. Did she not call you too?'

I think guiltily about how I've started putting my phone on silent at night, and the three missed calls I woke up to today.

Joely growls with frustration. 'She told everyone there would be no kids allowed at the service but a few of our relatives have gone mental about it. They were ringing her up all day yesterday to shout at her that she has to make an exception just for their children. They're acting as if it's their big day and they have a say. I know it's rubbish for her to deal with and must be a massive burden or whatever, but this is *her* wedding and I've heard her moan enough about it for ten lifetimes! It really isn't my problem. Lauren wants to get married on short notice, and also have the biggest, fanciest, most pretentious event ever, so she has to deal with the consequences. I told her it was a terrible idea to do this in six months and she should've given herself longer, but she never listens to anyone but herself. She thinks she can do anything she likes just because she's the *bride*, and we're expected to follow her around picking up the slack. Fuck the bride. She should just tell our idiot relatives no if she doesn't want their kids there! Why is that so hard? She loves saying no to us; why can't she say it loud and proud to bitchy Aunt Martha? And either way, I don't want to hear any more about it, you know? She's taking over my life. Everything in my life is suddenly about weddings and I'm not even getting married. Before all this, I was quite close to becoming a two-naps-a-day person, did you know that? That is the dream, the absolute dream, and now I don't even get one proper nap because she'll wake me up with some inane problem.'

I nod awkwardly. Naps are important.

She goes on: 'I haven't even had time to do my blog properly over the last few weeks because I've been so distracted. My fake boyfriend dumped me because I kept missing our set-up dates. I've had to settle for some *Big Brother* star from 2010 for my next publicity relationship. My followers keep asking if something's wrong and one girl commented on my last photo that I looked like I hadn't slept in a month! I'm going to start losing followers soon, just because Lauren's too self-obsessed to see that no one gives a shit about her wedding. I'm over it, Lil, totally bored of it. She's acting like she's the first person to ever get married. Newsflash, dickhead, everyone does it and no one cares! As if anyone's interested in table plans. Just fuck off already, Lauren.'

171

A voice full of ice cuts through the middle of us, from behind. 'Well, it's good to know what you actually think.' Joely and I whip around as one, and Lauren is standing there, red-faced and completely, absolutely, totally furious.

Oh no oh no.

'Lauren, it wasn't . . .' I begin, horror filling me as I try to count up the many terrible, destructive words she just overheard. Oh God, what did she see me doing? What was I doing? Nodding? Agreeing? I can't think – I was on autopilot. How was I reacting? How many supportive noises did I make while Joely was talking? Shit.

Lauren immediately stops me before I can say anything else, holding up a hand to my face. She's shaking with rage. 'Don't even bother, Lilah,' she snaps. 'I heard everything she said, I know exactly how she feels now. I suspected as much, and now I know. She's a spoilt princess and I'm sick of her selfish nastiness. She thinks the whole world revolves around her and it doesn't. She's just a fucking *blogger* – it's not even a real job – and she thinks it makes her better than us and too good to help her friends. But it doesn't, it makes her a pathetic, sad bitch, and everyone is laughing at her.'

Joely's shocked mouth snaps shut and she is suddenly just as angry as Lauren. 'You know what?' she spits, standing up straight to her full six-foot height, and towering over her averagely sized cousin. 'I'm not even sorry you heard all that, Lauren, because it's high time you got some home truths. *I'm* the princess? I've never known anyone with such a princess complex. You've been such a nightmare these last few months and I'm so sick of all your irrational demands. Everyone is. Do you even hear yourself sometimes? It's about time someone told you to cut it out. We are not your wedding slaves and we are not your hen do minions.' She turns to me. 'Lilah, did I even tell you that this cow told me to lose weight for the wedding?'

Lauren takes a step towards us. 'That's bullshit, Joely, and you know it. I was pissed off that you'd put on weight just before the bridesmaid fittings, and I made the smallest, tiniest little comment about you dropping a few of the kebabs on occasion so you could get into the dress. Believe me, I was seriously holding back, you have no idea. You think you've been restrained over the last few months – I'm the one who's had to hold my tongue. You're so rude and unhelpful. You seem to go out of your way to make me feel shit about asking for help, even though you know full well I'm dealing with all of this on my own. I haven't even asked for that much but you have deliberately looked bored and been useless at every single one of our wedding meetings. You haven't even had the decency to bother trying to disguise it. It's pathetic. This is my *wedding*, Joely. The biggest, most important moment of my life, and you're meant to care about that and be there for me. Not just as my bridesmaid and one of my best friends, but as my cousin too. You're family – you're supposed to be there for me. But no. No, because it's not all about you and your stupid cocking Instagram profile and stupid wanking blog, you can't even pretend to care, can you? You are unbelievable.'

Joely throws her head back and laughs sarcastically. 'Oh, Lauren. This is incredible. You are the most self-obsessed, un-self-aware person in the entire universe. I had no idea how badly you've climbed up inside your perfectly bleached bum hole! I can't believe you actually just said all those things out loud. You have been demanding our full attention every waking moment for months now. No one's allowed to talk about anything else. We can't even go for a drink together anymore – it has to be a stupid wedding meeting. Have you asked me anything about my life lately, Lauren? Can you think of even one moment you've considered doing that since May? Do you know anything about how I am? Do you know, for example, that I got dumped recently? Because I can't remember you asking even once. Yes, your wedding is important. Lordy, do we know it's important. But it's not THIS important. It's not meant to require your friends giving up their entire lives for you for months on end. That is absolutely insane. And Lilah feels the same, don't you, Lilah?'

Uh-oh. I have been watching their shouting match get louder and louder, and nastier and nastier, with growing terror. I knew I was going to be dragged in at any moment, and as they both turn to face me now, panting with anger, I just stand there, frozen, with my mouth hanging open. I am a rabbit caught in headlights, as the oncoming furious, unstoppable traffic thunders towards me.

Lauren turns back to Joely when I don't answer. 'Don't try to bring Lilah into this, you bag of shit,' she screams. 'She loves helping me, she's not an unhelpful, resentful bitch like you. And she's MY best friend, not yours, so if you think she's going to take your side over mine, you have reached a new level of absolute dumb. You've been trying to steal her off me for years, and especially lately, but you can just back off. You're only part of this group because we feel sorry for you, you stupid whore. We don't even want you as our friend, do we, Lilah?'

I whimper and Joely laughs spitefully. 'She is not your lemming, Lauren. She has her own opinions, her own life. Look at what you do to her, she can't even speak. Look – she was even too scared to tell you Will proposed to her because she knows you'll lose your shit about her getting more attention than you for one second. Can't have that, can we? A huge, massive moment in her life and she didn't tell you. What does that say about you? I know that Lilah's sick of you, just like I am. Come on, Lilah, tell her the truth for once – tell her you're sick of it.'

I have no idea what to say, so I stand there looking from one to the other.

'Lilah?' Lauren says impatiently.

Joely crosses her arms, bright red and livid. Her perfect, lovely features are contorted with fury. 'Lilah?' she snarls like an echo.

'I don't know what to say,' I reply eventually in a small voice. I really don't. I don't agree with anything they've said, but then I also agree with all of it. They're both wrong and they're both right. And I know nothing I could say right now would make either of them happy.

Joely rolls her eyes angrily when the silence stretches on. 'Right, OK, Lilah, maybe you *are* Lauren's lemming after all. You're too chicken to actually say what you think. But I know you're sick of her behaviour too. I *know* you are. You've been on the receiving end of her demanding nonsense even worse than me and I'm close to murdering my whole family just to escape her.' Joely glares at me, as Lauren starts in on me too.

'Lilah, tell her you don't feel like that. Tell her right now. I'm serious, Lilah, tell her to sod off and that I haven't been demanding too much of you.'

I am breathing so hard, my whole body is hot and sweaty. I blink rapidly and swallow down tears. I know I am close to full-on bursting into sobs and I know this would be the wrong moment to do so. They're waiting, both staring at me with hate-filled expressions and still I say nothing.

'Screw this,' mutters Joely. 'I'm sick of it. I'm leaving. I have better things to do than deal with you two. Don't call me, don't text me – either of you. I can't deal with your demanding shit –' she points at Lauren – 'and I can't deal with your cowardly shit.' She points at me and then she turns on her heel and storms out.

Lauren turns to me. 'I don't know what the hell is going on with you, Lilah, but I'm sick of it too. You're meant to be my best friend. I have always had your back, always stood up for you and protected you, but you couldn't do it for me even once today. You've clearly been slagging me off behind my back with her, and lying to me about stuff with Will. Why wouldn't you tell me that he proposed to you? Do you actually think I'm that much of a monster to have been annoyed? I would've been thrilled for you! But you decided to hide it, act like I'm some unbearable ego villain, and then surprise us with it today, months later, when I'm more stressed out than I've ever been in my life. Did you say no because of me? Did you? Because I never asked you to do anything like that, I never would. I would've been happy for you if it's what you wanted. Well, thanks so much, Lilah, now I know how you really see me.' She pauses, and my mouth opens and shuts. She goes on, and her voice is sad and hateful. 'You know what? I don't need your help with the wedding anymore. You clearly don't want to help and I don't need you. You're no longer my maid of honour. I thought you were my best friend, and I thought you'd be happy about being included in my special day, but clearly you're as ungrateful and selfish as Joely. Just . . . forget it. Delete my number.' She grabs her handbag furiously, and, after giving me one more awful, murderous look, she leaves too.

Wedding Number Ten: *Aakifah and Talal, The Granary Estate, Isle of Anglesey*

Theme: Garden party, which apparently means loads of elderly people holding teacups in a large marquee.

Menu: Smoked salmon starter, followed by chicken and a meringue dessert. Veggie option: stuffed red pepper with goat's cheese.

Gift: Honeymoon vouchers, because who really cares at this point @ £50.

Gossip: A very drunk pair of groomsmen stole all the disposable cameras from the tables and did an extensive genital-based photoshoot in the loos. Word is that the bride's dad later collected them all up to have the pics developed and made into a special album for his baby girl.

My bank balance: -£1112.12

16

'Siri,' I breathe out slowly, 'what am I going to do with my life?'

The cool, disinterested voice replies immediately: 'I didn't find any events about "life" in the next three months, Lilah.'

Oh thanks, Siri, you shady fucking bitch.

I try another question, desperate for some validation. 'Siri, is it OK to drink, like, a lot of alcohol, alone on a Sunday morning when my boyfriend is out at the gym again, I'm hungover from another lonely wedding where I knew no one, and I'm generally having a really bad time?'

Her reply is distant and disapproving. 'Here's what I found on the web for that, Lilah.'

The worldwide web, it appears, thinks it's probably not a good start to a Sunday and I close the booze cupboard reluctantly. I can't even get any warmth or comfort from my phone, and it knows me better than anyone.

I go for a wee and sit on the loo, drip-drying and thinking sadly about what is going on with my life.

It's been a week since Lauren and Joely stormed out of that wedding, leaving me high and dry – except not dry at all, because obviously I cried loads like the loser sap I am. After they left, I stood there awkwardly for ten minutes, my mind blank. I was probably in shock, still clinging on to my melting drink while I tried to process what had just happened and what I should do. I was peripherally aware that a few people nearby were staring at me – understandable, given all the shouting

– so I got out my phone and pretended to laugh at a couple of text messages. But then I lost it because I saw a text from Lauren, sent hours before, innocuously asking what I was wearing to the wedding and telling me she was bringing fabric samples along for my maid of honour dress.

That's when I ran out the building, barely holding it together. I couldn't stop replaying the argument over and over in my head. Going through what I should or could have said to calm the explosion. I'm still wondering that now, as I climb back into my cold, empty-of-Will bed, without any Sunday morning booze to warm me up. Whose side was I supposed to take? What could I have done to stop the horrible out-pouring at each other – and at me? A woman in the car park outside the wedding asked me if I was OK, and should she call someone for me. I assume she thought I was drunk (which I was), and I kept shaking my head, tears pouring down my face, and thinking that the people I needed her to call for me were the ones who'd just stormed off and abandoned me there. The person I was going through all this shit *for* was the one who'd just screamed at me and left. It didn't feel like the right time to reach out to Will to come get me – not after so much silence between us – and I knew my brother wouldn't even answer his phone.

So I got a bus home on my own instead, and cried against the window, watching the rain. There was the tiniest bit of comfort in the feeling that I was in a movie.

Since then, it's been a long, lonely, sad week of working, not sleeping, and feeling like dog shit. Will has barely been in the house at all, always at work or the gym – like now. I'm pretty sure he's deliberately avoiding me, and I kept all my crying for when I was alone. It says a lot about where we are in our relationship now, though, because even Rex

180

noticed I seemed miserable. On Friday he even offered me a bite of his Yorkie bar. But then he said maybe I shouldn't, actually, because he didn't want my sad, normal-people germs.

It was nice of him to offer, though.

I have tried exactly once to speak to Lauren and Joely. I rang Lauren's mobile on Tuesday evening, and her sweet little sister-in-law Simone answered the phone. She sounded mortified and said in a loud, awkward voice that Lauren couldn't come to the phone because she was in the shower. Then I heard a door slam in the background and she whispered in a rush of words, 'Sorry Lilah, she's still too cross to talk to you. Maybe just give her a bit of space for a few days? I'm sure she'll come around. You guys will be OK. You're such good friends, I know it will work out.'

Space! HA! We're not in an American sitcom. What is this space stupidity?

Anger at the humiliating rejection carried me through the next few days. I felt really annoyed with myself for even trying. Why *had* I tried? It's not like I did anything wrong! I didn't really do anything, did I? I was just standing there at that lovely wedding, an innocent bystander to the awfulness. This massive fallout isn't really my doing, is it?

Is it, Siri?

'I'm sorry, I don't understand the question, Lilah.'

Fuck you, Siri.

I made one other attempt – this time with Joely – sending her a WhatsApp message asking to talk things through, but it quickly became apparent that she'd blocked me. Which is gloriously melodramatic of her.

Annoyingly, the anger faded, and after over a week of silence – with nothing to show for it from either of them

181

– honestly, I just feel crushed now. Tired, sad and just . . . over all of this.

Meanwhile, I've still been getting calls and messages about the hen do, which is creeping ever closer and closer. Everyone's demanding confirmations and final payments for activities and events, not to mention the continuing questions from the hens themselves about things I've already told them five times. I don't know what to do about any of it. I don't know if I'm even still Lauren's maid of honour. She said I was fired during that argument, but surely she didn't mean it? That was just a heat of the moment thing, wasn't it? Oh God, I really don't know. Maybe she's already appointed someone else. Maybe Simone got promoted to the top job – I should've asked her. But if I'm not her maid of honour, there's no way Joely's still a bridesmaid either, right? So should I be cancelling her seat on the flight to Marbs? And mine? Should I be cancelling the whole thing? That would really show Lauren if I just full-on demolished her much-talked-about hen do.

Do I want to 'show' Lauren? Probably not.

I don't know anything at the moment and I feel so helpless.

So I'm doing the only grown-up thing I can do – I'm hiding. I'm ignoring the problem and hoping it goes away or resolves itself, somehow. And every day, with every missed call from a hen company and every ignored duplicated email from Katie Jacks, I feel the weight of everything piling higher on my shoulders, and the anxiety filling my stomach like acid. Every day I feel like more of a failure – as a friend, as a girlfriend, as a granddaughter, as a human being. There must surely be something I can do to fix it all, but right now I can't see it. I can't see anything much at all.

Just then, Will wanders into the bedroom. He's been to an early morning gym session and it hits me properly how little

I've seen of him lately. For once, I've been the first one to bed at night, and he's been gone when I've woken up, hitting the gym early, and working longer hours at the office than usual. He was supposed to come to the work-friend wedding I was at yesterday, but he cancelled over text at the last minute, saying he had to work. It was pretty mortifying having to explain his absence, but I can't blame Will for being sick of all this. I'm over it too. I wish I could explain that properly to him.

He doesn't smile or even look in my direction as he passes the bed, heading straight through to our en-suite shower. For a moment the sadness spikes in my stomach and I think I'm going to scream and cry in the middle of our bedroom. In front of the neighbour's cat, who always comes over on Sunday mornings for extra breakfast, even though Moira next door keeps pleading with us not to give it to her.

I really hate that this is the new normal for Will and me. Not speaking, not sharing, not even really seeing each other. I miss the touching, sure, but it's not even Will's physical nearness I miss. It's that thing you get with a nice boyfriend – the thing of having someone on your team. I miss talking over dinner about our mundane lives. I miss him being my partner.

You'd think with the sudden cessation of wedding messages and meetings this week, things would've been better between us. But it feels like it's gone too far now. He's not trying anymore. Neither of us are. I haven't even told him I've fallen out with my best friends. When I got back that night from the wedding, I couldn't bring myself to talk about it or tell him the things they'd both said to me. I told myself I'd tell him the next day, and then the day after that. But I still haven't and I'm not sure why. I miss talking to him so much, but this feels like too big a thing to start with. Maybe it's because we've hardly seen each other? Contestant auditions for next year's series have started with a vengeance again at work this week and I've been run off my feet with everything. I could've texted or emailed him, though. Or just stayed up until he got home in the evening, so we could talk. I guess, if I had to really self-analyse – which I seem to be doing a lot of at the moment – I think I'm worried if I tell Will what Lauren and Joely said to me, he might agree with them.

Because I think I agree with them. I *am* a coward. I'm a coward in life, too afraid of upsetting people or rocking the boat. And now it looks like my cowardice even extends to my relationship with Will. I need to talk to him about Lauren and Joely, and I need to talk to those two about him. These three are always automatically the people I go to when something major like this happens. But obviously I can't do that. It's very surreal when the people you would turn to most in times of trouble are the ones who've caused the trouble.

Or maybe I've caused the trouble? Oh God, I don't know.

I know, as well, that I've been avoiding Will because a conversation needs to be had. A big one. We are going to have to talk at some point about what's happening between us. And I don't think it's going to be terribly great. But yet again, I'm hiding and ignoring and proving to the world what a big stupid coward I am. If this was a movie, by this point in the story, the whole cinema audience would be screaming at me to just get killed by the villain already.

So yes, as you can probably tell, I feel pretty miserable and more than a little – OK, very very – sorry for myself. I've been trying to distract myself with yoga in the small moments I've had to myself. I've been to more early morning classes this week than in the last couple of months combined. I'm finally touching my toes, but once I was down there I re-alised it didn't matter. Why does it matter if I can see my chipped nail varnish up close or not? I've also tried to focus on Fuddy-Duddies United and went to view a possible new location we could hire for our weekly meetings. But it's so far away – there's no way our older members could get there without a lot of help – and it's too expensive without some kind of funding or subsidy. Actually, the only thing that's been good for channelling my upset this week has been the regular, shouty messages I've been leaving for Mr Canid at the council. We've had a couple of conversations on the phone, but he's mostly 'not available' to speak to me. Really, the man is impossible. I've never spoken to anyone more frustrating in my life. I've been working on alternative options for evicting us, and sent him another long email for a whole list of different locations he could use for his plan instead of knocking down our beloved building. I've been so helpful! But he's blocked me at every turn. He's refused to listen – I don't think he's even reading my emails at all, he certainly never replies – and has been as obnoxious in every possible way that he could be. I've had some really, truly cathartic shouting matches with him down the phone.

It's been fantastic, actually. I can't tell you how enjoyable it is having a bona fide dickhead around to take all my anger out on. It's anger I didn't really, entirely know was in me, under there, but it definitely is. Bubbling away furiously, ready to eviscerate anyone who gets in my way. Especially if they happen to be from the sodding council.

Will picks up a towel from the back of the door and I swallow a painful lump in my throat. My mouth is suddenly dry and it makes it hard to speak.

'You having a shower?' I say dumbly like a dumbo dumb-dumb.

He glances up, like he's only just noticed I'm there, and

nods. 'Yep. Just back from the gym. Bit sweaty.'

Small talk. Ugh. You again.

'Cool, cool. Well done you, getting up so early on a Sunday,' I say, a little of my desperation coming out in my voice. He makes a move towards the bathroom and I continue speaking urgently. 'Um, I'm going to yoga this afternoon, so I'm being good too. Hope it'll help me relax! I've had a really busy week again . . .'

I fall silent. He doesn't ask me about my busy week. He's heard it all before, I guess. And he probably assumes I'm still using up all my time – all *our* time – on Lauren, Joely and the wedding planning. And I kind of am. If not physically this last week, then certainly mentally and emotionally. It's all I've thought about.

He heads for the door and as he gets there, I say, 'Will.' And my voice breaks on the word.

He turns around and we look at each other for a long ten seconds. I think he might be about to cry. I am.

'Lilah,' he says softly, and I break. I bury my face in the duvet and he's suddenly beside me on the bed, arms around me. He smells of sweat and Will-ness, and it's so nice and safe and comforting. I just cry there for a few minutes, remembering how good his skin feels on my skin. I wait to cry it all out, to feel better, but the tears keep coming and I only feel worse and worse.

And then he pulls away.

I sniff, trying to regain my composure. 'I feel so sad,' I say simply, my throat raspy.

He takes my hand. 'I suppose we'd better talk,' he replies quietly, looking past me and out the window.

I nod, feeling afraid. 'I guess we should. Actually, I've been having a bit of a rubbish time these last couple of weeks. I—'

He interrupts me. 'I mean about us.'

I breathe in deeply and then we are silent, before I start slowly. 'I know things haven't been . . . great between us recently, and I know it's my fault . . .' I begin, knowing these words sound familiar. I've given him this speech before, and I did nothing to make things any better.

He shakes his head. 'Lilah, it's just . . . it's just not the same between us anymore. We used to be a team, it used to be so much fun. I feel like I've lost you.'

That's how I feel too, but I say nothing.

He falls silent and then drops my hand back onto the bed. 'I've always really loved your kindness and how thoughtful and sweet you are, but you've let Lauren and everyone else take advantage of that – take advantage of you. And it's not just about that; it feels like you've *chosen* all of them over me. I'm supposed to be the most important person in your life, and you've put me last, every single time. Even when I've asked you not to. I'm way behind everyone else in your priorities, and I have been for months and months. Really, I barely seem to register on your radar. I have tried over and over to make this better and talk things through with you about it. Get you to see it from my point of view, without being a big, demanding Neanderthal about it, but you're always either too tired, or not here, or you make big promises that you don't keep. Everyone else always wins over me. I thought we were solid and in the same place with this relationship. I thought we were both looking to the future as a couple but . . .' He stops again and looks at me, before continuing in a cracked voice. 'I wanted to marry you, Lilah. I was so sure. You're everything I always wanted. But I've been slowly realising I'm not what *you* want—'

I interrupt him, big, fat tears rolling down my face. 'But

you are, Will, you are what I want. I love you, you don't understand how much I love you. I wasn't sure before, but I am now. I know you're right about all this and I know I've been a terrible girlfriend, but I will put you first, I will. Please believe me, I don't want to ruin this. I didn't mean to ruin this.' I break on the last word but he's shaking his head again.

'I want to believe you, but it's who you are. You'll never be able to put me – or, probably more importantly, *yourself* – first. It's not enough for me, Lilah. I love you, but I think . . . I just think . . .'

'Please don't say it,' I cry. 'Please don't say it, Will.'

He looks up at the ceiling, tears glittering in his eyes. 'I think we're done, Lilah. I'm really sorry. It's over. We tried, but we have to break up.'

I pick up his hand again and kiss the back of it. My face is wet with tears on his skin. 'You can't mean that,' I say, aware of how pathetic and sad I sound.

He pulls away, gently but firmly. 'I do. I've spoken to Dan, and I'm going to stay at his place for a while. He has a spare room and it's close to work. You and I can sort out what to do about this place when the dust has settled. I don't think there's too much time left on the lease. I'll check.' He gestures around us at our bedroom, at the house – our home – and stands up. He swallows a couple of times, still staring up, and when he looks at me again, the tears are gone. He takes a couple of determined breaths and nods at me before retrieving the towel and leaving.

I sit there, staring after him, and feeling so hollow. I sit there until the tears have dried stickily on my face. I sit there as a steady ache in my front temple builds into a full-blown migraine, and then I rush to the toilet and I throw up. I feel like I've lost everyone and everything, and I don't know how.

I've lost Will, I can see that. He had that look I've only seen a couple of times. He's made up his mind. He doesn't love me anymore. There's nothing I can do. And I know it's my fault.

17

I really don't know if it's sweat or tears pouring down my face, maybe both, but I keep going anyway. Have to keep going. Focus on the next position, the next move, the next breath.

For once, I really do need to focus on my breath, because if I don't, I feel like I will forget to do it.

Don't think about Will.

Don't think about him. Don't don't don't.

I can't help it. The same thought just keeps circling my brain, like a loud, blocked plughole, gurgling angrily.

How have I fucked everything up so badly? I just keep wondering how it's possible.

Losing a best friend or a boyfriend would be bad luck. Losing both in the space of a couple of weeks? That's got to be my fault. I'm the common denominator here. Will, Lauren, Joely – they've all decided I'm not worth the effort, or their love. They've seen the real me and they don't like it.

I can't really be here, can I? This can't be real.

After our fight – was it even a fight? What does a fight with Will actually look like? – he took his shower while I stayed in bed, my mind blank and numb. He came back in, fully dressed a while later, wafting that clean shower gel smell and saying nothing. Then he packed his bag and left. Without another word.

I stayed there, unable to move, for the rest of the weekend. Then I called Aslan and told him I wasn't coming in. I told him that he'd have to handle things on his own for a few days. He sounded a bit stunned, but told me not to worry. He didn't ask many questions, which I appreciated.

And then I just lay there in bed, not eating and barely thinking. Just staring at my phone, waiting for it to do something.

Eventually I couldn't take the silence in our – *our* – bedroom anymore. And so I went into work.

I got Rex his tea, I laughed at Aslan's bad jokes, I got Sam to book more taxis, I put the contestants through the necessary audition hell. And here I am at yoga, breathing, breathing, breathing, like they tell us to.

But nothing feels real. It's like I'm walking through water. I'm on autopilot, looking and hearing everyone on a Skype delay. Everything's blurry around the edges and people are moving in odd ways. It feels like I keep having out-of-body experiences, where I find myself looking down at the room. I stare down at another version of me, a Lilah who's talking to co-workers and smiling like everything's normal. But nothing's normal.

I shouldn't have come to yoga today. There's too much quiet here in this room. Too much emptiness around me. The noise of work kept everything at bay this week, and now, here in the silence, it's all crept back in.

Will.

Lauren.

Joely.

Hen dos.

Weddings.

Engagements.

This many weddings in one year? What the fuck was I thinking?

My throat closes and I sit down on my mat heavily. The

people around me are suddenly too close to me, it feels claustrophobic. Bodies everywhere, moving and breathing and sweating. I need to get out, it's too hot, there's too much sweat. Too much happening in my brain.

I sit there for a long minute, trying to breathe. The instructor nods at me, checking I'm OK. I nod back, signalling that I am, even though I'm really, really not.

It feels like nothing will ever be OK again, actually. It's all so messed up.

Fuck. I shouldn't feel like this, it's not right. I have so many things happening in my life, so many people, and yet . . . I'm really totally alone. How can I be so busy, always moving, always going to parties and hen dos and weddings, all these friends talking and laughing, and still feel so isolated? That's not how lonely works, is it? It shouldn't be. I have 700 friends on Facebook, more on Twitter and Instagram, and yet none of it is tangible. I've been so scared of missing things, of not being included. Always saying yes, always running around trying to do the right thing and be a good person. I've forgotten what I need and what I want from my life. I've put everyone before me and this is where I've found myself. Alone, literally on my arse, totally broke, exhausted, and with nowhere to turn now. My best friends hate me, my boyfriend's dumped me and I could be losing Franny and the other FU ladies if we can't stop this demolition. We'll be scattered all over the place if we lose the building. Separated. My family.

There is so much to think about, so much to be sad and scared about. Maybe constantly doing things for other people and putting others first isn't the answer to it. Maybe it's about doing less. Beating my own path.

But what can I do? Re-train my stupid brain? I've been a

follower for so long, I don't know how to do things any other way.

I launch myself up off the mat and into a warrior pose, trying to ignore the thoughts. I want so much to focus, but now I know it's definitely stupid goddamn tears on my face I can feel.

18

You know who is amazing at horrible times like these? Franny.

You know who is even more amazing at horrible times like these? Franny with luminous, electric-blue hair.

'You are going to be OK, Delilah,' she's telling me, mid-speech about how everything happens for a reason. 'I know sometimes, when you're in the middle of something like this, it feels like there's no way out the other side. It feels like you're going to be stuck there forever. Like you'll never make up with your friends, and you'll never find love again. But of course you will. Because this is what life is: things going wrong and things feeling bad. If everything went smoothly all the time – if all of life was just moving from work to telly to bed for all time – you'd be bored senseless. You're doing it wrong if you're just *fine* all the time. Emotions are what life really is, my darling Delilah. Don't push it down and pretend it's not happening – *feel it*. Feeling miserable and then happy and then miserable again – it's all part of what makes this life fun. If you don't feel sad every now and again, how do you know what happy is?'

It's all excellent, wise, sassy grandma chat, but all I'm doing is staring at her shimmering, bright hair, winking at me as it catches the sun through the skylight.

So it turns out Franny and my runner Sam have been spending an awful lot of time together recently. Franny's been trying to peer-pressure Sam into smoking, while Sam has apparently been trying to distract Franny by getting her into Kylie Jenner. They've been exchanging non-stop You-Tube clips of *Keeping Up With the Kardashians*, and talking incessantly about lip gloss and bum implants. Franny is on the fence about bum implants but says she definitely really likes Kylie's many different hair styles. She especially liked the reality star's phase of dyeing her hair bright colours, so she's done her own usually silver hair exactly like that. Sam helped her with it yesterday lunchtime. Yesterday lunchtime, when Franny told me she had 'too much on' to share a 'disgusting' egg mayo sandwich with me. I am only a tiny bit jealous. It's fine.

'You know what would cheer you up?' Franny twinkles at me now, from underneath her metallic-blue fringe. 'We should go dancing. I can teach you how to slut-drop. It's awfully good fun, my love. Sam showed me how to do it, but her knees are better than mine. I can do it, but she gets back up a lot faster. I have to sit down on the floor for a little while immediately afterwards. We'll make a day trip of it: slut-dropping, followed by maybe a museum visit. Sam better come with us so she can show you properly how to do it. My legs don't go as wide as they used to.'

'I can't go dancing with you, especially not slut-dropping, and Jesus, I really hope you don't actually know what that means . . .' I try, but Franny's on a roll.

'Oh, I'm also going to send you some links on the old WhatsApp. Sam's opened my eyes to a whole new world of sexy stories. It's fan fiction written by very clever One Direction fans and it's very steamy indeed, my darling. That'll get the engines roaring again, make you forget Will or Julie, whichever one it is that you fancy more—'

'Joely,' I interrupt vaguely, trying not to smile, and then realise Franny will think I was answering her, not correcting.

Either way, she's still talking, undeterred.

'The "fan fic", as they call it, is very arousing, and I *ship* Larry now. Although, if Liam and Harry – or is it Louis and Harry? – don't work out, I want to see Harry and Kendall getting it together one day. They would make such beautiful Snapchats together.'

I'm so lost but I'm also laughing a lot. It feels really good. She keeps going, delighted to see me smiling, musing, 'Do you think the 1D lads will ever reunite? The Twittersphere thinks it will happen, but they all seem to be enjoying their own thing now. Who would ever have pegged Liam for doing so well without the others?'

I have no idea what she's talking about, but it's cheering me up immensely. And I really, really needed cheering up. Because Will officially moved out this morning after a long week of very undignified begging on my part. He's being really nice about the breakup, but also seems very sure it's the right decision.

Unlike me.

The thing is, I know it's stupid, given how bad things were, but I feel blindsided. He's obviously been planning this in his head for a while now, while I've been so distracted wondering what colour shoes I'm supposed to be getting for the next wedding I have to attend. Ugh, I hate myself. I know I should've seen it coming, and maybe a part of me did, but I just decided to stick with denial. I've been in denial about a lot of things lately. Either way, it feels like he's had time to come to terms with all this, while I'm stuck ten miles behind, struggling to breathe properly whenever I think too hard about my life.

Oh. I guess this means he won't be coming with me to any more of the weddings we had coming up. And I guess that also means I'm no longer invited to his cousin's castle.

Another gut punch.

He's staying with a work friend, Daniel, and says he'll keep on paying his half of the rent until the lease is up in a few months. It's pretty miserable stuff, but he's being very decent about it all. Because, of course, he is. Because that's who he is. A decent, lovely, handsome man, who I drove away. Well done me.

The depressing situation really hasn't been helped by the continuing silence from my friends either. I thought about maybe sending them a message telling them I'd been dumped, but I don't want to guilt them into coming back into my life. Or maybe I do??

I guess maybe not. They need to work this all out in their own heads first. Look at how they've been acting and decide if it's OK. I can't force them to come back or they're just going to resent me.

Franny thinks they're being bitches, though, and that has really helped me feel better.

She looks at me lovingly now. 'I know things seem dark at the moment, my darling,' she says nicely, reaching over and taking my hand with her own wrinkly one. 'But life will be better when you come out the other side of this. The girls will come back when they're ready – or when they need something.' She rolls her eyes before continuing. 'And Will is a very nice boy, but things haven't been right between you for a while now. If he couldn't be patient for a little bit longer while you got on top of things and worked out those priorities of yours in your head, you would've ended up going down this path at some point anyway. It was inevitable. Him running away at the first sign of trouble is a very silly thing to do, very immature. Imagine if you'd ever gone through anything really traumatic! He would've been completely useless. Better to break up now, before you're in too deep.'

I think about what Will said about wanting to marry me. We were pretty definitely already in too deep and now I'm stuck alone at the bottom of this cold, dark, lonely well. If this wasn't 'in too deep', I never want to know what is.

I clear my throat, feeling the need to defend him a little. 'Will's a good man, Franny. This isn't his fault,' I say, lowering my voice as a group of frightened-looking contestants walk by in a huddle. 'I've treated him badly this year, I know I have. And maybe, actually –' I pause to consider my words – 'for the whole time we've been together. I got too used to him being nice about stuff and I've walked all over him. I ignored what he needed. And when things started to go wrong, I kept promising him I'd put him first and I just didn't. He's right: he was never my priority. And because he's so good and nice, he let me do it, for too long. This is on me, not him.'

She tuts and waves her hand. 'Maybe so, but, well, goodness, that's not just Will's trouble. The pair of you let people walk all over you, you always have. But that's not really the point. The point is, if you were ever able to actually have a good old shouting, yelling, screaming fight every now and again, maybe you could've raised and resolved these issues before they got as bad as they did. You could've cleared the air, talked about your feelings. But you don't do things that way, neither of you do. You're both too nice and too worried about hurting other people's feelings to speak up when you need to. Even though most people are dreadful and would deserve their feelings being hurt.' She looks at me a bit searchingly now before continuing. 'You see that, don't you, my darling? Most people *are* dreadful and only care about themselves. They'll be kind and nice when it suits them, but ultimately, it's about numero uno. You're so much better off looking out for yourself whenever you can, like everyone else does.' She pauses and leans even closer, like she is confessing a secret. 'You must see that your two friends, Lauren and Julie – wonderful as they are in many ways – are also absolutely dreadful? Absolutely dreadful, dreadful people! Demanding, selfish, awful people.' She pauses and then loudly announces, 'And I'm dreadful too!' She laughs at the alarm on my face, and then continues on before I can argue the point. 'Darling, of course I am, don't try and deny it! I'm dreadful. Look at the way I treat that idiot Andrea! I'm an awful human being! But I don't care. It's fun and I'm old, and I've earned the right to be awful. Lilah, you are surrounded by narcissistic, self-centred, self-important, difficult people. Me, your best friends, your parents, even young Sam is a fairly terrible person – or at least the telly she likes is terrible. Although heavens knows why I can't get her to start smoking – what happened to young people these days? They used to be up for a laugh.' She pauses for breath and I can see her fingers twitching for a cigarette. 'But, my darling Delilah, that's exactly why you like us. Because those nightmarish, loud, obnoxious types are also the very best types. We're smart and fun and so completely alive and kicking. I'm nearly ninety-one and I am as big of an arsehole as I ever was when I was twenty. And when I do die, I'm not going out in my sleep like some sap. I'm going out screaming. Maybe being tortured – what do you think? And, hopefully, just after snogging Tony Robinson in a bush somewhere. I may be a bit crumply in the face, but I can still snog with the best of them.'

I vividly picture this.

She goes on, hardly pausing for breath. 'People *should* be difficult and high-maintenance, Delilah. That's what life is all

199

about. Those people standing tall and causing trouble are the ones who get what they want out of life and have the most fun. They're the winners. And that's why you're so drawn to these people. You can see they're making the most of their life and enjoying themselves. It's also why you and Will couldn't make it work. You won't ever be able to work as a couple unless one or both or you learns to start shouting, putting yourselves first, and demanding more from life. You need to learn to start being louder about what you want, my love.'

I don't know what to say, but Franny is nowhere near finished. 'I'm not saying you should be needlessly cruel to those who can't take it – and, by the way, Andrea can take it, she loves having my attention – and I'm not saying you shouldn't help those in need when you can, but being selfish and high-maintenance is important too, to ensure you get what you deserve. And, my darling Delilah, you deserve so much. So so much happiness. You take on too much of other people, and you seem to forget that you matter too.'

She narrows her eyes and looks at me searchingly. 'Actually, I thought you were starting to get somewhere with all these angry calls to the council on behalf of Fuddy-Duddies United. You were actually standing up for yourself, even to me a little bit! But you don't seem to be taking that fire – that life lesson – with you into the rest of the world just yet. You have an opportunity here with all this drama, my girl. You have a chance to start anew. Clean slate. No ties. You've fallen out with everyone, which means you actually have five minutes to breathe. You can find your passion and start putting it, and yourself, first. And then I want you to start shouting over every person you meet who gets in your way. That's how we get things done in the Fox family, my darling.'

I'm silent for a minute, wondering if there is more to come, but Franny smiles softly and folds down into her seat a bit, clearly content. I realise we've both been sitting very straight but I can only sit taller. I am ablaze with everything she just said. I mean, it's almost certainly nonsense – I'm pretty sure people shouldn't be selfish dicks all the time – but it felt SO GOOD and empowering listening to it. Maybe it's not all right, but enough of it is, and it *is* time to put myself first for a while. What have I got to lose? Trying to be nice has seen everyone I love leave me, so I might as well try being selfish for a bit. I'm not sure I can ever be the hellraiser bad girl Franny wants me to be – I would really rather not take up smoking – but I'm done playing a supporting role in my own life movie. I want to be a lead character for a while.

So there.

What now, then?

What do I feel passionate about? I love yoga. I like my job. If it wasn't for Rex winding me up every day, I'd probably completely *love* my job. But I can't do anything about him – can I?

Unless . . . is there . . . should I . . . *murder him*?

No, probably not.

And then there's FU, of course. I love all the charity work we do and helping around the community. I know I'm a total do-gooder and Joely always takes the piss, but it's not like she's around to mock me at the moment.

Except the FU is probably dead in the water right now too.

But maybe there's more I can do. Because Franny's right about that too. Campaigning and fighting and researching on behalf of the club was the first time in years, maybe ever, that I felt in control and powerful. I felt like an adult, being taken seriously. And I loved getting angry with that damned paper-pusher, Mr Canid – or however you pronounce his stupid name. That's what I need to be doing more of. And maybe I can combine what Franny said about taking charge with my own people-pleasing instincts. I can get angry and make things happen *for* other people who need my help.

So where to start?

Mr Canid says we can't afford to stay in the youth club, and there's no money in the pot to stop it happening. So let's start there.

Wedding Number Eleven: Lyndsey and James, Rise Home, Hull

Theme: Autumnal. Table arrangements full of flickering candles on beds of crunchy leaves that kept catching fire.

Menu: Smoked salmon starter, followed by chicken and a meringue dessert. Veggie option: stuffed red pepper with goat's cheese.

Gift: Cash in a card @ £40.

Gossip: The bride was very clearly eight months pregnant, but no one was talking about it. She was literally pretending to drink her champagne and glancing nervously over at her furious-looking dad all day. Also, all the bridesmaids had acrylic toe nails, shudder.

My bank balance: -£1999.99 (Overdraft limit is £2k, must not exceed. Credit cards still don't count.)

19

Well. I guess this is, at least, relaxing.

Sort of.

Kind of.

It's not relaxing.

We're on a 'juice crawl', which, yes, is as bad as it sounds. It's part of our uni friend Millie's hen do and she's opted for what her head bridesmaid keeps referring to as a 'wellness day'. There are no strippers, no willy straws, and no inflatables at all.

It's a bit depressing, actually.

We're going from juice bar to juice bar – like a really disappointing bar crawl – and we're ending the day later on at a spa, where all fifteen of the hens are having a very much non-optional 'detox cellulite-buster seawood float wrap bath.' It takes two whole hours, and then it's followed by a super healthy cucumber-based dinner.

I don't like cucumbers. Or being touched by strangers. Or seawood, probably, whatever that is. Is it, like, wood they found in the sea? I don't get it.

The whole thing is ripped straight out of Goop – fuck you, Gwyneth Paltrow – and I knew when I saw the itinerary that I'd be bloody starving by this point in the day. I have some strawberry Pop-Tarts in my bag and I had planned on fisting handfuls into my mouth during breaks in the tedium, but after three extra healthy, extra mandatory juices in quick succession – all featuring six different types of spinach and kale

– I'm not sure my stomach can take anything else. It's making some really disturbing noises, like a clogged swimming pool being drained. Actually, similar noises can be heard echoing around the room and everyone is beginning to turn the same colour as the smoothies. There better be a decent toilet in the next place we go to, that's all I'm saying.

OK, so yes. The big elephant in the room: Lauren and Joely are both here. Oh, wait, not that they're elephants! Don't tell Lauren I called her an elephant. Joely would be fine about it, but Lauren would kill me.

We're still not speaking and it is, as you can imagine, pretty awkward. We arrived at the same time earlier, all three of us twenty minutes late, and I could see they'd been thinking the same as me: get there late so you can slip into the crowd unnoticed. Lauren stopped short when she saw me and some unreadable expression flared up on her face. For a second – half a second – I thought maybe she'd smile and we could hug it out. Hug out the awkward. But she turned away instead and began stomping away in the direction of the crowd. It was just as Joely came in, so instead of making a dignified exit, Lauren almost barrelled into the only other person in the room that she desperately didn't want to see. They glared at each other, clearly still just as furious as they'd been during their last encounter at Ravi's wedding. And then all three of us splintered off in different directions to hide from each other and away from the bad feelings. It was a depressing start to a depressing day, capping off a truly depressing few weeks.

We haven't exchanged so much as a glance since then, and everyone else here has been too caught up in their own stuff (by 'stuff', I mean bowel movements, tbh) to notice that we three former best friends don't appear to be talking. It's awful and I have been mostly quietly playing Candy Crush on my phone and making small talk with this girl next to me called Flora, who keeps asking me if she should make her boyfriend spray-tan his balls.

'Like, the rest of him is really tanned,' she says now. 'And it's quite weird that his balls are so white. The only trouble is that they're quite shrivelled, so we'd have to really stretch them out flat to get an even colour. Oh, and then we'd have to hold them in place while they dried off, and I'm not sure that would be very comfortable, or good for our relationship. What do you think?'

I look thoughtful. 'What colour is his anus?' I say, reaching for a question that is equally as over-sharey, to prove I'm fine with this topic and that I care about this man's shade.

She nods enthusiastically. I've asked the right thing.

'Yeah, see, that's the other problem. He waxes and bleaches his anus, so that is actually super white and hairless.' She looks worried. 'Would that look weird, do you think? If he was that white at the back end but then really tanned at the front?'

I make a face like I'm thinking about it some more. 'You know, I reckon it'll look fine,' I say nicely. 'Because not many people would see him naked anyway, would they? Unless you go to a nudist beach? Also, you'd really have to part his butt cheeks to see the difference, wouldn't you?' I pause before adding, 'But I also don't think you should worry too much. There's too much pressure on men these days to be metro-sexual and look a certain way. I think you should let him be however he is, and not worry about what society thinks of your boyfriend's shrivelled balls.'

She looks a little offended. 'They're only a bit shrivelled,' she says primly.

'Oh, God, yeah, sorry, I'm sure they're lovely balls,' I say emphatically. 'And anyway, all men's balls are shrivelled, aren't they? I mean, my boyfriend . . .' I trail off, feeling winded by a low punch somewhere deep in me.

I haven't got a boyfriend.

Will hasn't been in touch much at all since he moved out, and my few desperate messages about anything I could think of have only been curtly replied to, usually a full day later. I got a thumbs up emoji the other day, which is when I think I knew it was probably definitely over. He doesn't usually use emojis, never mind a thumbs up.

I'm finding it quite difficult. Very difficult, actually. My life is strange and different without him in it.

There are so many things I want to tell him about – stupid, mundane, life things. How a woman outside the train station yesterday got her heel caught in the grate and then screamed and cried in the street about them costing £300. How Franny took me out for dinner the other night to cheer me up, and we accidentally ended up in a zombie-themed pop-up restaurant, where Franny attacked the waiter because she was convinced the apocalypse had genuinely arrived. I wanted to tell him how I've caught Sam with Jessica, one of the interns, twice now, snogging in a studio. I wanted to tell Will about all of it, and how I think they're falling in love. How cute it is when children (I know they are both over twenty and fully-grown women, but still) fall in love.

I haven't really slept properly since he left. You get used to having someone there next to you, don't you? The feel of someone shifting in their sleep, someone breathing hotly in your ear beside you. There were so many nights back when we were together that I would lie there, sweaty and uncomfortable, wishing I could sleep alone and really stretch out my limbs. I wanted to erase his big bigness taking over my side of the bed and stealing the duvet all the time. And now I have all the sides, and all the duvet, and all the space I could want, and there are moments I really don't think I can stand it.

I'm spending a lot of those hours in bed staring at our – my – ceiling. I've spent endless hours following the intricate, white floral pattern that trails across the ceiling of the whole room. It's funny, I'd never really looked at it much before. There were always better things to do in bed.

I'm talking about sleep, by the way, not sex. But sometimes sex too.

When I close my eyes now, I can see the pattern. It's imprinted on the back of my eyelids, like when a camera flash goes off in your face in a dark room.

I've also been listening to a lot of music. I don't think I've listened to this much music since I was a teenager. Actually, my neighbours on the left put a note through the door about all the Celine Dion. They were really nice about it, but they said could I at least play more than just 'Think Twice' on occasion. I can't oblige them with that, so now I'm using headphones all the time instead.

Flora leans in closer now and whispers in a desperate voice, 'Do you think today is going to get any more fun? It's quite dry so far, isn't it? I mean, I love Millie and I know she's into her healthy foods and fads, but I don't think I can have any more of these juices. I thought I had a cast iron stomach until today. And what are we going to do about dinner later? No one likes cucumber, do they? Is there not going to be any booze at all? Do you think Millie is pregnant or something? Because I don't think I can do yet another baby shower this year, they're so dull.'

'Probably,' I agree sadly, eyeing the bride's flat belly across the room. 'Although, I heard a rumour in the loo earlier that the spa serves alcohol, and that the grandparents and in-laws are heading home about seven o'clock. You never know, things might get more interesting then.'

'Fingers crossed.' She nods, staring with haunted eyes at the green drink in her hand.

Things definitely do get more interesting then. Four hours later and the baby boomers have left the building. The moment the door closed on them, all the bridesmaids pulled out hip flasks to the biggest cheer I've ever heard. And to make sure all alcohol bases were covered, we speedily ordered several bottles of eye-wateringly expensive bottles of wine from the in-spa menu. And then we powered through all the booze with a determination never before seen.

Obviously, we all got drunk incredibly quickly. We've had barely any food all day and I can personally attest to those juices passing straight through the human digestive system without touching the sides. Sorry to be so gross, but that loo experience is going to be with me a long time, and everyone says it's important to share your trauma.

Also, the cucumber-based dinner was left mostly untouched, which should surprise exactly no one. So now we have eleven women in a fancy spa, on a high from the departure of elderly supervision, drunkenly shouting at each other across a pool.

We're all spread out around the room, half lying across, half sitting on the loungers, with a couple of girls in the pool getting dangerously close to drowning.

And I can't believe how much more fun I'm having now! A spa hen do is a brilliant idea after all! A *drunk* spa hen do, I hasten to add. Obviously, I'm really, really wasted, and nothing I'm saying means anything at all, but it also means everything and I think that's the important thing here. I really love it, and I really, really think Flora is my new soulmate. It was like we were meant to meet here today. She's my new best friend, and she is just so great, even though I'm not sure we actually have anything in common. I don't need Lauren and Joely because Flora is better than both of them combined. She even likes *Sweet Valley* and we had a big chat about how Todd is the dullest man who ever lived and how it's mad that both Elizabeth and Jessica fought so hard over him.

Actually, that chat made me a tiny bit sad because *Sweet Valley* is mine and Lauren's thing.

Anyway, Flora and I are best friends forever now (until I sober up), and we've told each other about our whole lives. She laughed loads about my dreadful parents and mostly AWOL brother named after Tom Jones. And she told me about her work as a jobbing actress and talked some more about her boyfriend – Pete – and his pale testicles. And I actually really like all the boyfriend ball chat! It's SO interesting, y'know? So insightful. Like, we, as women, have all come so far in the last few years that we can discuss anything in public. We can even talk about our boyfriends' testicles to strangers-turned-soulmates without fear of reprisal. Not so long ago, we were all trapped in a totalitarian theocracy, where women were treated as baby-makers with no rights – oh wait, that's *The Handmaid's Tale*, isn't it? Close enough. And still, the ball chat is really what feminism is all about and I'm so so happy to be a part of it.

Ooh, the room is spinning. Fun!

I could really do with a nap, actually. God, I do so love a drunk nap. I do have the teeniest, tiniest, barely-worth-mentioning habit of passing out when I'm drunk. I have previously fallen asleep in multiple public toilets, four kitchens while cooking whatever form of pasta happens to be available, and one time, directly into my garlic dough balls at Pizza Express. The waitress was really nice, though, and didn't even charge me for the dough balls, even though I'd apparently requested sixteen extra pots of garlic butter.

For a moment I feel a lump in my throat. Lauren used to keep a count of these incidents. She said one day I would end up on one of those ITV2 docu-series about how Brits abroad are shaming the country. And then a picture of me collapsed in the street with my skirt over my head will appear splashed across the front page of the *Daily Mail* as an example of how Britain's female population is going to hell and ruining everything. She used to say all that in a proud way, while she was posting the photos on Instagram. I'm proud too – @UnconsciousDelilah has nearly 3,000 followers and the garlic dough balls picture got 407 likes! I sneak a look across at her now, on a sun lounger chatting to the bride. She looks happy. She's happier without me, I think, with a pang.

I give myself a shake. No more self-pity. I've had enough of that to last a lifetime in the past few weeks. And anyway, I have whatshername here now, as my new best friend. I don't need Lauren or Joely. Have I said that already?

Oh hey, maybe if I have a power nap for ten minutes now, I'll get a second wind when I wake up. Maybe I could even take a swim with those drowning girls. Wait – is that one actually dead? Oh, I'm sure she'll be OK, there are probably lifeguards here somewhere, right? I look around, noticing through a wine fog that all the other non-hen guests around the pool have left. Do you think that was because of us? We are being quite loud, aren't we? I feel bad for a second, but then everything is good again. I breathe the chlorine fumes in deeply and feel better than I have in ages. The ceiling pattern is gone from my eyelids.

Out of the corner of my eye, I notice a staff member approaching one of the hens a few pool loungers away. The hushed but tense back and forth conversation echoes around the large room.

'I'm so sorry to bother you,' the staff lady says really nicely, 'but I'm afraid we need you all to calm it down a little bit. Please could you stop shouting quite so much? We've had several complaints from other clients.'

'Complaints about WHAT?' slurs the hen. She might be the drunkest of all of us, which definitely makes her the wrong choice for the lady to speak to reasonably about this.

The nice staff member clears her throat, pulling nervously at the collar of her soothing avocado-coloured polo shirt. 'Unfortunately, I've been told to tell you that you're making a lot of noise and this is a spa, not a pub. We are all about tranquillity and serenity here, and our other guests have reported that they don't feel terribly tranquil and serene with you making so much noise. And I'm sorry, I'll have to ask you to collect up those empty wine bottles floating about in the pool, please.'

'That sounds like bollocks,' shouts a familiar voice, and I hide a giggle when I realise it's Joely. She's wearing the tiniest bikini you can imagine and is rippling beautifully in every direction. I recognise her eyes as Drunk Eyes, and watch in amused horror as she staggers over to the lady.

'Come on, Fiona, we're just having FUN,' she shouts at the confused-looking staff lady, who may or may not be called Fiona. I don't know where Joely's getting that from. She puts her arm around Fiona (TBC) and rests her head on her shoulder. 'Fiona, you have no idea what today has been like. It's been so fucking boring, I can't even tell you. We weren't allowed alcohol and there were cucumbers and everyone had the shits. But it's fun now, at last! We're finally letting loose and having a good time. Does your spa have a policy on people not having fun, Fiona? Because that would suck and my millions of follo-hiccup-wers would love to hear all about that. Sorry, I'm not taking it out on you, Fiona, babe. I know you're just doing your job, but we should be able to have fun, y'know? This is meant to be a hen do, for god's sake.'

Fiona (TBC) looks even more alarmed. 'A hen do? You're a hen do? We weren't informed that you were a hen do. We don't allow hen dos in here. We have a level-one policy about it. I could get in so much trouble.'

The original drunk girl pipes up again. 'Well, Fiona, love, we're not leaving. So off you pop, and bring us more wine, will you? We're paying through the nose for it, so you might as well take advantage of our loose credit cards while you can.' She waves an empty bottle in the air before lobbing it into the pool, narrowly missing the maybe drowned girl.

Fiona (TBC) looks panicked, her brow furrowed. 'I'll have to get the manager,' she says. 'I don't know what to do. I might get sacked. I certainly can't bring you any more alcohol. Stay here, I'm getting Darren. He's right upstairs. He'll know what to do.'

She scurries away in a panicky blur of pale green and the hens all look at each other.

'What shall we do?' slurs Millie, the bride. 'I don't want to leave, I'm having too much of a laugh. We only just got rid of my stupid great aunts. I don't want this to end. Can Fiona and Darren really make us leave, do you think, Joely?'

Joely squints at her. 'Who's Fiona?' she says, confused.

'Shall we hide?' shouts Lauren from the other side of the pool, and she's laughing. I feel warm inside at the sight, it's so nice to see. 'Come on, let's all hide!' she roars, jumping

213

delightedly up off her lounger. The whole room erupts with giggles as we all leap up and run in different directions. Even the drowned girl is alive again and running. Everyone is sprinting and shrieking and laughing. This is going to be hilarious and work out totally fine. There is no chance this won't be fine.

So we got arrested. The whole lot of us. They rounded us all up one by one – I was hiding in the showers with Flora – and marched us out. I passed out in the police van, and when I woke up we were in a drunk tank. I didn't even know those things existed anymore, I thought it was just for TV shows. Maybe they don't call it the drunk tank, but sure, everyone here is drunk. It's a large, windowless room that works as a kind of cell, with a loo in the corner. We're all crammed in here with a few other older women who may or may not be sex workers. That is not for me to say.

A bunch of the hens are crying, but most of the party seem to be unconscious, sleeping off the intensive binge-drinking on the cold, cement floor. I feel surprisingly refreshed but I think it was the nap rather than the spa. I flash back to that awful never-ending 'detox cellulite-buster seawood float wrap bath' and my skin itches.

I look blearily around until I spot Lauren and Joely. They're a few feet apart, backs turned on each other, but they're both wide awake. Lauren looks livid to be in this situation. Her arms are folded, and she has streaks of black mascara criss-crossing in every direction across her face. Joely is more joyous-looking, still head to toe soaking wet from when she jumped into the pool to escape the police officers.

That was glorious, actually. Two of them had to go in there

to fetch her out and the whole lot of us sang 'Fuck Tha Police' as she was escorted out, sopping, in handcuffs.

I should admit here that I was too scared to sing the swear words, so I just mouthed them, and then stopped altogether when one of the police officers looked in my direction.

Anyway, I know it was completely insane but I felt so proud of Joely. Especially when she screamed, 'I know my rights!' and the police officer said, 'OK then, what are your rights?' and she didn't actually know them so she started singing again.

I feel a sudden stab of something in my chest. These two are my best friends. For all their flaws, they are my best friends. Yes, Lauren is difficult and selfish, but she's also fiercely loyal and thoughtful. Joely is rude and spoilt, but she's also hilarious and warm. These are my favourite people in the world, apart from Franny.

Surely there is something we can do here. Surely this is the moment to say sorry and make amends. We're likely going to be stuck here all night. Couldn't the three of us talk things out? Figure out where things went wrong? Are we really going to stand here, backs turned, and ignore each other all night?

Just then, one of the possible sex workers (not for me to say) trips over one of her own stilettoes and staggers backwards into Lauren. Lauren shrieks as she falls like a domino into Joely, who remains standing, an immoveable force. They both turn on each other simultaneously with a growl, and the two of them stand there for a long moment, panting at each other.

Joely is the first to break the silence, snapping, 'Don't you dare touch me, princess.'

Sigh.

OK, it doesn't look like this is going to be the make-up chat I was hoping for, then.

'I didn't do it deliberately,' Lauren snaps back. 'She knocked me over.' She points at the woman, who shrugs vacantly and sits on the floor, examining her shoe for damage.

'It's always someone else's fault, isn't it?' Joely hisses. 'I don't care, Lauren, just leave me alone. I want nothing to do with you.'

Lauren takes a furious step closer and they are barely centimetres apart as she shouts back, 'What is your problem, Joely? Why are you being so pathetic? You're the one in the wrong here. Why do you get to be the one acting like such a cow? I should be the angry one; you should be bombarding me with apologies.'

Joely takes a deep breath, ready to launch into everything again, and that's when I snap.

'THAT IS ENOUGH!' I shout. A couple of the hens asleep by my feet sit up, startled, before immediately passing out again. Lauren and Joely both stop talking and turn to me, looking shocked. 'That is e-fucking-nough,' I say again, still loudly, but steely this time, calmly.

'I'm done listening to you two tear each other to pieces,' I say through gritted teeth, and my voice is more forceful than I remember it ever being before. They gape at me, but say nothing, so I keep going.

'You can both stop that right now. I'm sick of it. The truth is, you've *both* been behaving absolutely horrendously. And I'm not having it anymore,' I say, in full-on scolding teacher mode. 'You want to know which one of you is in the wrong? You're both in the wrong. You said you wanted to know what I think, whose side I'm on? I'm on nobody's side because the pair of you are being dicks in equal, terrible measure.'

216

I breathe out and turn on Lauren. 'Lauren, we know this wedding is important to you. It's important to us too, it really is, but Joely was right, you were going over the top with it all. The calls going on all night, the endless meetings, the constant demands, the way you would change your mind about everything every five minutes and panic-spiral. We all want to be there for you, we love you very much and we want your big day to be perfect. But you've been treating us like we don't have lives of our own and that nothing matters more than your wedding. And we do have lives. Or, at least, we had lives before all this took over.'

Lauren opens her mouth to reply but I put up my hand to silence her, before turning on Joely.

'And you,' I say, still stern, and she looks down sulkily at her dirty bare feet. 'You, Joely, have been behaving like a spoilt brat for ages now. We know you're a big-shot, famous person now, and that's really cool, but that doesn't mean you get to throw that in people's faces every day. Nobody cares about Calum Best, OK? Literally no one. And a million followers on Instagram might mean something to you, but it means nothing in the real world. You are still just Joely Bolt, the girl who crashed our school valentine disco to snog the coolest boy in our year, Dean Clark, and then got your period all over his white jeans. You are still that person, and you are still supposed to be our friend. A friend we really fucking need, OK?'

They are both looking at the floor now. Lauren is pouting, but I can see they are listening. I can see I'm getting through.

'And neither of you had any right to turn on me like you did at Ravi's wedding,' I continue, my voice breaking. 'I've been trying to do the best I can, the right thing, trying so hard to be there for you both. And I really, really needed my best friends in these last couple of weeks. I broke up with Will and neither of you were there for me.' I pause for a moment taking in their shocked expressions. Lauren's jaw falls open but I don't let her say anything. 'You were so self-obsessed. So sure your problems were bigger than everyone else's, and they're not – they're fucking not. Everyone has shit they're dealing with, and you don't get to scream at me and storm off when I needed you in my life. I've always tried to be nice and unquestioningly supportive . . .' My voice softens a little. 'But I'm realising now that maybe that wasn't totally the right thing to do. You didn't need unquestioning support, you needed a real friend who is prepared to tell you when you're being idiots.' I take a deep breath. 'So, OK, maybe this fallout was my fault too. I've been too worried about upsetting you guys to actually say anything while you both lost yourselves. I said nothing. I sat here, silently watching you get carried away and forget what's real or important. My job in this friendship group has always been to keep you two down to earth, to keep you from getting too self-obsessed. I know I'm meant to keep you grounded and I haven't been doing that lately. I failed you both.'

There is a long silence, and for a minute, I think they might start screaming again. Speaking my mind, telling them off, this is a brand new thing from me. None of us had any idea what that would look like before today, or how it would be received. And looking at their blank faces now, I'm aware it could go either way.

They both look at me. Lauren's mouth falls open again, and I see more of the same anger.

'Why the hell wouldn't you tell us you broke up with Will?' she starts to spit through gritted teeth, and just then the drunk sex worker (poss?) throws herself dramatically against the door of the cell, banging her broken shoe ineffectively.

'When are you going to let me oooooooout?' she wails, slurring at the police officers outside, pointedly ignoring us. 'I don't want to die in heeeeeeere with these morons who are having a tween argument.'

She waves in our direction and I stifle a giggle.

Joely catches my eye and lets out a snort. 'It would be a pretty undignified way to die, wouldn't it?' she says. 'Locked in a drunk tank with strangers on a hen do. We'd make the front page of the *Mail* with that one, for sure. Never mind your @UnconsciousDelilah Instagram.'

I smirk. 'The night's still early,' I say, and a ceasefire hangs in the air.

Joely clears her throat. 'Personally, given the choice, I'd rather eat myself to death, off my fucking nut on Valium, watching re-runs of *The X Files*. That Mulder, ooh . . .'

I see Lauren crack. 'You're already eating yourself to death,' she mutters, and Joely punches her in the arm. But it's playful. They smile shyly at each other.

I breathe out, relief flooding my body.

'Jesus, I'm really sorry about Will,' Joely says, awkwardness in her voice. 'I had no idea. Are you OK? It seems so out of the blue. Did something happen? I thought it was going well – with the proposal and everything. Why didn't you tell us if things were going wrong? You never said anything about you guys having problems and it must've been going on long before everything blew up at Ravi's wedding.'

Lauren stares down at the ground and then over at Joely. 'We haven't really given her much of a chance to share her life with us, though, have we? Because we've been so caught up in our own stupid shit.'

We all fall silent again, and Joely looks between us. 'Screw it,' she says. 'Guys, I'm so sorry. Lauren, you must know I was just venting at the wedding. I didn't mean it. I'm sorry. I really am so excited you're getting married and I'm thrilled about your amazing big day. I was just a bit tired and frustrated. And you know what I'm like! I say stuff for attention. I didn't mean that no one cares. Of course they do. Of course *we* do. We really, really do. And I'm so honoured to be a part of your wedding.' She looks awkward for a moment and then adds shyly, 'That's if I still am a part of your wedding? I'd really like to be. I want to be your bridesmaid, and your friend again. More than anything. I'm sorry.' She turns to me now. 'And Lilah, I can't believe the things I said to you too. I didn't mean any of it, you know I completely adore you and I'm sorry we stuck you in the middle. Lauren's right, I am always trying to steal you off her to make you my best friend because you're bloody fantastic, and kind and generous. I'm so lucky to have you. I can't believe I tried to wreck that or make you feel bad about yourself. And you're right about my ego getting out of control. I'm sorry. It was all just a joke to begin with – the whole "don't you know who I am" bit. I thought it was funny to pretend to be a famous person, but then it started getting a bit too real. I believed the yes men and my smarmy agent a little too much. I'm going to get a handle on it, though, I promise. No more shouting at shop assistants, or threatening people with bad blog posts. I know it's mean and unfair. I'll remember who I am and not let things go to my head so much. And if I ever forget again, I'll trust you to keep telling people the story about the time I got my period on Dean Clark.' She takes a second to smile widely, and then she adds aggressively, 'But you're wrong about Calum Best. Everyone loves Calum Best.'

Lauren sobs suddenly, 'I'm really sorry too.' Her already

ruined mascara is blobbing together into one large eyelash above each eye. 'I know I've gone mad these last few months. I can feel it happening but I don't know how to stop it. There's just so much pressure. The moment I got engaged, it was like my life became open season to comment. It's like I became public property. And it's not even just my friends and family – actual strangers come up to me on the street to ask me how much the ring cost! And then they demand to know every detail of the wedding: exactly what I'm doing, how much I'm spending, how many people I've invited. It's so competitive and aggressive. And everyone is so judgemental. This woman the other day practically shouted at me in Waitrose because I'm not having an "unplugged wedding". I didn't even know what that was!'

She looks at us, bewildered and confused, as Joely leans in. 'Oh, I know that one,' she says helpfully. 'Apparently it's when you confiscate everyone's phones before they come into the service, so pictures and details don't leak onto social media. It's supposed to mean you have complete control over the day. It's part of the whole tech backlash, which is very fashionable right now. Lots of celebs are throwing away their phones altogether, and they all insist on the unplugged thing at their weddings. It's very cool, and it also keeps their *OK!* magazine exclusive safe.'

Lauren nods tearfully before continuing. 'That makes sense. The woman said Pippa Middleton did it and then she screamed at me that I clearly don't care about my special day if I'm not doing it too. But I don't want to take everyone's phones away! I don't mind if the pictures "leak". What's the point of getting married if people aren't taking photos of you from every angle like you're a queen? Why have I been starving myself on this wedding diet if people aren't documenting that? But now I feel like I should care. Do you think I should? I don't even know what I think about anything anymore. Do I like phones? I thought I liked phones?' She stops momentarily for a long wail. 'And I had no idea how much work was involved in a wedding. Every time I think I've ticked something off the list, another thing gets added or will fall through. I've had to re-arrange the table plan forty-four times because all my relatives hate each other.' Joely nods at this, like she has something to say about their relatives too, but Lauren doesn't stop for breath. 'I bought a whiteboard just to try and arrange the tables more easily. And I keep thinking I've cracked it, and then I come back in the living room and my sodding parents have moved it around again. They keep putting their own friends closer to my table even though I don't even know their dumb friends! I want my friends by the top table! Why can't I have what I want? Oh, and of course everyone wants their bratty kids to come along and apparently I'm a tyrant for not wanting them there. Everyone thinks they should be the exception to the wedding rule. I hate it. I thought this would be fun, but it's turned into a nightmare. And I'm not even finished planning! There's loads left to do and no time to do it. I lie awake every night worrying about what disaster the next day will bring. Things are dreadful between me and Charlie too. We fight like cat and dog. I don't think he even wants to marry me anymore. And I don't blame him – I've turned into such a monster! I feel like I'm getting everything wrong and everyone hates me.' She stops for a big, ragged deep breath. 'And I know I took it out on you guys. I'm sorry. I needed an outlet for my fears and my freak-outs, but you didn't deserve any of it. And, worst of all . . .' She gasps for air between sobs. 'I had to spend last night in a Travelodge because a giant spider ran under my bed and wouldn't leave.

222

Charlie wouldn't help me get it out because we'd had a huge fight over entrees earlier. But I knew it would climb onto my face and into my mouth in the night while I slept if I stayed there. So I had to leave. I'm so pathetic – I can't even win a fight with a spider. He's driven me out of my own home.'

With this last pronouncement, Lauren fully bursts into loud, devastated tears. The type of crying you only see when someone has spent six months trying not to cry.

Joely and I are quiet, trying to take in the magnitude of her long speech.

Poor, poor Lauren.

And Jesus, that spider situation sounds awful.

We pile in for a long hug, and stand there until Lauren cries herself out.

I definitely do not want to glamorise prison, but this whole thing has been so totally exactly like an episode of *Orange is the New Black*. It was brilliant! After our little emotional reunion, the whole lot of us hosted a mini *X Factor*. Only about a third of the group were willing to actually sing as contestants, so the rest of us acted as judges. We had five Cheryl TweedyColeFernandezVersiniPaynes, three Simon Cowells, two Dannii Minogues, but I was the only Sharon Osbourne. I don't know why – I always thought she was the coolest judge, and her weirdly LA-cockney accent is so fun to do. The final came down to two contestants: Joely and one of the possible sex workers (not my place to comment). Possible Sex Worker truly nailed 'Don't Stop Believin'' by Journey, but in the end, Joely won the final vote, taking us to church with her rendition of Mariah Carey's 'Hero'. She dedicated her win to me and Lauren, all the starving children around the world, and the penis on the *Big Brother* star she's currently dating. It is – apparently – a really lovely penis.

It was truly magical.

Sadly, though, our wonderful evening in prison has come to an end. Cut too short because the stupid arse bride's fiancé came to collect us. Selfish.

I'm completely wiped out, exhausted but really happy. The police were pretty nice in the end and let us off with a stern telling-off and a caution. Actually, one of the officers gave Joely his number and then she disappeared, and when she came out from behind the station ten minutes later, she looked even more tousled than before. Flora giggled and whispered that they'd 'probably snogged'. It's really sweet that she thought that's all Joely had done.

I'm feeling amazing – flying on such a high. The relief and happiness I feel about working things out with the girls is incredible, but I'm also proud of myself for being so honest and standing up to them. Actually, I'm still a bit trembly when I think about what it took to speak to them like that. But I think it really got through. It feels like the air has been well and truly cleared, and we can get back to being best friends again. It matters so much.

Lauren's Uber pulls up at the curb and we hug each other goodbye, with a bonus, two-minute mini cry.

'I'm so glad we sorted this out,' she whispers in my ear as she climbs in. 'It's such a relief, and I'm sorry again – y'know, about everything. You have no idea. I'm so happy to have you as my maid of honour. Sorry I temporarily fired you. Can't wait for the hen do – it's going to be fantastic.'

She laughs as I wave her off, and my hand freezes mid-air.

The hen do. The panic is hot as it creeps up my spine.

Shit.

I'm maid of honour again. I'm in charge of Lauren's hen do.

The hen do I've been hoping would go away or magically solve itself. The hen do I've pointedly been ignoring. The hen do that is in a few weeks and I've done nothing to sort since we all fell out. I've pretended it wasn't happening. I didn't know if we'd work things out as friends or if I was meant to be cancelling everything, so I buried my head in the sand. Shit, what if our confirmations have all fallen through? What if I've lost everyone's deposits? If this hen do doesn't go ahead, I really will lose Lauren forever. Could she forgive me if I ruined her only hen do and lost everyone's money? That could be it for us. Again.

I need to get home and onto my emails immediately.

20

'Looking good, Franny.' I grin at her in the mirror and she winks back at me, wiggling her newly threaded and shaped HD brows.

'What colour do you fancy, lip-wise?' Gilly, the make-up artist, cocks her head, a very serious expression on her face.

Franny purses her lips, thinking about it. 'Well now, Gilly,' she says hopefully, 'you wouldn't happen to have any of the Kylie Jenner lip glosses, by any chance?'

'Ooh, Franny, you know what, I think I do!' Gilly looks delighted, her nose ring sparkling. 'I confiscated one from my daughter this very morning. It's been used once by a twelve-year-old – is that all right?'

She pulls a cherry red gloss out of her pocket and Franny delightedly snatches it off her. 'This is perfect!' she declares, handing it back and pouting carefully as Gilly applies it with precision.

'Oh Gilly, I look absolutely wonderful,' Franny sighs as the studio's make-up artist stands back at last. 'I could pass for your sister today, Delilah,' she adds, climbing out of the tall chair and giving her blue hair a final swish for the mirror.

'Um, I mean, maybe an older aunt,' I say, a little miffed. 'If someone wasn't wearing their glasses and was looking from a long way away.'

Franny ignores me, making kissy faces at the mirror. I gesture for her to follow me. Time to join the rest of the Fuddy-Duddies.

Honestly, I still can't believe this is really happening. We're going on air in less than an hour and I'm nervous AF but also absolutely buzzing with energy and excitement. OK, sure, I'm also buzzing with a whole lot of what-the-hell-am-I-doing-this-is-all-going-to-go-horribly-wrong-isn't-it. But it's too late now to stop this train, so I might as well enjoy it.

We pass Calum Best in the hallway outside the green room and give him a nod. I wonder if he's seen Joely yet today. Maybe they can finally make their faux-love work.

So here it is: the production team has been desperately trying for weeks to come up with an idea to add a little pizazz to *Quiz Monster*'s end-of-series live celebrity special. And we got nowhere. My researchers are all adorable geeks who think the clever questions they come up with are the only thing that matters on a quiz show (bullshit, guys, bullshit). All of Sam's suggestions involved some form of slow, brutal death for the celebrities, which would've been entertaining, no doubt, but might have complicated things. Aslan was even less useful. After he finally stopped trying to charm his way out of helping, he admitted he just didn't have any ideas. Which is fine. It's not like it's a big part of his job or anything. OH, WAIT, IT IS. And then, just when I was giving up hope and preparing to be fired, it hit me. Right in the middle of a Fuddy-Duddies United meeting.

Brainwave. Lightbulb.

A way to raise money for the club – to convince the council to keep us open – and also solve the show's problem.

The next day I cornered Rex, took a deep breath and I pitched.

Fuddy-Duddies United vs celebrities, live on *Quiz Monsters*. A bunch of brainy old ladies with an offensively acronymed name, renowned for acing every pub quiz they've ever done, whose whole raison d'être is trivia. And a team captain who was once a member of Mensa. Them versus the likes of Calum Best and Professor Green. 'Real people geniuses' are very in right now on quiz shows, and the public love seeing a celebrity shown up on TV. Even better when it's courtesy of a group of innocent-looking old ladies who are trying to raise money to keep their club alive. It's a fun twist, and seemed like a possible combined solution to both my problems.

Rex loved it, said it was brilliant. He loves old ladies – they're his staple fandom – and he said it was like *Eggheads* meets *The Chase* meets *University Challenge*. He was so enthusiastic he even insisted on coming along to our next FU meeting to break the news personally to the ladies. He barely got out alive.

Anyway, afterwards we had a bit of a chat. I told him that he needs to start using the runners and interns for things and treating me like the experienced professional assistant producer I am. I told him that I'm not going to be his dogsbody anymore. And because I was feeling extra brave, I told him he also had to stop speaking to me in such a patronising, insulting way.

And, weirdly, he said . . . no problem. He said he didn't really give a crap who fetched his tea and booked his waxing appointments. He just thought I liked it. Thought I enjoyed the honour and privilege blah blah of being his personal assistant. Then he asked why I hadn't said anything before.

I felt a bit stupid then. Why didn't I say something sooner?

As Franny and I arrive back in the green room, I'm hit by a wall of nervous energy bouncing off the walls. Annabel is skipping on the spot, chatting animatedly to Ethel. Sam's going from lady to lady, ferrying cups of tea and plates of Battenberg around. Franny joins them and they all excitedly ooh and aah over her glamorous new look. But, you know what? They all look great. I've never seen them so happy.

Although, is that . . . has Molly got a drawn-on beauty spot? Bloody hell. Might have to speak to Gilly about that, seems a bit excessive. She looks like she's been dressed for a period drama.

Sam beams at me as she passes. 'This is going to be so great,' she whispers, offering me a slice of cake.

I take one, hoping she's right.

Lauren and Joely are also around here somewhere. They volunteered to help with herding and babysitting the FU ladies, but last time I saw them was an hour ago over by the dressing rooms, chatting up the celebs. Lauren was asking for selfies, and Joely was explaining how she is 'one of them'.

They seem happy, like nothing happened between us. Lauren hasn't mentioned her wedding once today and when I asked her how things were going, she just smiled and said, 'All fine. Pretty much sorted now. I'm finally sticking to my choices and Charlie's actually been pitching in to help me at last.' It feels like she's learned some kind of major life lesson, but I hope we are still allowed to be included in these last bits of planning. I'd hate for her to think we don't want to be involved or help at all. That's not what I wanted.

I feel such a swell of satisfaction looking around the room at my ladies now. It's funny, really. It seems like all I hear in the news lately is that different generations hate each other and have nothing in common. They're pitted against each other, encouraged to blame each other for the world's problems. They hate the way the other votes, they hate how they live their lives, they hate what they stand for. Millennials blame baby boomers for having all the money, and baby boomers blame millennials for wasting their lives on touch screen technology. But look at Sam laughing over there with Annabel right now. There's easily fifty years between them, but they have so much in common. It's amazing seeing these women helping each other, working together. It seems to me like we all need each other more than we ever have before. The world is a tiny bit fucked up at the moment, and this is when people need to lean on each other the most. I know saving my small club isn't going to change the world, or help more than a few people. But maybe if I can keep Fuddy-Duddies United open, perhaps we can do more. We could expand the club, even make it nationwide. Encourage generations to get more interconnected.

Or maybe just sack off the Mother Teresa act and get them their own badass TV show! We could make it like *Charlie's Angels* but in a quiz format and with old women?

A delighted-looking Franny springs over, fluttering her excessively long fake eyelashes at me.

'How are you feeling?' I say and she nods happily, pulling out the Kylie Jenner lip gloss she has stolen from Gilly.

'Bloody excited, Delilah. I can't believe you made all this happen. I'm so proud of you,' she says, liberally applying and missing most of her top lip entirely. We might have to revisit Gilly en route to the set.

Sam comes over, the Battenberg is gone and her headset is on. 'Ten minutes until show time, guys. Oh, Granny Franny, what have you done to your face? You've already been through make-up twice. Can you stop messing around?'

Franny giggles and Sam stomps off to find a tissue.

My grandma pulls me close and we lean on each other for a moment.

'I mean it, my darling, I'm so proud of you.' She sighs, holding my hand tightly. 'You've done so well. And if this doesn't save Fuddy-Duddies United, nothing will. Oh, and it's nice to see your girls, Lauren and Joely, are here too, supporting you on your big day. I'm so glad you've made up. I know I called them dreadful bitches and I stand by that, but they are also very special. Although I'm not sure I've seen either of them actually do very much of anything today. They're both still princesses, I suppose – good-hearted, but definitely princesses nonetheless.'

I smile and she tilts her head, looking kindly at me. 'And what about the hen party, Lilah? Have you had any word about that yet?'

My stomach flips over and my chest squeezes. I open my mouth to explain but Sam is suddenly back with us, shooing Franny out of the room.

It's time.

HERE WE FUCKING GO.

Wedding Number Twelve: Millie and Mazi, Church of St Mary, Surrey

Theme: Irish Catholic meets Nigerian, which means nothing, except a lot of bright colours and loud families.

Menu: Smoked salmon starter, followed by chicken and a meringue dessert. Veggie option: stuffed red pepper with goat's cheese.

Gift: Coins in a Tesco carrier bag @ £20.

Gossip: The videographer caught the MIL slagging off the bride, who saw a rough edit a few days later. Bride now knows that her new mum thinks she is a 'cunt'.

My bank balance: -£2045 (Friendly, non-threatening voicemail from the bank and letters from credit card companies I'm not going to read because they don't count.)

21

'Come on, you lot, keep up,' I bark, feeling all authoritative. Some grumbles echo around behind me, but I ignore them, keeping my stride long and decisive.

I'm on such a high after Friday, I feel like I can take on anything. Rex was beaming with joy when I got to work this morning. The ratings were brilliant for the live show, and he's had fantastic feedback on Twitter all weekend. Which is the main thing he cares about. That's not to say everything went without a hitch. Truth be told, the whole thing was a nightmare and I spent most of the show peeking through my fingers and avoiding eye contact with my producer. But live stuff is always unpredictable and throw in a bunch of maverick TV-newbies – not to mention Granny Franny with her penchant for disobeying anything that sounds like an instruction – and things were bound to be a bit out of control. But the audience loved it! Especially when Franny detached her buzzer and lobbed it at Calum Best. And when Molly made Professor Green cry. Oh, and they *really* went nuts when Annabel sat on George Galloway's lap and got him to purr. It was just great TV.

Rex leapt on me this morning when he got in, shouting that I was 'bloody fantastic'. He says he wants me to lead all the brainstorming sessions for the next series – and he didn't ask me to make him a coffee! Oh, and my producer has agreed to give me a raise. In fact, don't tell Aslan, but I'll be getting more than him – to 'reflect my extra experience and compensate me for having previously been on less'. I'm even getting a series bonus. It means that I can consolidate my mess of credit cards and hopefully actually start paying them off. Maybe one day I'll even crawl out of my overdraft.

I said one day, let's not get ahead of ourselves.

Rex ordered me to take the rest of the day off, and said we can start working on the next series tomorrow.

I'm also on a massive high because GUYS, THE HEN DO IS GOING TO BE OK.

I didn't think I could handle it, but I totally could. I am amazing and I can handle anything.

OK, maybe not anything. Actually, it was a pretty close call as to whether I could handle this. At all.

When I got home from prison/making up with the girls the other week, I panic-rang up all the Marbs venues to try to get our bookings back. But everyone was so unhelpful. They just kept saying they'd have to check, and that I'd probably lost everything. The bookings, the apartments, even the deposits. It was so so awful and I was so scared. I called Franny and cried a whole bunch (predictably). She calmed me down and reminded me that I'm totally one of the most organised people in the world and if I've learned anything in the last few months, it's that I can stand up for myself and get shit done.

So I did.

I called them all back and refused to get off the phone until it was sorted. I was nice, I was horrible, I was generous, I was threatening. I threw in Joely's name and, when that didn't work, I promised Rex Powers would tweet something nice about them all.

(He owes me one.)

(And I have his Twitter password in case he says no.)

And it worked. I was still waiting to hear from the final place on Friday, but it's all OK. I have my itinerary and confirmations all there, in black and white, on my email. It's on. It's really happening. Honestly, I'm still sweaty with relief. Thank God, really. The idea of having to tell the hens it was all off . . . it still makes me feel wobbly. They didn't even know anything was wrong and they never will. They don't know I fell out with the bride and they have no clue they were on the verge of losing their holiday – not to mention their money. I am so happy I haven't ruined this. I think it's going to be brilliant. I hope it is.

I sent out a quick WhatsApp to the ten remaining hens this morning, which was obviously a giant-ass mistake.

Lilah Fox created group 'MARBS HEN DO'

Lilah Fox added 10 names

Lilah Fox: Hey everyone, Lilah here. I've set up this WhatsApp group so we can stay in touch and all start getting EXCITED for the hen doooooo! I can't wait. Everything is confirmed, and you all have the itinerary in your email inbox. Sooo, that's it! See you at the airport on the 5th. WAH!

Lilah Fox: PS. Is everyone following @BestWeddingEverCharlieLovesLauren on Instagram? Please do!

Joely Bolt: YAY. Thanks Lilah, you're my hero.

Simone Sweets: Can't wait!

Katie Jacks: Sooooooo excited!

Katie Jacks: Sooooooo excited!

Katie Jacks: Sooooooo excited!

Katie Jacks: Sooooooo excited!

Joely Bolt: No, Katie, NO. STOP IT.

Simone Sweets: I also have an exciting investment opportunity I'd like to talk to you all about while we're out there.

Katie Jacks: Lol wait what?

Joely Bolt: DON'T DO THAT AGAIN.

Simone Sweets: Are you talking to me?

Simone Sweets: It's an amazing opportunity, I promise. Going to get my whole trust fund back, and you'll all make loads of money.

Katie Jacks: Sooooooo excited!

Carlie Hodkins: HOW DID YOU PEOPLE GET MY PHONE NUMBER?

Carlie Hodkins has left the group

Katie Jacks: Sooooooo excited!

Katie Jacks: Sooooooo excited!

236

Joely Bolt has left the group

Lilah Fox added Joely Bolt to the group

Joely Bolt: Fuck you Lilah.

Katie Jacks: Lol wait what?

Katie Jacks: Lol lol lol why'd you leave Joely??? Also, I'm not on Instagram?????? Should I join???? I can follow it on Twitter????? Lol.

Simone Sweets: I'm just going into the gym, abs day lol. What's everyone else up to?

Katie Jacks: Lol lol just heading to Marks and Sparks for some yum yums for dindins lol.

Joely Bolt has left the group

Lilah Fox added Joely Bolt to the group

And so it went on. Three hours later and I can still feel my phone buzzing against my bum with messages.

But never mind that, because I'm here to take care of some mo' bid-nizz. We're on our way to see Mr Canid, because enough's enough – I need to speak to him face to face. We've had enough angry chats on the phone, and he's ignored my emails, so it's time to face the dickhead down. Look him square in his podgy eyes and tell him he's a podgy-eyed dick-toilet. Or maybe something less likely to get us thrown out. Either way, it is ON and I'm raring to go. I've got a speech and everything.

Because now we have leverage. We're not just a small group of confused old ladies with their pushover token youth – now we're a small group of confused old ladies with their not-going-to-take-your-shit token youth *and* the support of the nation. The *Quiz Monster* special wasn't just a success ratings-wise. We told the audience about the council trying to knock down our building and how we have nowhere else to go. We told them about the work we do in the community and how much we want to stay together. It's been incredible. We've had the most unbelievable outpouring of support and donations, from all corners of the country. #SaveFuddyDuddiesUnited was actually trending on Twitter! For maybe four seconds, but it still counts. And the most important messages of love have been from our local area. We heard from people we've met as a group over the years, people we've helped, and people we now desperately want to help if we're allowed to continue. Everyone was so nice and encouraging, and donated whatever they could. It's proof that we're needed and wanted. I've spent the whole weekend trying not to do that Sally Field speech, but sod it:

YOU LIKE ME, YOU REALLY LIKE ME!

Us. I mean us.

It has to be enough to save FU.

So we're all marching over to the council offices now, unannounced, to take on Mr Canid. The building isn't too far away from my work, and I wonder for a second why I haven't turned up here before to try to speak to him in person.

I guess I was too scared.

Duh. Of course I was too scared.

I walk taller now, thinking how much braver I've become

in the last few weeks. You do one small brave thing, and then you feel like you can do a slightly bigger brave thing. And then, before you know it, you're leading a pack of people to confront a scary bureaucrat with a stupid unpronounceable name. Without an appointment.

Ooh, I'm such a bad girl, somebody arrest me already. Again.

I'm at the front of the group, striding confidently, and behind me trails Franny, Ethel, Annabel, Lauren and Joely. Molly is also with us, even though she wasn't invited. She's trawling alongside the group on her mobility scooter, shrieking at everyone to go faster.

We turn the corner and there's the ugly, sixties block of a building.

Here we go.

I breathe deeply and head towards the revolving doors.

Everyone piles in at once.

'Oh, come on, guys, don't do that,' I say weakly, shoved up against the glass as six people try to cram into the same section of door. 'We don't all have to come in at the same time. This is how people die in revolving doors.'

There is some panicked pushing and shoving, and from outside behind us, Molly shouts at everyone to wait for her while she parks the scooter.

Nobody does, and after some limb rearrangements, we all make it into the foyer. The security desk is manned by two amused-looking men, who have watched our stupid Laurel and Hardy routine with the doors. I suspect it hasn't inspired the professional air I was hoping to arrive with.

'We're here to see Mr Canid,' I say, trying to sound official and important anyway. 'Please tell him Delilah Fox is here to speak to him and it's vital he come down to see me immediately.'

The nearest of the two nods and picks up a phone, speaking in a low voice.

'He says you can go up,' he says, and there is mild surprise in his tone. I guess I'm not coming off as quite so important as I'd hoped. 'He's on the twenty-second floor. He'll be waiting for you by the lift doors.'

He is, and I'm surprised and more than a little bit disappointed to find Mr Canid is neither fat, nor old. In fact, there is, inconveniently, nothing really physically wrong with him that I can pick on. I had planned to get so personal when this descended into a shouting match, I had my list of insults all ready. My parents have given me very little in the last few years, but they've definitely improved my insults vocabulary.

'Ms Fox?' he says to me, and there's that familiar voice I've come to know and truly loathe.

I take his hand, nodding sternly.

Actually, if I could see through my hatred, I might even say Mr Canid is quite attractive. Mid-thirties, dark hair, nice shirt. But obviously I hate him, which makes him hideous.

'Mr Canid?' I say, as politely as I can.

'It's *Canid*,' he says and I bristle. But he's smiling.

'Follow me,' he says, peering around, a little confused at the whole group. 'Er, all of you, this way.'

He leads us down a beige council-offices-type corridor and into his large office. Franny and I take the seats in front of his desk, while Molly, Annabel and Ethel collapse loudly on the sofa. Lauren and Joely hover nearby, and I note with irritation that Joely has that look on her face she gets when she fancies someone and is close to taking her bra off to throw at them. In fact, she is definitely wearing fewer clothes than

240

she was in the lift and I don't even know how that's happened because she was already fairly skimpily dressed. What a traitor. At least Lauren has my back, just like she always has. She gives me a steady nod and a wink, as I turn to face the dickhead.

'Thank you for seeing us, Mr Canid,' I say, and I clear my throat, readying my speech.

'Oh, no problem,' he says cheerfully. Too cheerfully. 'It's nice to put a face to the name, Ms Fox. Here's a fun fact for you: did you know my surname means a mammal of the dog family? That includes foxes. I feel like we're practically related!' He laughs nicely and I shift uncomfortably in my seat. This is all a bit too bloody jovial and friendly. I need to stay on message: he's a prick and I hate him.

'Right, well, that's as may be,' I say, sitting up straight. 'But that's not what we're here to talk about. In fact, I expect you know why we're all here.'

He nods encouragingly, so I carry on. 'I don't suppose you saw Friday's episode of *Quiz Monsters: Live Celebrity Special*, but—'

He leans in. 'Ooh, no, I didn't. Was it good? Should I get it on catch-up?'

'Well, yes, you should . . .' I am flustered. 'But that's not the point either. I mean, yes, watch it, definitely because it was promoting our cause and it's a really good show that everyone should watch anyway. And Twitter was full of—'

'Twitter, eh!' he says happily. 'I'm not on Twitter but my little sister loves it. She's always trying to sign me up. She's called Annie. Let me show you a picture of her.'

He leans across the desk with his phone held up and I sigh with frustration. This is so annoying. I had my whole speech thing ready. I was going to call him all the bad words. My parents' hatred was finally going to be useful. Why's he being so nice? What an unbelievable arsehole.

'Oh, she's beautiful!' Ethel, another traitor, declares from the sofa.

'How lovely. What age is she?' Annabel throws in.

I hastily cut the conversation off before he can answer. 'Look, Mr Canid, we're here about the youth club building and Fuddy-Duddies United. I'm here to tell you face-to-face that you can't shut down our building. You've been unreasonable on the phone and ignored all my emails with alternative suggestions, so—'

'Your emails?' He looks surprised.

'Yes,' I say impatiently, and he leans into his computer monitor, clicking through and then leaning back in his chair.

'Oh, bloody IT,' he moans, and it's the first hint of the grumpy cat I thought I'd be meeting. 'They promised they'd fix my spam filters. I can see you've sent me quite a lot of messages, Ms Fox. I'm sorry. You must've thought I was a right prat ignoring you!'

Wait, what?

Oh FFS.

I put my head in my hands. All that research and time spent looking for options. All that wasted emotional energy thinking he was deliberately blanking me. But he was still horrible on the phone . . . er, wasn't he?

Um. I mean, I probably wasn't really in the best frame of mind for our very few conversations. Falling out with my best friend, sabotaging my own relationship, panicking about work and the FU . . . It's a tiny bit possible I was projecting some hostility onto this perfectly nice chap.

'Having said that,' Mr Canid says, firmly but nicely, sitting forward in his chair again, 'I still can't help you, I'm afraid.

It's too late, the order is in. Everything is already underway to demolish the building. I wish I could do more. I'm sorry – I can see you've done a lot of work trying to get this project changed.'

'Wait, please listen to us before you say that,' I say, pleadingly. 'Look, we've been inundated with support since we went public with this. People don't want to lose Fuddy-Duddies United. We're important to this community. And there's so much more we could do if we had the chance.'

I scramble for the piece of paper in my pocket, unfolding it and pushing it across the table to him.

'This is how much we've raised so far on our crowdfunding page. That's since Friday and the donations are still coming in. Ask your sister about all the tweets we've had.'

He looks at the figure written down and then up at me. He cocks his head.

'The community donated this much to a trivia club?'

I shake my head. 'We're not just a trivia club; we're way more than that.'

'Yeah, we make jam too,' Ethel shouts unhelpfully.

'I mean, we do a lot of charity work as well,' I add, rolling my eyes. 'Which I think is probably more in need right now than ever before. Look, people care.'

Beside me, Franny nudges me, ever so subtly.

'Oh,' I say hurriedly, 'and of course Granny Franny is pretty well known around here. She's kind of a big deal, so that helped draw in donations too.' Franny puffs up self-importantly and a rumble starts behind me from Molly, so I quickly add, 'Er, as are *all* the wonderful women at FU. Especially those members here today. Molly here –' I turn to gesture at the ladies on the sofa – 'she worked in the local post office for forty-five years. Everyone knows her. Ethel there was a volunteer with Amnesty International when she was younger, and travelled all over the world helping with humanitarian crises. She's a hero in the community. Annabel has volunteered in the local homeless shelter for half her life. She's the reason we started doing our charity work in the first place. These women matter and they can't be thrown out onto the street like they don't. It's not right.' I take a deep breath and look Mr Canid dead in the eye. 'Last week I saw young people working alongside pensioners, all for a common cause, and it was wonderful. They loved it. It expanded horizons on both sides of the age divide. There was so much connection, so much excitement and interest. I feel like we can learn so much from each other . . .' I falter, knowing I've crossed over from normal levels of enthusiasm to Tom Cruise jumping up and down on Oprah Winfrey's sofa.

But I keep going anyway. 'I want this to be our chance to expand the FU group, open it up to younger members. I want us to include more of the community again – and Molly won't stop us this time.' I pause to pointedly ignore Molly's har-rumph. 'I want us to get out there and help each other. I want to give the club a makeover, to get the youth and the elderly to spend time together. If you shut us down now, we can't do any of that. It would all be a waste. All those connections made will fade and people will forget how important this was – how important it *is*.'

Mr Canid has been listening carefully, watching my face as I talk. He sighs now and looks down at the figures on the scrap of paper again.

There is a long, tense silence and everyone holds their breath.

'OK,' he says at last, resignation in his voice. 'I think there might be something we can do. You're very convincing, Ms Fox, very passionate! I'd offer you a job on the council if you'd take it.' He smiles. He isn't serious, but I still feel the warmth of the compliment.

'It's clear people around here care about your club, and I don't want this new park to get in the way of such a wonderful thing—'

Molly interrupts from behind me. 'Wait, young man, did you just say . . . park?'

He nods slowly.

I turn to see Molly's eyes have both started watering. 'You mean . . . you mean, you want to turn the youth club building back into . . . fields?'

Molly, Ethel, Annabel and Franny all look at each other.

He smiles. 'Well, I mean, it's a park, not a field,' he says. 'But yes, we at the council feel that too much land has been overtaken by unnecessary and derelict buildings in the area. We'd like to see a bit more of what we used to have around here – more open spaces – don't you think?'

The women behind me are close to tears. If they were thirty years younger, they'd no doubt be trying to have sex with Mr Canid on his desk right now.

Actually, I'm surprised Franny isn't.

'Anyway, you were saying . . . ?' I prompt him.

'Well,' he smiles again, 'how about if we build you a new youth club, in the park? We can make it bigger and nicer, with better amenities. That place you're in at the moment is a mess and practically falling down. We can make the new building your official Fuddy-Duddies United headquarters, and you can use it to work on this idea of yours to expand the charity and youth-centric side of things.'

245

Is this really happening?

He hands me back the piece of paper. 'I'm really impressed with your fundraising efforts, Ms Fox, but you can keep the money. Invest it in the club.' He looks thoughtful. 'Maybe we could even work together on it? I'd like to talk to you more about that – bringing the young and old together. It sounds intriguing. I've been looking for something like that as a charity project to work on. It could even be a nationwide campaign. Would you be willing to work with me on this? I might actually really offer you a job, Ms Fox.'

We smile at each other and the group cheers behind me, talking excitedly among themselves.

Mr Canid leans across the desk to me. 'Ms Fox, I'm sorry we've had issues over the phone. I know I've been difficult. I've been told I have very bad BRV.'

Oh God, what on earth is that? Is it some kind of medical condition that I should know about? Maybe we could donate some of the funds we've raised towards helping BRV?

'Bitchy Resting Voice,' he adds, and then he barks out a laugh.

I beam and put out my hand to shake his. He looks at it.

'Oh,' he says, and I swear he sounds a little disappointed. 'Are we finished then? I should've dragged this meeting out a bit longer, shouldn't I?'

He is twinkling at me. Twinkling as he slowly shakes my hand. He is FLIRTING WITH ME.

'Oh, I, er . . .' I stutter. I am wholly unprepared for flirting. Wholly unprepared. Especially flirting from someone I thoroughly hated until about twenty minutes ago. My hand buzzes against his palm – it literally buzzes, I swear. Like static electricity. I fight the urge to take off my clothes.

'We better go. I have to get back to . . . life,' I say, standing up.

'Right then,' he says, coughing and suddenly looking a bit vulnerable and awkward. We look at each other and I realise I'm still holding his hand. I let it go and he looks disappointed again.

We all stand and crowd out of his office, shouting happily at each other. Ethel, Annabel and Franny race each other to the lift, while Molly grumbles behind them. Lauren and Joely sing 'Eye of the Tiger' in loud, out-of-tune voices at each other.

Mr Canid and I bring up the rear. I have never been so aware of another person standing near me before. He clears his throat as we follow everyone slowly down the corridor.

'Well, now that's settled,' he says in a low voice, his hand tingling on the small of my back, 'Ms Fox, would you con-sider . . . do you want to go on a date with me sometime?'

'What?' I say stupidly.

Franny glances back at us and smiles. She's twenty feet away; there's surely no way she could've heard him.

I think fast as he continues. 'A date. A drink. Dinner, maybe, if you're into eating food in the evenings.'

'Are you serious?' I whisper, bewildered.

He stops walking and I stop too. 'Completely serious,' he says, studying me. 'I'm told I don't have a sense of humour, so I must be serious.' He smiles again. 'I know it's a little unconventional and I would probably get into trouble for asking while I'm on official business, but there we go.' My stomach goes a little funny. 'Honestly, Ms Fox, I've really enjoyed our phone conversations, impassioned as they were. They've been a bit of a highlight for me. You won't be sur-prised to hear that things can get a little dreary in the council

247

offices on occasion, so you've brightened things up a bit. I even told my sister Annie about you! I've always liked people who aren't afraid to tell me what they think and stand up for themselves. I also very much enjoy a good shouting match from time to time.' He pauses and I see a flash of amusement. 'Plus, I really like how you pronounce my name. It's so exotic.'

I think for a second. A date. Dinner with this man who isn't Will.

I have to admit, I've been oddly enjoying our phone arguments too.

Maybe I should go for it. Maybe this could be . . .

Will's face flashes in front of mine for a moment and guilt fills me.

No, I can't do it. I'm not ready. I'm not ready to let Will go just yet. Even if he's long since let me go.

'Um, my situation is a little bit complicated at the moment,' I say reluctantly, fiddling with my shirt buttons. I go on. 'I'm kind of in the middle of a breakup. Sort of. I mean, I got dumped a few weeks ago, but I'm not sure I've fully accepted I've been dumped yet, if you see what I mean.' I feel flustered, and add, 'Sorry, you really didn't need to know that, sorry, sorry.' I feel myself going red and stutter as I continue. 'I am very flattered, and think you're . . . well, you're . . . And at another time . . . if you asked me . . . It's just not really the right moment for me to be dating. I'm sorry.'

There is a moment of silence before Mr Canid takes a step away.

'OK, I understand,' he says, his professional face back in place. 'I guess we'll have to cancel the Fuddy-Duddies United plan after all.'

I gape at him, and for a second I think he's serious.

Then he laughs. 'I'm just joking!' he says, his hands raised defensively. 'Maybe I do have a sense of humour after all.'

That is debatable.

22

'The truth is . . .' Elizabeth pauses dramatically before shouting, 'I'M NOT REALLY ELIZABETH.'

We all gasp and Lila Fowler – AKA Lauren – doubles over, laughing so hard she is genuinely struggling for breath.

'Elizabeth' whips off her blonde wig to reveal her own brunette hair underneath, and we all break into applause on the street. She fixes the group with an evil stare and continues talking loudly. People walking past stop to watch. A man holding a pint of beer in a plastic cup shouts, 'Get your tits out.'

Elizabeth ignores him, shrieking in her most dramatic voice, 'That's right! I've been living as Elizabeth for the last few months but I'm really the evil Margo. And I'm going to murder the real Elizabeth because, basically, that uptight frigid bitch can suck it.'

Elizabeth/Evil Margo (or even her real name, *Simone*) has done very well with her big reveal. Although I'm not too sure about the ad libbing there at the end.

So basically, the theme for Lauren's hen do is . . . wait for it . . . have you guessed? Maybe you worked it out the moment I mentioned Lila Fowler. Lauren's hen do is all themed around the book and TV franchise, *Sweet Valley*. That means *Sweet Valley Kids*, *Sweet Valley Twins*, *Sweet Valley High*, *Sweet Valley University* – as well as all the hundreds of other *Sweet Valley* spin-offs/money-making enterprises.

It was Lauren's favourite thing when we met at school and

it's continued to be an inside joke throughout our friendship. In fact, we're basically friends because my name is Lilah and that's her favourite character's name.

It has turned out to be absolutely epic, even if I do say so myself. All the hens are dressed up as different characters from the books – I had a lot of fun assigning those roles. Elizabeth's twin sister, Jessica Wakefield, is being played by Joely, who said it was bitchy typecasting but was clearly pleased with her starring role. A girl called Nicola is Elizabeth's dowdy best friend, Enid Rollins, and later tonight, Nic is going to switch wigs and become Enid's sexier university alter ego, Alexandra Rollins. She's then going to get really into drugs and sleep with Elizabeth's boyfriend, Todd Wilkins, just like in the books. Nicola said she's planning to get as method as possible with her role, and since I'm here in drag playing Todd, I'm pretty intrigued to see where the night's going to take us.

Oh, that girl Katie Jacks got stuck playing Elizabeth and Jessica's 'mom', Alice Wakefield. The other girls insisted on that as a punishment for all those 'fucking annoying' emails she kept sending. Katie Jacks doesn't seem to mind, though – she is the most enthusiastic person I ever met.

I've written a very loose, very short script for all the hens. The idea is that it's not just a theme for the weekend, it's a SHOW! Each hen gets one big dramatic reveal about her character during our three days here in Marbs. We all get a 'scene' – we all have our big moment in the spotlight. Tomorrow, Jessica/Joely is going to announce she's joining a cult – she has been rehearsing her monologue for weeks. And earlier today Katie Jacks performed a totally believable – but if I'm honest very much over-acted – storyline where Alice Wakefield got kidnapped at a spa and an old college friend tried to steal her face. Which, come on, has happened to all of us at some point, hasn't it?

They are all genuine storylines plucked from the books but, given there are hundreds of stories in the series, even die-hard fan Lauren has no idea what to expect. She seems to be finding the whole thing hilarious and you should've seen her face when we presented her with her purple Unicorn Club outfit. She's never been happier. I reckon she might wear it out again. Like, all the time.

I feel super proud now, surveying the scene. Everyone's so into it and has really gone to town with their costumes. There are so many different wigs, girlish Alice bands, and an array of pale pink early nineties jumpers – as well as our sashes that declare us to be members of the Unicorn Club.

It's a hen do, so obviously there are many arbitrary rules involved in our *Sweet Valley* game – like, we're only allowed to refer to each other as our character names, or there are drink penalties and forfeits. If anyone breaks character, they have to take a shot from the 'penalty liquid'. The penalty liquid is some awful high-alcohol-content liquid I'm carrying around in my bag, which is – as far as I can tell – essentially blue petrol. But it's doing the trick, and it's vital to ensure we cram in the maximum amount of drinking as we move from bar to bar. I've never been wholly sold on a lot of the hen do traditions, but the heavy drinking side of it is one I will always be more than on board with. It's actually really lucky that so many of the characters in the books ended up being terrible drug addicts or alcoholics. It makes staying in character for the drinking games a lot easier.

Anyway, the whole thing has been very very fun and very very funny. But also, admittedly, incredibly confusing. Especially for me, whenever someone calls Lauren 'Lila'.

But there was no question that bride-to-be Lauren would be Jessica's rich, snobby best friend. Lila is not only the best character in the books by far, but she's also the leader of the Unicorn Club, so duh. But I keep having to drink whenever I accidentally respond to my own name.

Very drunk now.

Of course, the best part is that Lauren seems to be having the silliest, awesomest time ever.

She's like a different person, like the old Lauren. It feels like she's let go of all that fury and frustration that was building up in her. It's like there was a big wedding-shaped knot in her stomach and talking to us has untied it. She's laughing and enjoying things again. And – shock horror – talking about the rest of life going on around her. She's even complaining about work again. Apparently she's mostly doing tampons now, after they lost their sanitary towel client.

The wedding is just weeks away but she seems more relaxed than ever. I feel a bit bad, actually, because I really haven't done anything to help in weeks. Every time I ask about it, she says it's all sorted and not to worry. In fact, she's barely spoken about the wedding at all. She's more chilled out than I've ever seen her – even when Joely's latest reality star boyfriend turned up here earlier today to surprise us. I thought she'd be livid about a boy on her hen do, but she was delighted. Turns out she was a fan of that series of *Big Brother*. His name is Brian and he loves telling people he was in *Big Brother*. He's told us over and over. And over. He told everyone here, he told all the other guests in our self-catering apartments, he told everyone around the pool, he told all the staff, and he told some guys in the loos – and then he came out of the loos and told us he'd told them.

He came to Marbs to surprise Joely, which is super sweet and she looked genuinely excited to see him. He even got into the spirit of the theme by bravely taking on the role of class clown, super geek Winston Egbert. He looks adorable in glasses and his Unicorn Club sash. He's said he'll even do a scene for us! I jokily suggested he perform Winston's dramatic death – where Winnie got drunk and fell from a balcony. Brian said yes way too enthusiastically and now I'm worried he is going to jump from a balcony for real. I picture him sailing through the air, screaming, 'I WAS IN *BIG BROOOOOOOOOOOOOOTHEEEEEEER* ...' Splat.

Anyway, he's really fun, and I don't want to speak for Joely, but I have a sneaky suspicion she actually genuinely really likes him. And I don't think it's just for publicity stunt purposes. They're not officially together or anything, but since things slowed down on the wedding planning front, Joely's had so much more time to spend with Brian. They've been doing everything together and I see them on the MailOnline homepage constantly. They seem happy.

He's gone off to do a personal appearance and a DJing gig now, but he'll be back in the wee hours for his death scene (hopefully not for real?) and then he's flying home with us tomorrow night.

Joely is making the most of him being gone, and is heroically flirting with every group of stags we come across. Which is a lot. This road – this area – is officially hen and stag do central. She says she's just being in character and it's what Jessica Wakefield would've wanted from her – which is no doubt true. She's on the other side of the street now, making her way around a pack of about seventeen men dressed like babies. They're in actual nappies and are each carrying a giant milk bottle, presumably filled with something like our blue lighter fuel. It's possibly the least sexy thing I've ever seen in my life, but I don't suppose they were aiming for sexy. Stag dos are about humiliating each other, right? Making sure the groom is properly and thoroughly brutalised, so he comes back traumatised and feral.

Oh, and if there's a fatality, that's a bonus, apparently.

Either way, the nappy-fashion is not stopping Joely. I can hear her signature flirty giggle tinkling across the road now, as the guys all fall over themselves to get her attention. Have you ever seen a groom in a giant baby bonnet trying to do a handstand? Because it's not a pretty sight. The whole street smells like hormones.

As Joely/Jessica says goodbye to the stag-baby group with a cutesy wave, I vaguely try to herd everyone towards the next bar, where we have a sizeable array of cocktails waiting for us. Oh, except we seem to have lost the bride again. Lauren is very drunk and keeps wandering off. I've twice now found her having wees behind bins. Even though, both times, we only left the last bar seconds before.

'Lauuuuuurrrrren?' I call ineffectively. She's nowhere to be seen, but to be honest, everything more than three feet away is pretty hazy. I am very drunk. Bloody blue penalty liquid. Bloody drinking games. Why did I do this to myself?

That's right – because it's awesome.

Joely joins me on the pavement and I note vaguely that her make-up is everywhere. There's actually lipstick on her eyelids and in her hair. I briefly wonder if she did that deliberately. Her whole job on the internet is to spark new trends and lead the pack. Maybe hair and eyelid lipstick is now a thing?

'Lauren's gone again,' I say conversationally. For once, I'm not worried. I feel quite peaceful, actually. We're all adults and I refuse to get anxious this weekend.

'Didn't you microchip her?' Joely giggles, rubbing her cheeks absentmindedly.

Oh, there you go! Her hands are covered in lipstick – that's how it's spreading so fast.

Wait, is hand lipstick a thing?

Joely continues, oblivious: 'Oh, and you didn't call her Lila, so you have to take a shot. Come on, Todd.' She takes the penalty liquid from me and pushes it into my face. I happily take a swig of the thick blue liquid inside. Bleugh.

Joely laughs at my pain and links her arm with mine. 'I'm sure I saw her wandering off that way,' she says, pointing up the street. 'She's probably having another piss behind a bin.'

We find Lauren ten minutes later, a little way up the road, in a tattoo parlour. It turns out she'd accidentally started following a totally different hen party, thinking they were us. It's an easy mistake to make, except that this hen party are all quite clearly Japanese and all wearing very obvious sailor hats. Lauren didn't notice they weren't her hens until someone started tattooing an anchor on her wrist. She realised at that point but still got the tattoo anyway. And then a bunch of us decided we should get them too! Because why not! It hurt a lot, but I think it probably looks super cool. I can't decide. I'll decide when I sober up. I hope I like it! I hope so, because I think tattoos are forever, aren't they? But that's OK, forever's not that long. And my friend Jamie had her tattoo lasered off last year and it wasn't that bad. It only cost her thousands of pounds and took months to do. They sort of boiled it off her skin across a series of sessions, but that probably won't hurt that much . . . Oh God, what have I done?

It'll be fine.

Don't think about it.

Either way, we're all back together again now and hanging out with the Japanese sailor hens – they are brilliant girls! Even though they don't actually speak English. But we're getting on *really* well! I think we'll stay in touch! Maybe we can all be pen pals?

When I was eight I had a pen pal I found on Ceefax.

Hey, remember Ceefax? My loyalties were usually with Teletext but BunnyLover456 said in her letters that she preferred Ceefax.

Am I rambling? What was I saying?

I'm really happy.

Lauren's absolutely buzzing – I think she's even happier than me. She's dancing on the pavement near me now, sweating a lot. She keeps telling us how much she loves us and talking about how much she fancies Jeremy Vine. She's never mentioned it before, but apparently she really, really fancies him. She's crying about it a bit, actually.

She's also chewing her cheeks a lot and her pupils are all black.

Hold on, who gave the bride drugs?

And where can I get some?

23

I feel lightheaded as we float through the arrivals lounge of the airport. We are one huge, singular mass of exhausted hen party. Half of us are still drunk and the other half is dangerously hungover. I'm somewhere in the middle, thanks to one final sickly sweet wine on the flight back. It was definitely a mistake, but it's staving off the worst of it for a few more minutes. I catch sight of myself as I shuffle past a reflective surface and look away quickly. My hair is sticking out in all directions and I am basically yellow from all the drinking. Why are airports full of mirrors? Oh, I feel rank.

But it was worth it.

We had such a good last day. Such a good weekend generally. After our amazing *Sweet Valley* Saturday, we stayed up all night dancing in the street outside a bar, while the stag party in nappies gave us shots from their baby bottles. And then that segued seamlessly into an all-day pool party today at the apartment. The baby lads joined us, and so did the lovely Japanese hens.

And guess who I got to come along for our last few hours? Shiny Naked Man!

Shiny Naked Man, it turns out, is called Stanley. And he's not training to be a world famous doctor or anything, he just likes taking his clothes off around Spain and partying with drunk women. Also, he's not twenty, he's thirty-one, but he uses a lot of Botox. So that makes me feel better. And maybe a little sad.

Stanley was a last-minute addition to the festivities. I had planned to avoid the more intense hen do rituals – I swore I would – but then I thought . . . fuck it. Strippers and willy straws are a tradition for a reason – because they're funny! I don't have to take it all so seriously. It was only ever my own stupid awkwardness stopping me having a good time at those other hen dos. So I decided for our last day, we would embrace some of those classic hen tropes. Shiny Naked Stanley was in the area and said he'd updated his insurance so he could actually serve us drinks, so everyone wore willy headbands and spent the day brandishing rude inflatables with a shiny, naked butler. And it was really great.

I feel like we ticked all the hen boxes in the end. Every single one of us was sick at various points, we all have blood-ied feet and knees from falling over and walking around the streets barefoot. There was snogging and arguments and passing out. Simone sold a bunch of timeshares to the baby stags. Katie Jacks announced she wanted to try MDMA for the first time but we didn't think she should be allowed to get any more hyper, so we gave her a Nurofen. She still went mad, though, and ended up kissing everyone in the apartment complex – even a guy with a cold sore, so she definitely has herpes now. And then she accidentally killed the apartment concierge's pet fish – it's a really long story – so we had a fish funeral and I made a speech. It was everything a bride-to-be – and her weary maid of honour – could ask for.

By the time we had to leave for the airport late this after-noon (we were asked to leave by apartment security and a very cross concierge), we were all totally spent. And Lauren was floating unconscious in the pool, on top of a giant inflat-able willy.

We waved goodbye to the baby men and the Japanese

sailors, while Shiny Naked Stanley performed the last of his butlering duties by bundling us all into our cabs, promising to stay in touch.

It was the perfect end to a brilliant hen do, and I'm so relieved and happy that it all worked out. It was worth all that effort and time and fear.

But ugh, here comes real life, and a very real hangover, which I can already feel will last all week.

'Lilah?' a voice interrupts my haze as we pass through customs and out into arrivals.

'YES?' Lauren jumps automatically a few feet ahead of me, only just conscious but still trying to be in *Sweet Valley* character. She is grey and drawn. She looks worse than me, I note, with satisfaction. I have performed my maid of honour duty fully and Lauren is definitely broken.

'Er, Lilah?' the voice says again, and this time I register the familiar note.

Jesus Christ, it's Will. Will's standing awkwardly behind the arrivals barrier, staring at me.

Will's here. Why is Will here? My breath starts coming out in ragged gasps.

I haven't seen him in ages. Not even once since he moved out, not a glimpse.

He's been coming to get his stuff bit by bit from the house when I'm not there. It's been like being slowly robbed in the saddest way possible. Everything that made the house 'ours' gradually disappearing on a drip feed. It's made me cry every time I've noticed yet another stupid Marvel comic souveniry thing I never liked anyway was gone.

We've not spoken on text much either. I ran out of excuses to message him, and the replies were not enthusiastic.

I realise now that I'd given up hope of him coming back. I

hadn't processed the split yet – too busy and distracted – but deep down I'd given up on him.

And now he's here. In the airport, of all places.

Why is he here? He's just standing there, like this is normal. He looks smart and nervous. He's wearing that nice blue shirt he wears for job interviews.

Shit. Is he here meeting a girl? He must be picking up a new girlfriend or something. The idea of that hits me squarely in the chest, the picture of him moving on without me. An image flashes across my brain of him kissing someone else and I catch a sob before it can get out. I couldn't handle it if he were here for a girlfriend. I'm not ready.

Before I can react or say anything, a commotion breaks out a few feet further along the crowd. Cameras are flashing and a group of men are shouting for Joely and Brian. Oh my God, it's photographers – paps!

'JOELY, OVER HERE, BABE! BRIAN, LOOK THIS WAY! SMILE FOR US! NICE HOLIDAY, GUYS? ARE YOU OFFICIAL NOW? ARE YOU IN LOVE? LOOK THIS WAY, WILL YOU, GUYS? DO ONE TOGETHER, CAN YOU? ARE YOU ENGAGED? JOELY? BRIAN? WAS THIS A BABYMOON, EH? MAKE OR BREAK HOLIDAY? WHAT'S GOING ON WITH YOU TWO? SMILE, WILL YOU?'

The men are all shoving each other for space as the general public around us crane their necks to see what's going on. What famous people have they missed? The whole arrivals procession slows to a halt.

What on earth are the paps doing here? Oh my God, it must've been Brian! He obviously called them, I think furiously. He's such a bastard! I thought he seemed all right. Poor Joely, trying to have an anonymous holiday and really connect with him, and he's tipped them off just to make a scene! How awful is that!

I can just about see Joely and Brian in the crowd up ahead trying to move their way forward with their cases. They both have their sunglasses on and are wearing harried, upset looks on their faces. Expressions like they're used to this but can't be doing with it. They don't get too far, though, before Joely suddenly stops.

She throws her bag dramatically to the floor, in full view of the cameras. She turns to Brian, who looks surprised, as she screams, 'That's it! I'm so done with you, Brian. I won't take any more of your cheating! We were deeply in love and committed but I realise now that you are a scoundrel and I am better than this.' It's a bit wooden but the photographers are eating it up, their flashes going off like mad, blinding the onlookers/audience.

I look back over at Will and he is staring at the commotion too, bewildered.

'What are you talking about, Joe?' Brian is shouting back. 'What's going on here, babe? Did you call them? I thought you wanted to do this for real? I thought you liked me?'

Joely starts shouting over him. 'Shut up, you! I knew you couldn't keep it in your pants for long. I can't believe this, after you told me you LOVED me and wanted to MARRY me. I was a fool to believe you, Brian. I saw the pictures, Brian! And I know you did it with that girl from *Love Island*! How could you? We're over for GOOD, Brian! Never call me again. I'm going to date P DIDDY and he says he HATES you.' As she shouts, Joely repeatedly glances over at the photographers to check they're taking note. They most certainly are.

'What girl from *Love Island*?' Brian looks genuinely perplexed. 'What pictures? Are you really dumping me, babe? I promise I haven't done anything! I thought we were getting serious? And how do you know P Diddy?'

Joely storms off and away from the group. She whips off her sunnies for one devastated, tear-streaked final look at the cameras – and they go crazy.

I note that she's re-done her make-up on the plane.

We are witnessing the most public, overly planned and set-up dumping possible. Poor unsuspecting Brian.

Bloody Joely, she'll never change.

I turn away from the shouting and back towards Will. For half a second I'd forgotten he was there.

Why is he here?

He gestures at me to join him at the barrier and slowly I comply, pulling my case behind me with dread. My wrist throbs and I try not to think of the stupid tattoo sitting there under my sleeve. It's probably in the process of becoming infected. The hand will no doubt have to come off.

The creakings of my hangover are burrowing into my brain as I stop short in front of Will and I feel a tug of horror at how terrible I must look.

I've thought about this moment – the moment I'd get to see him again – so many times. Those bits of sleep I've managed to catch in the last couple of months have been full of that image. But even during the worst of the anxiety-filled nightmares, I've never imagined myself having to face him while coming out the other side of three solid days of drinking. Ugh.

We stand face to face, staring at each other silently for a moment.

He looks surprised to see me.

I clear my throat, waiting for him to speak. He should be the one to speak, shouldn't he? He's the one here in the airport. He's the one who called me over. I open my mouth and then shut it again. I can't find any words in my brain.

He laughs suddenly, but it's humourless. An uncomfortable noise to fill the silent hole between us.

'How are you, Lilah?' he says, and his voice cracks a little.

I nod. 'I'm OK,' I say, my voice hoarse. 'Bit hungover. It's been a long few days. But I'm well enough.'

We fall silent again.

'And you?' I say, sounding a bit desperate.

'Good! Good,' he says, and he trails off there.

'What are you—?' I start to ask why he's here but he interrupts, suddenly talking urgently. 'Actually, Lilah, I'm not good. I'm terrible. I'm a mess. I'm so sorry for showing up here like this, but I still had your itinerary and flight details on my computer. I know it's creepy to just turn up, but I couldn't wait any longer to talk to you. I nearly flew out to Marbella to find you guys but I knew that would be ridiculous . . .' He trails off again and the room starts spinning.

Is he . . . ? What is happening?

He swallows hard and keeps going, studying my face intently as he speaks. 'I've spent the last few weeks hiding away, Lilah, trying not to think about you. But it's all I can do. Daniel had to confiscate my phone weeks ago, just to stop me messaging you. He admitted the other day that he'd even replied to a few of your texts.'

Maybe that was where the thumbs up emoji came from. From what I remember of Daniel, he's much more of a thumbs up emoji type than Will.

He's still talking. 'I need . . . I have to . . . Lilah, I miss you so much. I know things weren't great between us, but I should've been more understanding of what you were dealing with. I know it's only because you care about everyone and

264

wanted to help. I was so selfish. I wanted you all to myself and it was so . . . I'm so sorry, Lilah.'

He takes another big breath and I feel my mouth drop open. I close it.

He laughs shakily and goes on. 'I know it's a ridiculous cliché to turn up at an airport, but it worked in *Love Actually*, right? There's an airport in that, isn't there? It's been a while since I saw it . . . Oh, I don't know what I'm doing, I really don't. All I know is that, Lilah, I love you. I want us to get back together. Please can we get back together? Take me back?' He stops, and then, stuttering, he says, 'More than that, I want us to be together forever. I . . .'

He glances at the crowds around us. They're still distracted by the Famous People commotion to notice our intense exchange.

And then Will gets down on one knee.

Oh my God. This can't be happening. This cannot be happening.

'Delilah Mary Fox . . .' he begins, half smiling, but he is white with fear. He looks more uncomfortable than I've ever seen him. This is not Will at all. He doesn't do public displays. He is a person who can't even talk to Joely when we're out, because he's afraid of ending up in a fan picture. He hides from the TV when I'm watching ITV2 shows because it's all 'too much' for him. He cannot be down on one knee proposing to me in an airport. This is all wrong, wrong, wrong.

He clears his throat and looks up at me, shaking. 'Lilah, will you marr—' he begins and I grab him, pulling him up.

'Get up, Will,' I whisper. 'You don't want to do that. Not like that, I know you don't.'

His face turns a shade paler – he's practically green now

– but he looks intensely relieved. I pull him in for a hug and over his shoulder I glance around, breathing out.

No one noticed. Or if they did, maybe they thought he was tying a shoelace or something.

'You don't have to do something like that,' I say into his ear as we stand there hugging. 'We're not in *Love Actually*. This is real life.'

He makes a noise and sags into my arms, suddenly becoming a stone heavier.

'That was the stupidest, worst thing I've ever done,' he whispers into my neck. 'Worse than actually breaking up with you. I'm sorry. But I thought it would be what you wanted. Daniel said it's the kind of thing all girls want – a big public proposal. I said it wasn't really you or me, but he seemed so sure. I just wanted to prove to you how much I want this. I know that was dumb and impulsive, but I do . . . I do want to marry you, Lilah. I want us to be together and live in our house and have a life together forever. You're all I want. I've missed you so much. I feel broken without you, like half of me is gone.'

A whispered, awkward proposal in my ear feels much more like Will, and I feel his warmth seep through me.

This would be such a nice life. A nice life with my lovely, nice Will. Spooning him and popping his spots. I could say yes right now and that would be so wonderful.

But.

But.

Oh fuck.

I don't know what to think. The yes should be out of my mouth already and yet . . .

Look, I didn't want to break up with Will. I tried so hard to make him change his mind. I begged him to stay and talk.

266

I cried every night for weeks. I haven't slept properly in ages. But now he's here. And he's saying all this lovely stuff I thought I wanted to hear. He loves me, he's missed me like I've missed him. He's offering me everything I should want. I thought I definitely wanted a life together.

But I'm not sure.

Because I know now that he was right to dump me. I didn't make room for him in my life. And not just in the last few months – I never did. Even before the crazy year of weddings began, I was slotting him around my life instead of making him his own place in it. I let him skirt the outsides of my universe, but I never really let him in. I never made that effort. And Franny was right too, when she said we had problems we weren't dealing with. We weren't able to argue and be honest with each other – and you should be able to argue with your partner, shouldn't you? I always thought us never arguing was a good thing, but I think there should be fallouts, at least once in a while. There should be easy, fun bickering. I should be able to tell Will when I'm upset about something without fear of making him sad.

And why am I so sure I don't want to marry him?

I pull away a little from our hug and he lets me.

I sigh, looking at his sweet face. 'Will, I need some time to think about this,' I say slowly. 'This is all so nice, but I feel very overwhelmed. It's really good to see you, but . . . I don't know what I think. I'm sorry.' I press my hand to my forehead and stare at the high white ceiling above us. 'It really doesn't help that I'm both drunk and also hungover right now; it's hard to think straight. This has come out of the blue, Will. I've heard nothing from you, I thought it was over. I do still love you but . . . I . . . look, I've had no sleep in three days. I barely know where I am.'

He looks wounded, but puts his hand on my shoulder.

'I get it,' he says, nodding slightly. 'I am so sorry about everything, you have no idea. I want this – us – to work, though, and I'm prepared to be patient. I know we can make it, I'm sure of that now.' He pauses. 'Do you have to go? Can I at least give you a lift home?'

I shake my head. 'We've booked taxis, and they're here, waiting for us all. I need to pay my share, so I'll go with the girls.'

He nods again, silently, miserably, and I give him another quick hug before slowly turning away, pulling my suitcase along behind me. I look back once and he's staring after me, looking sad. I made him sad. But that's OK. Life is sometimes about making other people sad so you can be happy.

Lauren and Joely are waiting for me by the car. They look frantic.

'What the hell happened?' Lauren shrieks at me excitedly. 'We saw you with Will – it looked really intense. Are you OK?'

I wince. The hangover pain is real, and so are the emotions.

'I'll explain in the car,' I say, giving her a tired smile.

'Are you all right, though?' adds Joely nicely.

I think about it. 'Yeah, I'm surprisingly all right,' I say, as I load my suitcase and climb into the back of the cab.

I turn to her. 'Are *you*, though? What was that scene back there? It looked pretty nasty. I thought you were actually starting to like Brian for real?'

Joely looks horrified. 'Oh God, no,' she says, shaking her head. 'Don't accuse me of having real feelings, ever, please. No, no, I just thought if I seemed enthusiastic during the trip, one of the other girls might sell a story on us. Y'know, tell the *Mirror* how happy we seemed right before the end.'

'Did he really cheat on you, though?' I say, confused.

'Oh, probably!' she says dismissively. 'But who cares? It's over now. I don't want a real boyfriend – too much hard work. Plus, my agent gave me David Walliams' number, so we have a date lined up for next week.'

She gives me a thumbs up and the driver starts the engine.

24

We're meant to be at the hotel right now. We're meant to be getting ready and pulling those last-minute details together ahead of Lauren and Charlie's wedding. We're meant to be getting our bridesmaid dresses on. Then we're meant to be making our way over to Charlie's dad's place to ooh and aah at the giant marquee. And then we're meant to be watching Lauren get married.

But an hour ago we got a call.

The fuckers have eloped.

So apparently, she and Charlie had a big talk last night. Their first proper conversation in ages, by the sound of it. Lauren admitted how carried away she's been getting with all this wedding stuff. She finally told him a lot of what she told us in that drunk tank a lifetime ago. How she feels like she's lost herself a bit and – worse – how she feels like she's lost Charlie. The actual celebration of their relationship got lost in the planning and Lauren confessed that she didn't even really want this big elaborate wedding in the first place. She doesn't know how it happened. Her first instinct, back when he proposed, had been a little wedding with just her closest loved ones. But she'd let everyone else's opinions and judgements get in the way.

She told Charlie how she'd ended up dreading the whole thing.

And Charlie totally got it. In fact, he said he was absolutely delighted to hear it and then immediately booked them a pair of tickets to Vegas. He said he'd only suggested having a quick engagement because he was worried about this very thing happening. He said he'd seen it happen to loads of his friends who got engaged and he didn't want Lauren to have to deal with all that pressure. He didn't know how crazy things had become, because she'd been pretending everything was in hand. Pretending everything was great and fun. Like she did with us for ages.

So they're in Las Vegas right now, getting ready for a wedding ceremony that will be performed by an Elvis impersonator. They'll have strangers for witnesses and literally not one friend or family member present. Lauren's not even wearing one of those nine different wedding dresses she had ready. She says she's going to wear her favourite £55 green dress from Topshop. The one she wore for her birthday last year.

I can't stop laughing. I'm so pleased for them.

Of course, everyone back here is going mad about it. Lauren is kindly redirecting questions to me – my final duty as maid of honour – and I've had so many messages this morning from angry guests. I understand that both sets of parents are especially livid. And I get why they're angry, but I also think . . . fuck them.

Just a little bit!

But yeah, fuck them.

I know they've spent a huge ton of money, but their anger doesn't even seem to be about that. They're angry because they saw this wedding as being *their* big day. They saw it as their moment in the sun.

And this is one of my problems with weddings – how buried the bride and groom get in all of it. So often, it doesn't really get to be about them and their relationship, it becomes about everyone else. Everyone has an opinion to offer and

271

pointed suggestions and demands. People feel a weird right to comment on every aspect of a wedding.

Today was supposed to be a day for Lauren and Charlie. It was supposed to be about celebrating them and their commitment to each other, and by the end, it wasn't anymore. It was about everyone else and what they wanted. All this anger from the guests – who don't get to put on a fancy hat, talk about 'who's going to be next' and single-shame Joely – proves that.

Ultimately, Lauren and Charlie wanted to get married and they're doing just that. Without any of the craziness. And I'm really, really proud of them.

Plus, Lauren promised she'd FaceTime us from the ceremony – yay.

Joely and I are sitting on the floor of my living room now, drinking the champagne we'd planned on taking to the hotel with us. No point wasting it, right? Joely's just put her dark green bridesmaid dress on, because she said she wants to wear it at least once. It looks great on her – I mean, it should, since she chose them for us.

She's on her computer, writing a slightly tipsy blog post about elopement and how everyone should 'totally do it immediately'. She looks up thoughtfully.

'Maybe I should elope with David? Just for the LOLs?'

'By LOLs, do you mean attention?' I say, smiling.

'Yeah, yeah, I do mean that,' Joely says, laughing. 'We could do it drunk, with drawn-on cat whiskers, like Ross and Rachel, and then get an annulment.'

I hold my glass aloft, struck by inspiration. 'No, wait, plot twist. Why don't you elope with Calum Best! Leave David heartbroken. And then you could run off with Brian when you get back!'

'Yesss!' she says, standing up unsteadily. 'This is perfect.' She starts texting.

Oh, she's actually doing it.

I was only joking.

Lauren's going to be so mad if Joely steals her elopement thunder.

My phone rings and I answer it on autopilot.

'What's new, pussycat?'

Dad.

'Hey, Dad, how are you?' I say, feeling a spike of irritation at that tired greeting. 'You got the message, right? The wedding's off? Don't come to Charlie's house – they're pulling down the marquee right this second.'

Truthfully, that was another reason to be happy about the elopement. The idea of my parents being in the same room for a whole day, without causing some kind of awful scene, seemed incredibly unlikely. The idea of it has filled me with dread ever since we got their separate confirmed RSVPs.

'We did indeed get the message, pussycat,' he says cheerfully.

We? Who's we?

He pauses and then says importantly, 'I have some news, actually.'

'Oh?' I say, intrigued. He hasn't launched immediately into some tirade about Mum, so we're already in new territory.

He hums happily. 'Your mum and me . . .'

Here we go.

'We're getting back together!'

'WHAT?' My shock comes out louder than I'd intended, but I can't contain it. 'You're what? What do you mean? You can't be.'

I can hear Dad's smiling as he goes on. 'We started talking

273

yesterday – well, if I'm honest, Delilah, it was more *arguing* than talking—'

'Shocking,' I interrupt dryly, but he misses it.

'We thought we should talk when we realised we were both going to Lauren's wedding. I was angry at first that she was going, because she was being such a bitch, and I couldn't believe the Bolts would invite her when we all know I met them first! I remember distinctly – it was a Tuesday back when you were at school. We said hello, shook hands, and it was definitely at least three or four days before your mum met them. So I should have priority status with them. Anyway, we had a bit of a fight about it. And then your mum said we should try and make an effort to be cordial for this one day only, since it was Lauren's special party. And then we started talking properly and realised we should get back together!'

You have to be kidding. This is insane.

'Dad, that's ridiculous,' I say. 'I thought you hated each other.'

He makes a scoffing noise and says, 'That's all behind us now, pussycat. Your mum is the one for me. I'm moving back in this week.'

Oh, great, they're taking it slow then.

I sigh. 'OK, cool. Well. I guess, congratulations? And thanks for letting me know.'

'Thanks, pussycat,' he says happily. 'I better go, but tell Lauren and that boy of hers congrats on the elopement.'

Just as I hang up, my phone rings again. It's Mum this time.

'Lilah?' she says excitedly when I answer. 'You'll never guess what!'

I give it a beat. 'You and Dad are getting back together?' I say, unenthused.

There's a shocked silence before she answers. 'How did

you . . . ? How could you possibly . . . ?' She pauses and then shrieks, 'He told you already? That bastard! He said we would take one child each – he'd ring Tom and I could tell you. I can't believe him! I wondered why you were going straight through to voicemail. He is a lying arsehole. I can't believe I ever thought he'd changed.'

Well, then, this didn't last long.

I clear my throat. 'Hold on, Mum, I'm sure he was just too excited to wait, and I bet Tom didn't answer his phone so he—'

She cuts me off. 'Hold on, I'm calling that piece of shit and putting him on conference call. Stay on the line.'

'No, wait,' I say, panicky. I really don't need to be involved in this, but she's already muted me.

I sigh. I can't keep doing this.

They return a minute later and they're already shouting at each other.

'We had an agreement!' Mum shouts. 'You are a liar, just like you always were.'

Dad shouts back, 'You've got it wrong, you stupid bird-brained cow. Don't blame me for your stupidity. I said I would call my pussycat and you could try and get hold of the other one.'

'Why would I agree to that?' Mum shrieks. 'We both know Tom won't answer, that's why you said I could do Lilah. I thought you were finally being thoughtful and putting some-one else first. But you could never change, could you, you dung monkey?'

I'm not sure they even remember I'm here, and I consider just hanging up and letting them go at it. But curiosity gets the better of me.

'HEY,' I shout over them, and they are momentarily quiet.

275

'Are you not getting back together after all then?' I say, and there's a deafening silence.

Dad speaks next, at a lower volume this time. 'Why on earth would you say that, Delilah? Of course we are. We love each other. We've always loved each other.'

Mum joins in, and she sounds happy. 'We really do, Lilah. Oh darling, we're just sorting through our issues now, and then we'll live in harmony together for the rest of our lives.'

I let out a short, sharp bark of a laugh. 'You will not,' I say, and I realise I'm about to give them some shit. I'm ready for it, it's time.

'I'm delighted you're back together,' I say, not feeling particularly delighted at all. 'I'm very happy for you, but please don't delude yourselves that this will stop the arguing. You'll be as bad as ever, torturing each other.'

'Why would we want to stop the arguing?' says Mum, and she sounds genuinely confused. 'That's the best part of us, Lilah. It means we still care and feel passionate about each other.'

Dad agrees noisily. 'You obviously don't understand how relationships work, Delilah. Maybe you're too young, you haven't seen enough people in relationships get older and become indifferent. That's the killer, that dreadful indifference, as couples drift apart. So many of our friends who've been married a long time barely speak to each other at all. They just sit there in separate chairs, wallowing in their boredom. Sleeping in their separate beds, in their separate rooms, barely communicating, barely even looking at each other. They don't see each other as humans at all after a while. It's not that there's hate – at least that would be an emotion – there's just total disinterest. They have nothing to say and no

276

interest in each other. And yet they stay together. That's so sad, don't you think?'

I think about it for a second. 'I'm not sure your way of doing things is better,' I say cautiously.

They both stay silent for another moment and then Dad says quietly, 'But it makes us happy, Delilah. It works for us.'

I nod. OK. To be honest, I know all of this really. They like their drama, they thrive off it. The shouting makes them happy. It makes them miserable, and that makes them happy.

But I don't have to be at the centre of it anymore.

'OK, Mum, OK, Dad,' I say, feeling a speech building. 'I am genuinely pleased you're back together and I wish you many serene years of screaming at each other. But here's the thing: you have to stop putting me in the middle. It's so unfair. I'm your daughter and I love you both. I can't keep listening to you two bash each other night and day. Do it to each other, by all means, if it's what works for you, but I'm not here for that. It hurts me, do you understand that? It makes me sad and anxious, and I can't have that in my life. I can't let you do that to me anymore. I'm in a happy place right now, and you will not ruin that for me. Why do you think Tom doesn't take your calls? He doesn't want to deal with this – with you two being awful about each other.' I breathe out slowly, and continue. 'Look, I want you both to know that I understand, and I know it's hard. I know you're human beings, and we're all flawed. But I also need you to be my parents, at least a little bit. So, please, no more calling or texting to complain to me. Save it for your therapist.'

The silence is a little shocked. They're not used to me speaking up for myself. Honestly, I'm not used to it either. I've never told my parents off before. I've never said any of this. I've spent years quietly listening to them being selfish, putting up with it like some idiot. But I'm done with that now. A new Lilah is in town.

'OK, pussycat,' Dad says in a low voice. 'We hear you. I'm sorry. I hadn't really thought about how our problems would affect you. I didn't think, I'm sorry.'

'I'm much sorrier than he is!' Mum interrupts, and then stops herself. 'No, sorry, ignore that. We love you very much, Lilah, and you're right, it's incredibly unfair what we've been doing to you. But everything's going to be wonderful between us now anyway, so we won't need to moan to you anymore.' She laughs. She knows that's not true. 'Either way, I promise we'll stick to normal parent chat from here on out. Life, work, the weather. Do you forgive us?'

I giggle, relieved and feeling empowered. 'Of course I do. But while we're here, Dad, please can you stop answering the phone that way? It's really annoying. That Pussycat song is so patronising. And can you just call me Lilah? Because you do know that Delilah song is about a woman cheating and then getting murdered with a knife, right? You've actually heard the song, haven't you? It's such a weird choice to name your only daughter.'

Mum laughs heartily and Dad harrumphs.

'I told him that too!' she says happily. 'I'm sorry I couldn't stop him, Lilah, I was out of my tree on labour drugs.'

Dad sighs. 'You two just don't appreciate the genius of Tom Jones. It's got many layers, that song. But fine, OK, I'll stop.'

I breathe out, smiling down the phone. 'Thank you. Thank you both for listening. I want you to know I am here for you if you need to talk about anything. I just don't want to hear any of that mean stuff anymore.'

'You got it,' Mum promises, but she sounds distracted. 'Hey, Harry, what are you doing right now? Do you want to come over? You should see what I'm wearing . . .'

Nope.

'Right,' I interrupt, mortified. 'I also don't need to be here for this, thank you very much. I'll catch you two later. Enjoy your reunion. Love you both.'

'We don't need therapy, though,' Dad mutters as I hang up.

Across the room, Joely is grinning at me. 'Bloody hell, well done, Lilah,' she says. 'Now text your chicken shit little brother. Give him a good telling off for abandoning you with your folks all the time and ignoring your messages.'

Ooh, good idea. I like this, I'm on such a roll.

'Dear Tom,' I type, reading it out loud for Joely, who is pouring herself more fizz before topping me up too. 'You are my brother and I love you dearly, but it's time to stop being a chicken shit. It's time to stop hiding from real life. We are both grown-ups and real life is happening over here. You have to share some of the responsibility for our annoying parents (who – shocker – are getting back together, by the way. Did you know?).' I stop to take a sip from my drink, feeling the fizz flood through my sinuses. It always makes me burp through my nose.

'Tom,' I continue, 'I need you. I need my little brother. I want us to be close, and we can't be close unless you decide to answer my messages or even pick up your phone occasionally when I ring. I only hear from you when you need money and that's not enough for me. What do you think? Please text me back.'

Sent. Done.

Ooh, it feels good telling people off. People who really deserve it. Even if it is only in digital form.

I feel like I've had a to-do list hanging over me for ages – years, maybe – and I'm finally ticking things off. My parents needed to hear some home truths, and so did my brother. Now, if he still doesn't make any effort and if my parents are still selfish arseholes, at least I know I asked. I tried.

I really feel like a different person in recent months. Like I've been unleashed. I think it all started with Mr Canid and arguing with him. He's really opened up a can of wormy kick-ass. I know I'm mixing my metaphors there, but that's fine.

We're still fighting, by the way. I'm still having lots of arguments with Mr Canid – I can't get used to calling him Oliver – but it's much more like fun bickering lately. The hate is definitely gone. Oh, except when he says I still don't know how to say his name right. But even then, I'm mostly just pretending to be annoyed.

We've been working together on the Fuddy-Duddies United Youth Project, and we just heard it's got proper government funding! We're going to be launching events around the country to bring communities together. We're going to help vulnerable young people spend time with lonely older people. It's about connecting those who need connecting, and I feel so excited and passionate about it.

As for the situation with Will . . . I still don't know. We've met up a few times since his shock appearance at the airport. We're talking a lot and I do still love him, but – and I don't know if I really want to admit this out loud, even to myself – I think maybe I don't want to get back together. I think it's that cliché thing people say: I love him but I'm not in love with him.

Basically, I feel like I want more from a relationship. More excitement. More arguments. More passion. I've realised that I was kind of . . . settling with Will. And he deserves more than that. Everyone around me was getting serious and making big life commitments and I thought I had to as well.

Like, it was the right *time* when he came along, so he must be the right guy. But much as I like him as a person, I think, more and more, that we weren't quite right for each other. Plus, he wants to get married, and screw that.

It seems stupid because, really, I have everything I need with Will. He's good and kind, and we have our lovely life together. My friends and family all like him. I like him so much! I know he would make me happy and we would have a nice life together.

It's not as easy as knowing one path would be the right path, because life is more complicated than that. Every path is right and every path is wrong. I'd probably be happy enough with Will. I feel sure we'd be fine. But maybe it wouldn't be that much fun . . . I don't know, I can't know, because life doesn't work like that. No one can know what will happen.

So, for now, I'm not making any decisions. I'm being a really awful person and keeping him dangling a tiny bit. And I don't even feel bad about it! I feel great.

The thing is, I've spent so much of my life worrying about other people. Worrying whether they liked me, worrying how I looked and worrying what everyone thought of my decisions. I worried about being lonely, I worried about not being included, I worried about social media. I scrolled through Instagram, convinced everyone else had it all figured out. Convinced I was getting my life wrong. I was afraid to say no and thought I had to put everyone else first. Even when people treated me badly or continued to behave selfishly, I let them. I encouraged it, even, because I thought it made me a good person to let them treat me that way. I thought being a nice person was the only important thing to be.

I mean, it definitely *is* important, and I still want to be a nice person wherever I can. Obviously I want to make the world a better place in my own small way – maybe with Fuddy-Duddies United! – but I think I can do that without worrying and caring so much. It doesn't require giving over my whole self to other people.

I think this world has a way of making us distance ourselves from our own lives. We present this image online of who we want to be, rather than who we really are. It makes us feel like we should strive to be everything to everyone, and we forget what's actually real.

I want to keep some of myself back from now on. Keep some of me just for me. And I'm trying to embrace being a bit more difficult for a while, like Franny says. It doesn't come naturally, but I've got a lot of people around me – cough, Franny, Lauren, Joely, cough – to offer up some selfish inspiration.

Plus, I'm finally learning how to say no! I've already turned down three wedding invites for next year! And I'm not even panicking about it. The thing about FOMO and all that sad stuff is that it's a bit of a vicious circle. The more you do things you don't really want to do, the more left out you feel and the lonelier you get.

But that's silly and unnecessary, because I have so much in my life. I don't want to be like that, and I don't have to be. Saying a hearty no whenever you need to is a big part of that and things are going to be better now because of it.

After all, look at everything I've helped happen in the last few months: Lauren and Charlie are off having the actual wedding of their dreams; Fuddy-Duddies United are moving into their new headquarters, and it's bloody fantastic. Ethel, Molly, Annabel – they're all doing brilliantly. We got together to check out the new building last week and it was so much fun. They're all so excited about the field (park) that surrounds it too, I can't even tell you. The final touches will take a little bit longer, but we've been temporarily hosting our meetings around Franny's house. She doesn't like it and keeps screaming at people to get off her rug, but she's also happier than I've ever seen her, dancing in all the attention her blue hair and newfound Kardashian knowledge brings. I asked her the other day if she minds that people are always looking at her and talking about her. She told me that it doesn't bother her in the least, but mostly everyone's just concentrating on their own lives and their own issues. People – even the kindest, most thoughtful people – are really only thinking about their own problems.

I've been thinking about those words ever since. It strikes me as somehow quite wise. I've spent too much time worrying about how people see me, but even that was my own problem I was worrying about. And I needn't have, because most of us only really see ourselves. It's like that thing when you have a spot on your chin, and it's all you can think about. You walk around with your head down, not making eye contact with people because you're convinced you look so terrible. And then you ask Joely and she confirms she hadn't even noticed it until just then. But then she insists on taking a close-up picture of it on her phone and sending it to Lauren.

I'm not saying that's how the world should be. Obviously it would be a better place if we could look at each other more, and be kinder, but we are flawed human beings. And it does mean that whatever happens in my life only has to matter to me. I can focus on myself without fear of being thought of as a bad person. And whatever happens in my life now – whether I get back with Will, whether I get a promotion at *Quiz Monsters*, whether Fuddy-Duddies United takes off – I am excited about all of it. I love my work, I love my friends – I even love pretending to have a perfect life on Instagram. It's all part of who and what I am. And that's cool.

Next to me, Joely knocks over her glass and swears loudly.

'Sorry about your carpet, Lil,' she says, but I'm not worried about it. It's only a little prosecco. I fill her glass back up and she asks me if we should make a toast.

'To weddings!' I say, and we clink our glasses.

Wedding Number Thirteen (lucky for some): Lauren and Charlie, Elvis' Lagoon, Vegas

Theme: Everyone-can-back-off-this-is-about-us theme.

Menu: Chips and curry sauce, apparently.

Gift: A cheerful Skype congrats.

Gossip: Lauren claimed their Elvis officiant was flirting with her, but then Charlie admitted the dude tried to kiss him in the loos at the end of the night.

My bank balance: £62. YES, I AM BACK IN THE BLACK, THANKS TO A CONSOLIDATING LOAN. THIS WILL LAST ABOUT EIGHTY SECONDS. Oh, my rent just came out, never mind.

From: DelilahMFox@gmail.com
To: 10+ contacts in your address book
Date: 22 December

Hello awesome human beings!

I just wanted to say I'm sorry I didn't get to see you at Lauren's wedding after all, but I'm excited to see you at the elopement party in April! We're about to get stuck into helping Lauren organise that, so wish me luck. I think it's going to be pretty massive!

Thanks again for the best hen do ever. You guys were all wonderful.

Merry Christmas!

Love Lilah, AKA Todd Wilkins
Xx

From: Katie.Jacks@barclays.com
To: You
Cc: 30+

Hey Lilah,

Katie Jacks here!!!! Nice to E-MEET YOU! Lol lol lol.

Thanks for the email, how exciting!!! I'd soooo love to come, just checking what dates you reckon the hen will be????

Thank you soooooooo much, can't wait!!!!!
Katie xxxxxxxx

From: Katie.Jacks@barclays.com
To: You
Cc: 30+

Hey Lilah,

Katie Jacks here!!!! Nice to E-MEET YOU! Lol lol lol.

Thanks for the email, how exciting!!! I'd soooo love to come, just checking what dates you reckon the hen will be????

Thank you soooooooo much, can't wait!!!!!
Katie xxxxxxxx

From: Katie.Jacks@barclays.com
To: You
Cc: 30+

Hey Lilah,

Katie Jacks here!!!! Nice to E-MEET YOU! Lol lol lol.

Thanks for the email, how exciting!!! I'd soooo love to come, just checking what dates you reckon the hen will be????

Thank you soooooooo much, can't wait!!!!!
Katie xxxxxxxx

Where are they now?

Shiny Naked Man AKA Stanley Morris

Stanley decided to quit his work as a Butler in the Buff after a heart-to-heart with a 'weird' maid of honour he met recently in Marbella. He thinks her name was 'Delilah', but he doesn't think that can be right because who's called Delilah in this day and age? He is currently living with an older woman called Jill and is training to be a world-class heart surgeon.

Flora Ives

Flora decided that, yes, she would help her boyfriend spray tan his balls. They are both pleased with how it turned out and would recommend it to anyone thinking about doing it.

Rex Powers

Rex was recently scarred in a terrible chest-waxing accident and is suing the beautician who did it. He says he will never be contoured in the same way again, but his pores remain magnificent. His show *Quiz Monsters* continues to pull in impressive ratings despite his chest problems.

Petra Mooney

Shortly after attending a wedding in Scotland with some old school friends, Petra got caught up in an unfortunate incident at her local zoo. A pack of hyenas got loose and stampeded, and no one realised she was trapped in the middle of it all, because her cries for help sounded uncannily like a hyena mating call. Luckily the animals adopted her as one of their own and she was eventually rescued, three days later. She says the incident 'changed' her, and she has finally become a better person who cares about others and values the milk of human kindness. Oh, she's also getting divorced because Richard caught her getting off with his second cousin.

Tom Jones Fox

Delilah's brother is still living in his 'urban commune' but has recently become a much more active and involved member of the family. He says it's because his big sister gave him a kick up the arse, and he finds her to be much less 'boring' these days. In fact, he says he likes to 'wind her up' because she gets so cross now. Tom confirms that during his last visit she put him in a headlock.

Tom Jones

He remains a very popular Welsh singer with incredible hair.

Fiona (TBC)

It turns out the staff member at the spa is not called Fiona, she's called Natalie, and yes, she's still working there. She was recently promoted to deputy manager and is having a baby with her line manager, Darren. He hasn't told his wife yet, but all of Natalie's friends say they're sure he'll do the right thing.

Alice and Harry Fox

Their romantic reunion lasted three whole months before Harry caught Alice selling some of his old Tom Jones records to her ex-lover, Jack the gardener. He said it was a deal-breaker and wrote a really long update on Facebook about betrayal and loyalty. Seven people liked it. They later reunited but they're still fighting a lot. They often ring their son, Tom, to bitch.

Joely Bolt

Instagram recently had a crackdown on spam bots and Joely lost 300,000 of her followers overnight. She's really upset about it and doesn't want to talk right now. Come see her again on Friday night after she's had a few drinks. According to the MailOnline, though, Joely recently eloped with Calum Best, leaving her boyfriend David Walliams devastated. The marriage was annulled shortly afterwards and she's currently dating a non-celebrity teenager she met at a wedding last summer.

Lauren Bolt-Sweets

Lauren is in the process of looking for a part-time job in a pub to supplement her income, as she now owes her parents a 'significant sum' of money. Despite this, she and Charlie say they are very happy with their decision to elope. They regularly exchange emails with the Elvis who married them, and are hoping to visit again next year. Lauren is still writing adverts for tampons. Her latest innovation is to stop using blue liquid, because 'what the cock is that? Who is bleeding blue water?'

Simone Sweets

Charlie's younger sister is currently serving four years in a Nigerian prison for fraud charges, after she flew out to meet a 'prince' she encountered online. She was carrying £50,000 in a carry-on bag and, after a lengthy trial, she was locked away – mostly for her own good.

Katie Jacks
She still doesn't know how to work her fucking email.

Oliver Canid
Mr Canid has been taking improv classes in order to 'better develop his sense of humour'. He says it's going really well and he's considering a new side-line in stand-up comedy. His friends and sister, Annie, are all very emphatic that he should not do that. He's hoping the development of his personality will be enough to persuade Lilah Fox to go out with him on a date one day.

Dean Clark
Dean never did get those period stains out of his white jeans and his mum went mad at him about them because they were brand new from Burtons.

Will Hunt
Will quit his job and went travelling on his own. He grew his hair long and says the whole thing has been a life-changing experience. He still wants Lilah back, but he's happy to settle for being friends right now. He hates Oliver Canid.

Will's friend Daniel
He still sends people the thumbs up emoji and it really riles everyone up.

Sam
Sam just got a new job as a researcher at *Good Morning Britain*. She says Susanna Reid is a delight but that Piers Morgan is utter dog shit. Worse than Rex Powers.

Andrea

Andrea is on Guardian Soulmates and if you know anyone she might be right for, she is up for blind dates. She would also like you to sponsor her for the 1.5 km walk she's doing next summer.

Franny Fox

Granny Franny has recently been recruited as a regular on *Quiz Monsters*. Her specialist subject is the Kardashians and she's currently 'actively pursuing' Rex Powers as Husband Number Five. She says he reminds her of a young Tony Robinson with the spunk of a blue-haired Kylie Jenner. She's delighted with the new FU building and loves telling everyone how she single-handedly saved the club.

Molly

Molly recently received a parking ticket through the post thanks to a mobility scooter left abandoned outside the council offices last October without a permit. She seemed OK about it, but it's hard to tell because she recently had her tear ducts fixed and no one can tell how angry she is anymore. She still likes talking about fields.

Delilah Fox

Lilah was recently made series producer on *Quiz Monsters*. She's really enjoying it and is still having lunch with her grandma every day. She continues to attend the FU, and her latest youth outreach project has been picked up by branches around the UK. She's also getting kind of chubby again and she quite likes it.

She's still pronouncing Mr Canid's name wrong.

Acknowledgements

OK guys, bear with me here because I'm still in shock that this book thing is happening at all – never mind writing thank yous for my second novel in a year (pause for applause). The first people I should toast – given the subject of *What Fresh Hell* – are all my brides. You have never been any bother at all, I swear, and I truly loved being a bridesmaid for each and every one of you. So, thank you Lisa, Alysia, Lyndsey, Kate, Liz, Carey, Clair and Sarah. All of your weddings were my favourites.

Probably more importantly (though what's more important than a bride?) I would also like to raise a glass to my incredible publishers, Orion. You have been the best possible set of humans I could have asked for throughout all of this, and I'm so happy I get to keep working for you (this is a written contract and you are hereby agreeing to let me keep writing novels for you until the end of time). Thank you x a million to my clever, insightful editor Clare Hey. Sorry for that time I said I would have sex with your dad. Thank you to the dazzling and award-winning (pause for applause) Elaine Egan, you are my hero in all things. Thank you to Laura Swainbank, who has taught me that GIFs are everything. Thank you to Olivia Barber, Harriet Bourton, Jen Breslin, Krystyna Kujawinska, Hannah Goodman, Paul Stark, Mark Stay, Georgina Cutler, Loulou Clark and everyone else amazing who has worked so hard on this. And mega thank you to Katie Seaman, for y'know, everything. Also thanks to Jeremy Vine, just because

I'm trying really hard to make everyone think we're related.

Thank you to my fabulous agent, Diana Beaumont, who is as cool as her name suggests. I will never stop being obsessed with you and occasionally trying to lie in your lap. Thanks also to Luke Speed and Guy Herbert, whose laps I have been nowhere near.

Shout out to all my future bridesmaids for when I marry myself: Lynds H-D, Sarah C-A, Clair G, Jo U, Kate D, Katie H, Abi D, Shelly H, Daisy B, Angela C, Daniel K, Kate H, Emily S, Carey B, Becky V, Emma L, Kate W, Issy S, Rhiannon E, Emily P, Kelly A, Zoe B, Lynn R, as well as Lollipop, Tizz, and Boo. And thanks to Sam, who explained what a TV producer is and why that makes him special even though he's not. And a massive thank you to all my family, especially my mum, who made me a lot of food while I was writing this and is probably definitely one of the best people on the planet.

That's it.

Dude, why are you still reading this? It got boring three paragraphs ago.